In the Shadow of the Cities

A Novel

IN THE
SHADOW
OF THE
CITIES

A NOVEL

NEW YORK

LONDON • NASHVILLE • MELBOURNE • VANCOUVER

In the Shadow of the Cities

A Novel

Published in New York, New York, by Morgan James Publishing. Morgan James is a trademark of Morgan James, LLC. www.MorganJamesPublishing.com

ISBN 9781631953279 paperback
ISBN 9781631953286 eBook
Library of Congress Control Number: 2020946124

Cover and Interior Design by:
Chris Treccani
www.3dogcreative.net

Morgan James is a proud partner of Habitat for Humanity Peninsula and Greater Williamsburg. Partners in building since 2006.

Get involved today! Visit
MorganJamesPublishing.com/giving-back

To my mother, Teresa Fitts,
who taught me how to write.

Contents

Acknowledgments

It's hard to imagine that I am finally publishing my first book, and I know that without the support and encouragement I had along the way, it would not have been possible.

I am grateful to my husband, Yader, who supported my yammering about imaginary characters and plot ideas without telling me that he didn't want to hear about them anymore.

A very special thanks to my best friend, Lauren Sisk, who read through many of my manuscripts and inspired me to keep writing even when my life was "too busy."

To my family: I inherited my writing gene from my mom and grandma, so I want to thank them for that gift. Also, my mom and dad have been so encouraging throughout everything I have tried, including my writing. I appreciate knowing I have two parents who will always believe in what I am doing.

To the Morgan James team: Thank you for taking a chance on a first time writer. I appreciate the wisdom and guidance you have given me as I partake in this "published writer" journey.

Chapter 1

Scarlett stared out the window of her history class.

The Blue droned on at the front of the room, but Scarlett hated the story of the Government, not that she would dare say as much aloud. *Blah, blah, blah.* Citizens couldn't be trusted to share. *Blah, blah, blah.* They had been organized according to abilities and were allowed to live their best lives as long as they followed the rules. *Blah, blah, blah.*

Scarlett had never seen one of these Citizens, but she had been shown many pictures. They looked just like her, except for the fact they weren't as intelligent. But that wasn't always something you could see.

Scarlett shifted to a more comfortable position in her chair and dared a glance over her shoulder at Jaylin. Jaylin was staring intently at the Blue as though they hadn't been told this same story before, as though she might absorb some detail that she had missed during another account.

Scarlett sighed softly as her mind turned to what she would do when she was finished with her classes for the day. She had exactly two hours of free time before dinner. Free time was the only chance she would have to see Rhys because males and females weren't often allowed to mingle.

A piece of paper landed on her desk, and Scarlett's eyes flew up. The Blue was already moving on to the next desk. A quiz? On what? They hadn't learned anything new. Scarlett waited for the signal to turn her paper over and quickly scanned the questions. Then, rolling her eyes at the quick bout of anxiety, she raced through the quiz, circling the correct answers.

All of her other classes moved on to new material after a week or two. But history class—it was always the same. At least she was guaranteed a good grade. What Scarlett couldn't wait for was the "Life in the Cities" class. But she wouldn't be able to take that one until she was a Blue, and who knew when that would be. She had been a Green for three years, but she could continue to be a Green for another five if she wasn't able to meet the right goals. She could potentially remain a Green forever, but she knew that wasn't a real possibility, not with her dedication to the training.

A grating *beep* signaled the end of class, and Scarlett placed her book carefully into her satchel. Everyone remained silent until they exited the classroom, then Jaylin grabbed Scarlett's arm.

"Female! You have *got* to come with me. Miya and I are planning on participating in the Optional Fitness Program, and you have to join us."

Scarlett nodded, trying to match Jaylin's enthusiasm for the program. Scarlett enjoyed working out, and she often spent time exercising during her free hours. But there was something about having another program in lieu of choosing her own exercises that made Scarlett wary of joining.

"Thanks, Jaylin, but Rhys and I are going to practice in the shooting range today."

"You can practice tomorrow. The program is only four days a week."

Scarlett and Jaylin were old friends. They had been promoted to Green on the same day and had nervously learned to navigate the new waters together. Scarlett knew her friend wouldn't be hurt if she turned her down.

"I think I need more aim training than ab training," Scarlett said. They had reached the end of the hall. "I'll see you at dinner time."

Jaylin shrugged, making a pouty face that Scarlett knew was exaggerated. "Fine, female, abandon me then. Miya and I will talk bad about you behind your back."

Scarlett laughed. "Just don't wear out your lips from using them too much."

Scarlett hurried toward the front door, which led to the gate that separated the males' and females' training centers. There was only one way to pass from one to the other, and you had to be approved by the Blue guarding it. It was a fair process. Scarlett had never been denied entry.

She stepped up to the guard and presented her badge to be scanned. The guard nodded as the time flashed up on the board along with Scarlett's information. She entered the males' training compound, heading around the building rather than through it. Scarlett found most males maintained a horrendous odor, and it was best to avoid them in concentrated numbers when possible.

Scarlett entered the males' shooting range, scanning the pods for the familiar dark curls. Pod 3. The pod where they had met.

Scarlett checked out a longer rifle and headed toward the pod, adjusting her safety gear. She waited for Rhys to lower his pistol and bob his head slightly to let her know he knew she was waiting to enter.

Carefully, Scarlett slipped the sound-proof glass door open then closed. She stood beside Rhys, taking her position on the other shooter's mark. Rhys didn't hogwash her with boring questions of how her classes were. He already knew. He took the same classes, just in the males' training center.

"Five shots?" Rhys asked instead.

Scarlett raised her rifle. "I don't have my gun of choice. I thought I would go with something I hadn't practiced with for a while."

"All the better," Rhys responded, aiming and firing five shots in quick succession. Four hit the middle of the target. The other one missed by two centimeters.

"Why? Because you're assured of a win? Is that why you want to compete? Because you can't normally provide a challenge for me?"

Rhys smiled as he waited for her to take her turn. Scarlett hesitated, but she wasn't one to back down from a challenge. She turned toward the target and took her time aiming, the bulky weapon unfamiliar in her grip. Finally, she took her shots, pausing between each one.

"Two," Rhys declared bluntly.

"Yes, two. Thank you. My eyes are working very well."

Rhys laughed a little as he lifted his safety goggles and propped them on the top of his head. "Hey, I couldn't be sure after those shots. Besides, you agreed to it. I didn't force you into anything."

"Sure," Scarlett said, copying his move with the goggles. "The 'peer pressure' came on pretty strong." Scarlett looked toward the booth where she had checked out the rifle, wondering what had made her grab it. She hated being beaten.

Rhys laughed and turned toward the target once more. They had various competitions and "trick shots" they could try, but Scarlett had something else on her mind. She gazed through the pod toward the east. She couldn't see the Mound from here. The dorm's tall frame was too close, but that didn't mean it wasn't on her mind.

"Your turn," Rhys responded impatiently.

Scarlett shook her head "I have a better idea," she said, even as her stomach twisted into knots. "I'm ready to get over my fear."

"Of heights?" Rhys knew her well. He followed her gaze, then laughed, rubbing his coffee-colored hands together in enjoyment. "What are you going to do? Scale the dorm?"

Scarlett laughed. "Uh . . . no."

"Then what? There's nothing else taller than that, so if you don't scale the dorm building, then you're letting me down."

"There's the Mound," Scarlett said, referring to the large thing that lurked just outside the fence, just outside the area they were allowed to go. No one quite knew what it was made of, but it looked possible to scale.

Rhys gave her an incredulous look. "You're not serious. When?"

Scarlett shrugged, the nervousness making her feel weak. She turned to the target and took a few shots to calm her nerves. They were near the bullseye, close enough with the unfamiliar weapon that she felt assured again.

"Tonight."

"After lights out?"

Scarlett nodded. "Yes. The only question is . . . are you coming with me?"

Rhys cocked an eyebrow. "I never miss out on an adventure, but . . . I also don't break the rules. The rules are there for a reason."

The corner of Scarlett's mouth curved up just a bit. "What rule would we be breaking?"

Rhys shook his head. "I don't know. How about never leaving the training center walls? Or the one about staying in bed between lights out and morning wake up? Do you want me to go on?"

Scarlett sighed. "Those are Level 1 infractions; it's not like you've *never* broken the rules before."

"Yeah, but two Level 1 infractions?" Rhys sighed and inspected the pistol carefully. "I'll do it. I mean, for you. But I know I'm close to being promoted. I know I'm going to be a Blue soon, and when that happens, none of this. I can't risk being stuck at the training center for the rest of my career. I want to be in a City."

Scarlett nodded. "Okay, tonight. I'll see you an hour after lights out where the fences meet."

Rhys considered her idea for a minute. "Okay, I'll be there." The seriousness of their plan weighed on them as they continued shooting.

Scarlett couldn't back down. She had been considering the idea for weeks, and now seemed like the time to do it. After all, Mrs. said you should conquer all fears before entering a City. And that meant facing them. Now that the plan was in place, Scarlett felt nervous, like maybe she shouldn't have suggested it, like maybe they would be better waiting one more night. She glanced askew at Rhys. She didn't dare say anything to him now. He would never let her live it down. So, tonight it would be.

Chapter 2

Scarlett glanced at the other females as she donned her sleep pants. Females were grouped around the room, talking and laughing. Some hung from the bunk beds. Others were stretched out on the floor. They didn't suspect her of anything.

Keeping her movements slow and measured, she slid the leftovers from the pocket of her daily outfit into the pocket of her sleep pants. She pulled her sleep shirt longer to hide the slight bulge, her stomach knotting up. While she wasn't a perfect Citizen, she certainly wasn't used to breaking bigger rules, like sneaking out at night.

Jaylin's bed squeaked at Scarlett's side, and Scarlett whipped her head around. Jaylin leaned over, the metal bed frame pushing into her stomach.

"What are you doing?" she asked with a playful smile.

Scarlett shrugged nonchalantly and rolled her ankle in front of her, trying to keep her breathing steady. "Just waiting for lights out."

Jaylin made a silly face. "You're usually rushing in at the last moment. Strange to see you actually getting ready for bed before lights out."

Scarlett shrugged again, looking around the room for something to get Jaylin's attention off her. "Well, Rhys, big baby, said he was tired."

"Ah, that explains it." Jaylin nodded in confirmation. "Hey, we still have fifteen minutes. Want to play a quick game of cards?"

Scarlett nodded, as Jaylin was already moving to sit on the other end of Scarlett's bed. The bed above Scarlett creaked, and Miya's legs appeared. She peered down.

"Can I join?"

Jaylin nodded, and Miya lept off the bed, using the frame to propel herself onto Scarlett's bed without touching the ground. Scarlett smiled despite her nerves.

"You almost kicked me in the face."

"Aw, man, I was aiming for Jaylin," Miya said. As Jaylin dealt the cards, Miya looked at Scarlett. "It's strange to see you in here before lights out. It's usually just me and Jaylin."

Scarlett once again tried to take the attention off herself. "And these one hundred other females don't count?"

"I know, but I mean of our group," Miya said, bumping Scarlett's shoulder. Scarlett bumped her back. They started bumping each other back and forth, and Jaylin held up her hands for them to stop.

"You're going to knock the cards off the bed. Then I'll have to reshuffle. There's no time for that." The three females started into a lightning fast game of Sevens. The cards flew up, down, and around as they tried to get rid of them as quickly as possible. The one minute warning bell sounded, and they checked their current cards, quibbling about who would have won if they had had more time. Jaylin grabbed the set of cards and shoved them onto her bed, leaping after them just as the lights clicked off.

Scarlett lay down, staring at the lines of metal springs supporting Miya's bed. A few creaks and loud breaths were heard as they waited for when Mrs. would come check. She didn't always come, but when she came, you better hope you were still and sleeping. She didn't tolerate any noise after 10:00.

Scarlett found her eyes starting to droop shut as she studied the way the wiring met the springs at the end of the bed. Her eyes traced the faint lines over and over again, thinking about Rhys and what time it could be. She heard the tone of the room change as the random puffs of air and mattress squeaks were exchanged for regular breathing and soft snores.

Scarlett tested the waters by sitting straight up and waiting thirty beats. No mattress squeaked. No heads turned. She should go . . . and quickly. Scarlett reached for her jacket that she always left at the head of her bed, but it wasn't there. Scarlett tried to scan the floor for it, gently swiping her feet to see if it had fallen. But she couldn't find it. Oh well, it shouldn't be too cold out tonight.

Scarlett carried her shoes and padded across the cement floor to the door. She opened it as quickly and quietly as possible. Hopefully, if anyone heard anything, they would just think it was Mrs. coming in for a late night check.

She hurried down the long hallway, not wanting to pause to put on her shoes for fear one of the Blues would find her out of bed. Her heart pounded as she turned the corner and ran for the exit. Why had she and Rhys decided this would be a good idea? Well, she had pushed Rhys into it. But that's always how it was. She pushed to do the crazy, and when it actually came time for it, she acted like one of the Reds. She didn't want to think about what would happen if they were caught.

With the main door shut behind her, Scarlett still didn't feel safe. Anyone could peek out one of the many windows, and supposedly, there were a few people set to keep watch during the night, not that they were expecting anyone to walk right out the front door. As Scarlett scurried across the sandy yard, pebbles pricked at her feet. Time to put on her shoes. Crouching behind one of the few trees, she dusted her feet off and shoved them into the shoes.

She made it to their chosen meeting place and studied the landscape before her. She could not see much other than the thin wire fence separating the females' training center from the males'. Grass was hard-put to grow in the harsh climate. Rhys should be there at any moment.

Scarlett looked down at the standard issue watch and noted that he was eight minutes late. Eight minutes! When you're meeting after curfew, eight minutes can mean anything from fell asleep while waiting to caught and currently in isolation.

Three minutes later, Scarlett detected movement in the shadows that indicated someone was coming. By the subtlety of his movements, Scarlett knew it was Rhys. Her shoulders relaxed. She didn't realize how on edge she had been.

"Why are you late?" she demanded in a harsh whisper.

Rhys smiled good-naturedly. "Terry was dealing with something, and I had to wait for him to stop sobbing and start snoring to sneak out."

Scarlett rolled her eyes and tried to tame the smile. She was still mad at him for making her worry. She put her hand up to the chain link fence, looping her fingers through the holes and feeling the metal bite into her skin.

"Sure you want to do this?" he asked.

Scarlett nodded. "Come on. We've come this far. If we turn back now, sneaking out will all be for nothing." She didn't want to admit that she was hoping he would suggest they go back and give up on the plan.

"Hey, I'm not turning back. I'm just giving you an out if you want one."

Scarlett smiled and pulled her hand away, standing up slowly as she scanned the area. "Like I would wimp out of something. You're usually the baby."

Rhys laughed just loud enough that Scarlett looked around to make sure no one had heard. Not that there was anyone casually lounging around to hear, but still, they couldn't be too careful.

"Okay, sneak out and meet me by the acacia. I'll lead you after that."

Scarlett nodded and slipped toward her own escape route. Slipping unnoticed from the female to the male side was impossible, literally. The fence was always patrolled and re-secured often. But the outside fence, not so much—as though the Government thought nothing much could hurt them out there.

Scarlett shimmied under the loose portion and bounded toward the acacia, not sure why she felt so sick. Maybe something in dinner hadn't agreed with her. Maybe she shouldn't have taken a second helping either.

Rhys strolled up as though it were the middle of the day, and he was inside the compound. "Hurry up," Scarlett whispered to him angrily. He was always so calm when he shouldn't be, as if nothing could hurt him.

"I'm coming," he responded nonchalantly.

Scarlett rolled her eyes again at Rhys. They were both so different. Yet, somehow, they had become best friends. "Whatever you want to call it, I don't want to get caught." The two started through the desert toward the odd mound that rose like a giant finger poking through the earth. They had all assumed it was some sort of termite mound and rarely wandered near it when outside the training center walls. But after closer examination, Rhys had declared it bug-free. He said it was some sort of large rock. A large rock or not, it was at least four times their height.

Scarlett craned her neck back to examine the top. She could see the jagged edge pushing into the night sky. She wouldn't say she was afraid of heights, but they definitely weren't her favorite thing. Maybe that's why her stomach felt so strange. She knew the impending climb would use all of her strength, mental and physical. But still, she had to do it. They were told to face their fears, and heights was one of hers. If she could do this, then she could do anything.

"Come on," Rhys said, already halfway up. "We can't be out here all night or someone will notice we're not in our beds." Scarlett took a deep breath and began taking slow step after slow step. Rhys was making jokes above her. Heights clearly didn't bother him at all. She did the best she could to block out his voice and only focus on one movement at a time. When her fingers grasped the edge of the top, she saw Rhys standing above her, watching.

"Don't stand so close to the edge," she said.

Rhys backed up a half step and leaned down to pull her up the last bit. But Scarlett shook her head. A horrible image of her accidentally pulling Rhys off the edge and sending them both tumbling down the fifteen meters caused her to focus only on her hands moving further and further onto the cliff top.

"Did it," she said, letting out a deep breath.

"Now time to eat," Rhys said, motioning for her to hand over the goods. Scarlett unwrapped the food she had saved, and Rhys dove into it like they hadn't eaten a mere three hours before. Scarlett bit onto the edge of the pita bread, not sure her stomach could handle anything more.

"There. We did it," Scarlett finally said, trying to settle her stomach. "We really did it."

"See, I knew you could," Rhys responded. "And if you can climb up this thing, there's nothing else you could be afraid to climb because nothing else is higher than this."

"Well, I wouldn't go around climbing barbed-wire fences anyway," Scarlett responded. Rhys nodded in agreement.

Scarlett shivered just a tad, but Rhys caught it immediately. "Come here," he said, pulling his jacket off quickly. Scarlett reluctantly accepted it, the cloth warm against her icy fingers. She pulled the jacket around her shoulders and tucked her fingers under her armpits. Rhys laid on his back, gazing up at the sky and not at all bothered by the chill in the air. "Relax," he said, nodding toward the sky. "Take a moment to enjoy the view."

"Just for a minute," Scarlett said, "then we have to start down." Her mind didn't want to consider how that part of the climb would feel. The fact that she couldn't see where her feet would be placed, that she was just one slip away from death, was too much to consider. But as the fear built, her excitement did, too. Why did she enjoy doing things that frightened her?

"Mmkay," Rhys agreed. Scarlett settled onto her back on the ground, a few centimeters separating her from Rhys.

What felt like only a second later, Scarlett jerked awake. She knew she had fallen asleep, but she also knew something was amiss. The smell in the air had changed from fresh, sweet air to something unwashed. Scarlett sensed movement and sat up, her head spinning slightly.

A spindly male was standing before her, his limbs old and wrinkled. He didn't appear threatening, but his mere presence bothered her. She had never seen him before, and she knew everyone in the training centers, if not by name then by sight. He didn't look strong enough to be a Blue or anything higher. She had never seen anyone so old before. The male stared directly at her as she elbowed Rhys, hard.

He sat up, mumbling something, as his eyes blinked open and shut. Then, he pulled a pistol and aimed it at the male. Scarlett stared at him. Had he really stolen a pistol from the shooting range? That was a much more serious offense than sneaking out to climb some strangely-large rock. But at the moment, Scarlett wasn't considering the consequences. She was only wondering who this male was and what he was doing here.

He didn't seem at all fazed by the gun pointed in his direction or by Rhys, the one who was pointing the gun.

"What are you doing here?" Rhys demanded.

One of the male's eyes was squeezed shut, but he glared out of the open one. "I'm here to warn you," his grizzled voice announced. His voice shook when he spoke, but it wasn't from fear or insecurity. His words could not be more sure. "You," he said, pointing directly at Scarlett. He paused, but Scarlett couldn't take her eyes off him.

"Get out of here," Rhys said, motioning with the gun to the side of the looming rock. Rhys stood, towering half a foot above the bent, old male, and the male glanced at Rhys, clearly nonplussed. Scarlett took the opportunity to scramble to her feet as well. The old male turned his one good eye back to Scarlett and nodded confidently.

"You will kill him before two months are over." With that, the male turned toward the edge and disappeared over the side, not struggling with the climb despite his age.

Rhys lowered the gun, and Scarlett turned to him, trying not to let her fear show. "That . . . that was weird," Scarlett said. Rhys put his gun away and looked around. Neither of them felt sleepy any longer. They both needed to get back inside the training compound as quickly as possible. Who knew how much time had passed? Without any further discussion, they began the slow descent. Scarlett's stomach dropped as her foot scrambled several times for a foothold she couldn't see.

The two hurried toward the fence. Scarlett started to hand Rhys his jacket back but held on to it for a moment longer, looking for some sort of assurance against her worry.

"You don't think he was right, do you? He was just some freak, right? Maybe an escapee from one of the Cities who is slowly going crazy in the desert?"

Rhys shook his head, pursing his lips tightly. "He was clearly unstable. Part of why I want you to get back in your dorm as soon as possible. We can talk tomorrow, okay?"

Rhys walked Scarlett to her corner of the fence before going over to his side. As Scarlett sneaked her way back into her dorm room, she couldn't stop going over and over in her head what the old male had said. Rhys was her closest friend. She would never hurt him. Ever.

Chapter 3

When the morning bell rang, Scarlett's eyelids felt like lead. She tried to open them, but they seemed to be closing of their own accord. Miya hopped off the bed, poised and ready for the morning bell as she always was. Trainees were not allowed out of bed before the bell, so Miya always rushed to be the first into the bathroom.

Jaylin groaned from her bed, and she wasn't the only one. Scarlett heard echoing groans throughout the room. She forced herself to sit up and stretch. 6:00 a.m. was too early to be waking up, especially after her night. She had checked her watch when they stumbled back in, and it had been almost two in the morning.

Miya was skipping back into the room by the time Scarlett had grabbed her green training uniform and begun taking off her sleep pants. "You look dead," Miya said, laughing at Scarlett's apparent discomfort with the earliness of the hour.

Scarlett stretched her arm as she pulled off her sleep shirt, and Miya leaned closer. "Whoa! What's that on your arm?"

Scarlett turned her arm toward herself, squinting to see what could have drawn Miya's attention. There was a long bruise down her arm. She blinked a few times, not sure how to respond. Her brain was not fast enough in the morning to think of good excuses. She remembered slipping slightly the night before and banging her arm on one of the rocks. It hadn't really hurt then, but now, there was a long purple mark on it.

"Uh, I . . . hit my arm last night," Scarlett finally stammered out, focusing on pulling her training uniform on. The sleeve didn't cover the mark, and Scarlett wondered if anyone else would see it. Would they believe her story?

"What kind of dream were you having?" Miya asked laughing. Jaylin dragged herself to the edge of her bed and peered at them both through bleary eyes.

"Is Scarlett okay?"

"Yeah, I'm fine," Scarlett said, clasping her hands behind her back. "Just you know me, I can never lay still when I'm sleeping." Luckily this was true. Miya looped her arm through Scarlett's.

"Come on, let's go walk the halls until morning exercise." Scarlett trudged along, her energy not matching Miya's. She wanted to see Rhys and talk about what had happened the night before. It didn't seem all that real anymore, like something she had dreamed. But she knew it was real. The crumbs from their shared meal on top of the rock had been in her sleep pants pocket. But she wouldn't have a chance to see him until evening free hours. Before then, she had hours of training and classes to go through.

"Female, you look really tired. Are you sure you're okay? Is something bothering you?" Miya asked.

Scarlett pasted on a smile and tried to act as normal as she could. "Yes, I'm fine. Just tired. I had a weird dream last night."

"You remember your dream? Tell me!" Miya begged.

Scarlett shook her head. "No, it's just weird. I don't remember it fully."

"Well, whatever you remember," Miya insisted. "Come on. We still have ten minutes before we have to report in the yard."

Scarlett turned away so Miya couldn't see her roll her eyes. Then, she made up a crazy dream story about how the Reds and the Blues had switched roles, so the littles were in charge of the whole training center.

Miya was laughing, and even Scarlett felt like smiling by the time she had elaborated the whole thing.

As they lined up in the yard to start their blood flowing, Scarlett looked toward the males' training center. She couldn't see them doing their exercises. They were too far away, but she could imagine Rhys. He was so dedicated, fulfilling the routine to the fullest. He was on the cusp of being a Blue. While Scarlett didn't want to stay a Green for long, she couldn't imagine working any harder than she did now.

"Scarlett!" her name was shouted by one of the two Blues leading their exercises. Her eyes opened wide, and she sped up the pace, aiming to pass at least two runners before allowing her thoughts to wander again.

At five o'clock, they were given two hours of free time before dinner. After dinner, they were sometimes allowed free time as well. Other times, they had homework to complete for their classes the following day. If Scarlett was going to speak to Rhys, now was her chance.

She headed over to the males' training center, the guard allowing her to pass. When she reached the entrance, she pushed Rhys's number into the panel. She wasn't allowed to enter the males' dorm, but she could call him with his number. It would signal with a light on his bed that someone had come to visit him.

Scarlett waited almost ten minutes before deciding he wasn't in the dorm. The search began. Scarlett assumed he would be outside, but would it be the shooting range or the exercise ring? At the thought of the shooting range, Scarlett remembered the gun Rhys had carried the night before. Had he been able to return it or had he been caught? Why had he taken it in the first place? They could have easily taken that old male in hand-to-hand combat.

Scarlett stepped through the entrance to the exercise ring, several structures scattered throughout the area. As she looked closely at the dark green training uniforms, she realized none of them held Rhys. Scarlett sighed and turned away, but one of the males jogged up to her. Scarlett didn't recognize him, but he seemed to know who she was.

"Hey, you looking for Rhys?"

Scarlett nodded, crossing her arms.

"He's in the office with Mr."

Scarlett's arms dropped as she tried to control her facial expression. "Why?"

"I dunno, but it hasn't been long. He just got called there when free hours started." The male wiped his sweaty hands on his green training uniform and stuck it out. "I'm Dag, by the way." He seemed to remember she was a female and withdrew his hand.

Scarlett nodded, accepting his name. She hadn't really associated with any males aside from Rhys and didn't know what to say.

"You can wait here," Dag suggested. "He said he would come out here as soon as he was done with whatever Mr. wanted."

Scarlett pursed her lips and nodded, but she knew she couldn't just wait there and continue making small talk with this male. Her mind was rattling inside her skull, fear radiating down her spinal cord into her extremities. If they had come for Rhys, then they would be coming for her next. Unless, of course, it wasn't for anything negative after all.

"I'll be in the shooting range if he comes out. I'd like to talk to him."

"I will pass the message along," Dag promised, nodding to her as he turned back to the set of parallel bars. Scarlett hurried toward the shooting range, not looking at those on her right or left. She was one of the few females to come over and socialize on the male side. Many of the females considered the males to be juvenile and raucous. But Rhys wasn't.

Scarlett checked out a pistol and stood in front of the target. There was another male, practicing at the far end of the shooting range. Scarlett grabbed her pistol and stood in front of the target, staring at it but not really seeing it. Too much reverberated throughout her brain.

She adjusted her stance, opening her eyes wider instead of narrowing them. Rhys had taught her that while she was focusing on the target, she should always be aware of what was going on around her. Scarlett pressed her lips together and shot. The bullet just tagged the middle of the target, the bulk of it landing in the white ring around the center. Scarlett shook her head. She had to better her aim.

Five shots later, she was hitting the middle. Scarlett nodded and checked the time. She had been in the shooting range for twenty minutes. Had Rhys really been in the office that long?

Scarlett meandered toward the edge of the shooting range to have a better view of the males' compound. She saw a Blue and a few Greens, but none of them looked like Rhys from this distance. Scarlett sighed. Maybe he had been caught, and he would be put in isolation. She should just turn herself in. They always lessened punishments if you turned yourself in.

But then she noticed that the Blue seemed to be heading toward her. She looked closer, and her heart dropped. It was Rhys. He was a Blue? So, they hadn't found out what happened the night before?

Scarlett waved to Rhys then brought her hand down quickly as a couple of Greens turned to look at her. She didn't need any extra attention for the discussion they were about to have. Rhys reached her a few moments later, and Scarlett nodded to him. Males and females were not supposed to exchange physical contact. It had been awkward at first when she went from socializing solely with females to spending most of her time with Rhys, but she had adjusted by now.

"You're a Blue?" Scarlett asked, her eyes pointing to his training uniform.

Rhys nodded, the smile taking up most of his face. "Yes, I am. And we need to talk, Scarlett." Scarlett agreed. She didn't need to be told.

"Where?" she asked, nodding back toward the shooting range. "There's one male here, but he's at the far end."

"I've got a better idea. Check your weapon in," Rhys said. Scarlett did as Rhys asked, making sure it was locked into place before following Rhys. He led her toward the exercise ring, and Scarlett groaned. Was he going to take her there, with that awkward Dag again? Scarlett didn't actually know much about Rhys's male friendships. And while Rhys knew Miya and Jaylin's names, he didn't really know much about them either. Just as Rhys was about to reach the entrance to the exercise ring, he took a sharp right. Now, he was walking along the exercise ring, which had a strong concrete wall built around it. They reached the back of the exercise ring, where the concrete met the chain link fence. It formed a small alcove, and Rhys nodded to her.

Scarlett curled into the alcove, settling into the mix of sands and rocks on the ground. Rhys squatted next to her, fiddling with the rocks.

"So, what happened?" Scarlett asked, still feeling the need to whisper.

Rhys turned a stone over in his hands before throwing it down the way they had come. "I'm a Blue now."

Scarlett nodded. "Yes, I did figure that out. I've been pretty confident about my colors for at least a decade."

Rhys smiled just a little, but his large smile from earlier was gone. He seemed really serious now. "That means my daily duties will change drastically. I won't be training with the Greens. I'll be patrolling the Greens. I won't have free hours like you do anymore."

"I won't see you," Scarlett suddenly realized. She turned away, tracing the roughness of the cement wall.

Rhys nodded. He reached out and touched Scarlett's hand. Even though touching was forbidden, no one could see them here. And with the feeling of happiness that ran through Scarlett at his touch, she couldn't understand why it was against the rules. "I think it's good," Rhys responded.

Scarlett narrowed her eyes at him. He didn't want to see her. He didn't want another of their two-hour debates or one of their shooting competitions?

"That male last night," Rhys shook his head and let go of Scarlett's hand. "I can't stop thinking about what he said."

"So he was real?" Scarlett asked.

"Unless you and I are sharing dreams now," Rhys responded with a sarcastic expression. "I don't know where he came from or who he used to be. But at the same time, I can't just ignore what he said. I think it's good we will be separated. It will mean you won't have a chance to . . . shoot me or whatever."

"You know I would never do that anyway. You're my best friend."

Rhys licked his lips and shrugged like he couldn't believe it either, but he did. "I'd rather err on the side of caution."

"So, basically, you don't want to see me for the next two months."

"It's not that I don't want to, but I won't. I'll have different duties, being a Blue. And, why shouldn't we be more careful?"

"You're not being careful right now," Scarlett countered, mad at him. "Maybe I have a weapon hidden you don't know about. I could shoot you right here."

Rhys smiled halfway. "I know you don't. Don't be mad at me about it. I just want us both to be safe. And that means we can't go doing things anymore like last night. If I do that as a Blue, I could be demoted to a Green and never have the chance to go back up."

"Whatever," Scarlett responded, knowing she was acting like a Red who wasn't getting her way. They sat there a few more minutes, Scarlett bumping her fingers over the wall and Rhys shuffling through the rocks with his toes.

"Well, congrats on being a Blue," Scarlett finally stood, not knowing what else to say. She didn't make eye contact with Rhys. "Good luck with your procedure."

"Yeah, it'll be tomorrow." Another rough silence.

"I'll go get ready for dinner," Scarlett said, even though she had at least another half hour. She really just wanted some time to herself. She should be excited about her friend's promotion to Blue. But she couldn't help but feel left behind and alone.

"I'll walk you to the gate." They walked together, side by side, in silence, passing the exercise ring and the shooting range. They walked through the sandy area where morning exercises were done and reached the gate that officially divided the males' training center from the females'.

"Good luck," Scarlett said again, without making eye contact.

She hurried into the chain-link corridor, feeling the guard's eyes on her. Once she checked back into the females' side, she tried to find a place she could think. The history classroom was empty, so Scarlett settled onto the floor beside the map of the Cities. She felt its papery surface rustle against her training uniform as she curled into a ball, resting her forehead on her knees.

Once Rhys went through the procedure, it would be official. He could be sent out to patrol one of the Cities. He could be stationed there permanently. He would be. That was their purpose, to train until they were old enough and fit enough to protect the will of the Government. Rhys was just fulfilling his purpose. But if that were so, why did it hurt so much to know she could be permanently assigned to a different City? Or maybe she would be giving a permanent role here in the training centers, working with Reds or Yellows.

"You were created for a purpose," Scarlett told herself. "You will fulfill that purpose. You will not let Rhys distract you from that purpose." Even as she repeated the words to herself, she still felt a tugging that indicated she wanted something more from her life than just fulfilling her purpose. Her free hours were her favorite because she always spent them with Rhys.

The dinner bell rang, and Scarlett started. As she jumped up, the cool air alerted her that her face was wet. She rubbed the tears off her cheeks and pasted a smile on. She would fulfill her purpose. She would become a Blue and receive her permanent assignment.

Chapter 4

Scarlett sat in math class, rotely completing problems. Her mind was on Rhys. What was he doing right then? Had his procedure already been completed? Was he in any pain? She didn't know the details of exactly what happened during the procedure, but she knew it was part of becoming a Blue.

Every individual had a procedure when they became a Blue. The rumors around the center intimated they implanted a tracking chip in you. Other people thought they did something to your brain to make sure you would never question authority again. Scarlett didn't care what they did. She just hoped that Rhys was okay. Surely he wouldn't be completing duties today. Maybe she could visit him.

"Scarlett." Her name was spoken in an authoritative manner, and Scarlett looked up, alarmed. Had she missed something?

A Blue was standing at the front of the room, staring in her direction. "Oh, yes?" Scarlett said, standing beside her desk at attention. Her execution was awkward.

"Come with me," the Blue said. Scarlett gathered her education materials and satchel and walked toward the Blue as she tried to shove the education materials inside her bag. The Blue stared at her disorganized state with obvious disdain.

"Sorry," Scarlett said as she leaned the satchel on her knee and shoved the rest of the papers inside. "Okay." She felt her classmates' eyes on her as she left the room, following the Blue. Her surprise at being summoned and the embarrassment of everyone watching her had taken over those first few minutes. But now, as the Blue strode quickly down the hallway and Scarlett stretched her legs to match the pace, she had time to wonder where they were going. She hadn't been called out of class since she was a Red when she had gotten in trouble for using the adhesive on another classmate's head.

Had she been found out? It had been two nights ago now. Would she always live in fear that someone had seen something and had told the wrong person and now it would catch up to her?

"In here," the Blue said, stopping in front of a door with no windows. She punched a code into the panel, and the door popped open. Scarlett paused at the entrance. She had never been in this room before, and it certainly wasn't Mrs.'s office. Inside the room were some desks arranged in a circle. Eight Blues lounged in them, talking and seeming completely unstressed. The Blue who had led her there pushed her forward and closed the door soundly behind her.

The Blues in the room made eye contact with her. Scarlett gave a half wave before sinking into the nearest chair. What was she doing here? She didn't belong. Sure, she saw Blues all the time, and she recognized them. But she had never actually done anything other than take orders from them. But Scarlett didn't feel comfortable enough to raise any questions about what was happening. She hugged her satchel and listened as they finally turned their gazes from her back to their conversations.

"Vaely said she would be picked first, but you don't see her here, now do you?"

"I'm pretty sure she's going to get assigned to work with the Reds. She's not even good enough to work with the Yellows."

The other Blue laughed, and Scarlett averted her eyes.

"So, what's your name?" one of the Blues asked, raising her voice so that the entire room was drawn into their conversation. Scarlett looked up and found the Blue along with several others staring right at her.

"Scarlett," she said, trying to infuse confidence into her voice.

The Blue nodded. "Amirah."

Another Blue offered her name. "Jess."

Scarlett's eyes scanned to the other Blues, but they just watched without saying anything. "Are you sure you're supposed to be in here?" Amirah asked. Her question, while straightforward, didn't seem rude. It echoed exactly what Scarlett was thinking.

"I just followed the Blue who came in my math class."

Amirah nodded, her eyes thoughtful. "Because I'm pretty sure we're being sent out. And they never send out Greens. I mean, I've never heard of it."

The other Blues erupted in chatter, talking about the messed-up system if a Green got sent out without having to go through the tough Blue training. Scarlett remained quiet. Sent out? She was *not* ready to go into one of the Cities. Surely they wouldn't send her! She hadn't completed the proper training.

Mrs. appeared in the doorway, silencing everyone immediately. Mrs. was a formidable female, her brown hair pulled back into a tight bun. Her eyes were a light green color that seemed able to see into a person's soul. She stood at almost 1.8 meters, and her arms boasted of her daily exercise routine. Her eyes stopped on each of the females in the room. When her eyes reached Scarlett, she didn't seem the least bit surprised to see her in a room full of Blues.

"Follow me," she barked, marching down the hall. Everyone hurried to follow Mrs., and Scarlett noticed she was the only one with a satchel. Everyone else had free hands. Should she stash it somewhere and come get it later? She already felt out of place enough. She didn't want something else drawing attention, especially from Mrs. She stuffed the bag under the desk, rushing after the others to catch up with Mrs. Only when the door closed behind her did she remember it was a door that required a code to get in. Oh well, surely someone would unlock it for her later.

Scarlett matched her pace to Amirah's, staying just two steps behind her as she tried to surmise where they were going. They had left the classroom area of the building behind. They were passing through the Green dormitories and toward the front door. Were they going to do some sort of training exercise? Whatever they were going to do, Scarlett could not figure out why she was included. Her stomach turned over as though she had been caught doing something bad.

They headed down the chain-link passageway to the males' dorm. Mrs. turned around to face them once they had all reached the end. The guard checked them off the list one by one, and Scarlett saw the strange look on his face as he came to her, as though something was wrong. Scarlett tried to gain clues from his look, but after that moment, his face was a mask again as Mrs. began her speech.

"You will enter the screening room in the males' training center. There, you will be presented with the details of your mission. I trust you will make us proud." She made the common salute, three fingers pressed over her heart. "May the Government's wisdom and power live forever."

The girls repeated the blessing without thinking about it. Then, Mrs. turned and went back to the females' training center, leaving Scarlett and the Blues to find their own way to the screening room. Scarlett had spent many hours in the males' training center, but she and Rhys had never made it to the screening room. Rhys! At the thought of Rhys, Scarlett wondered if she would see him. Maybe after they did whatever they were sent over here to do, she could find him.

With that happy thought, Scarlett bounced forward with the other girls. A Blue took the lead as though she knew the place, and Scarlett wasn't about to try to take that away from her. People who took the lead usually needed to feel like they were in the lead, even if they had no idea what they were doing. Besides, what was she as a Green even doing here?

The Blue marched them into the males' training center and asked the first Green male she saw. "Where's the screening room?" The Green male looked them over for a moment as though surprised to see so many females there in the middle of the day.

After a moment, he responded. "Uh, I can show you." He turned and started walking. Everyone, nine girls in all, followed him. He stopped in front of a black door. "This is it."

"Thank you," the Blue smiled at him. He smiled back then scurried away. All nine girls, eight Blues and one Green, entered the screening room. Instead of darkness, like before a screening, the lights were on brightly. Two males were standing on the small stage, and the screen was rolled up. The first three rows were filled with males. They turned and watched the females entering. Scarlett's eyes skittered over each face. Then . . . her heart stopped. There was Rhys looking right at her. Her hand fluttered upward, as though to capture him, before she broke her gaze and turned away.

Why was he here? What were they doing?

The females settled into the fourth row and found the two males on the stage staring at them. One male was a White. The other male, guessing by his dress, was Mr. Scarlett had never seen Mr. before. But his sharp features and unforgiving eyebrows mirrored Mrs.'s look. His dark hair was slicked back with a product that made his hair glow, reflecting the lights back at them. The Whites, well, Scarlett had only heard rumors of them. She had never actually seen them. You could only become a White after five faithful years of service as a Blue. Five faithful years in a City, not at the training center.

Scarlett studied the White's face carefully. He had a fluffy beard, and his face was pock-marked, small caverns carved out of his skin. How had he become like that? Had he always looked so solemn? For the first time, Scarlett felt scared about fulfilling her purpose. She loved the Government and everything they stood for, but was she willing to suffer personal injury for them? She had to be.

Mr. cleared his throat, and all of the shuffling silenced immediately.

"Thank you for coming," Mr. thanked them as though they had had a choice. "We have a serious assignment in City 6 that all of you are needed for."

Scarlett's eyes dropped to scan the room, peering at the "all of you." Her mind had been on finding Rhys when she first entered. Now, her mind was on finding another stray Green. She was the only one. Surely there had been a mistake! But no, the Government made no mistakes.

"Brock has been sent from City 6. He will fill you in on the specifics of the situation in just a moment." Mr. paused. His words were slow and measured. No matter what was occurring in City 6, he didn't feel rushed or worried. The Government would work everything out. "First, I will walk you through your Code of Conduct on this assignment. You have been selected for a variety of reasons. One of those reasons is a constant demonstration of your responsibility to fulfill expectations and assignments. You will be expected to exhibit that same level of responsibility there. You will be instated in City 6 for a period of six months, approximately. That timeline may change due to unforeseen circumstances. However, if you do well, you will continue to work in a City, though not necessarily City 6. As you are being called onto an assignment before we would normally assign you Blues," Mr.'s eyes caught on Scarlett's, and he paused for a moment longer than necessary. "You will have a few specific regulations to follow.

"One. You are to accept any and all orders from a White as though they are coming from me. You will obey them exactly. Failure to do so could result in immediate termination." Scarlett's mouth dropped open a little. Termination? What could he mean by that? Death? "You *must* report any acts of subordinance from Citizens. Once again, failure to do so will be treated as traitorous behavior. However, you will have the chance at the end of two years to be promoted to a White. In two years, if you are advanced to a White, you will receive the benefits that go with such a status. You would receive your permanent position." Mr. looked at them each individually, making sure they were all paying strict attention to his words.

He ran a hand over his suit coat at his stomach, flattening it. "Brock, tell them a bit about City 6." Mr. took a half step back, and everyone turned their attention to the White.

Brock was not nearly as eloquent as Mr. "You could die in City 6," he started. "Right now, the Citizens are not appreciative of what the Government has given them. They are rebelling, wasting resources needlessly, and fighting against us. Your job will be to help them stay in their place. They provide resources, and we provide protection and equality. It's dangerous, but if you follow orders, you'll be fine."

Mr. stepped forward again. "Many of the Citizens will not appreciate your presence there, but I assure you that the Government pays you its highest respects. Your contribution is seen and appreciated. This evening and tomorrow, we will prepare you for your departure. You will be divided into squadrons. These squadrons will be your team while in City 6. You will work closely with them and report everything. There are no secrets. You will be divided into your squadrons shortly. Proceed to the exercise ring for your next set of instructions."

As one, the Blues and Scarlett stood, turned toward the back of the screening room, and marched toward the exercise ring. Scarlett glanced back several times to catch a look at Rhys, but she couldn't see him in the sea of faces.

They reached the exercise ring and spread out, some of the Blue males automatically reaching for a machine or something on which to busy themselves while waiting for further instructions. As Scarlett looked around, she realized no White was with them. Who was supposed to be leading them?

Well, Scarlett shrugged. If they didn't have a designated activity to do, then there was nothing stopping her from talking to Rhys. No matter what he had said the day before, she was determined to have a decent conversation with him. She also wanted to ask the details of the procedure. She was curious which of the rumors was true.

Chapter 5

Scarlett marched over to Rhys. He was looking toward the entrance to the exercise ring as he stretched out his arm awkwardly. "Hey," she said, startling him. He shifted suddenly and winced.

"Ohmygov, are you okay?" Scarlett said, almost reaching out before she remembered. There were others around. She stretched her fingers instead, trying to make the movement less awkward.

"How's everything?" she asked, her voice lower.

"I'm fine," Rhys said. He pulled down the collar of his blue training uniform and showed Scarlett a small opening, the red skin bunched together with what looked like thread weaving through it.

"Uh, oh, wow," Scarlett responded, surprised by how angry the mark looked. "Um, does it hurt?"

"It doesn't feel very nice. That's for sure," Rhys shook his head. "I can't lift my arm above my shoulder height. And—" he shook his head.

"What?" Scarlett asked.

"I don't know what else they did during the procedure, but I am having trouble walking."

"How can they expect you to go into a City if you're injured like this? This—"

Rhys shushed her, and Scarlett looked at him. He never told her to be quiet. They said whatever they wanted, and she never felt judged by him. What was going on? He nodded toward the entrance where three Whites were watching them all carefully. A few at a time, the Blues noticed they were being watched and stood at attention. Rhys winced as he clicked his heels together and put three fingers on his heart.

When everyone had drawn to attention, two of the Whites spread out, walking slowly and observing the Blues as though they were selecting which chicken would taste the best. The White combing the right side came to Scarlett and stopped. Her gaze made Scarlett nervous, and Scarlett looked down, no longer able to hold eye contact. The White stepped closer, entering Scarlett's circle of personal space.

"You're Green," the White said.

Scarlett nodded, glancing up for just a moment. The White's lips narrowed, and her eyes squinted. She turned on her heel and immediately went back to the White who was typing rapidly on a screen. They conferred quietly, and Scarlett caught Rhys looking at her. He looked worried, but they didn't dare talk. The White who was writing nodded and seemed to shove off the female's concerns.

"We will create ten squadrons. Listen carefully. I won't repeat myself," the lead White explained. Scarlett stood at attention as she listened for her name.

She heard it a few moments later. "Devon, Scarlett, Rhys, Malak."

Scarlett swallowed, her eyes combing the area for either of the two unfamiliar males. When the squadrons had all been announced, they were to begin the regular afternoon exercise routine with their squadron.

Scarlett turned to watch as Devon and a towering male approached Rhys and her.

"Hey, squadron," Devon said with a wide smile. He reached out and did a bro hug with Rhys who groaned just low enough that Scarlett heard him. Devon did the same to Malak. He came to Scarlett and reached out his hand for her. Malak wrinkled his nose.

"You can't touch a female, Devon," Malak reminded him.

Devon shrugged his shoulders like he could care less what the rules were and nodded toward Scarlett as though she should take his hand. Scarlett looked around, unsure what she should do. The Whites were gone. The Blues, whom she used to fear, were now being treated as her equals. There were no leaders to tell her what she could or could not do. Scarlett took his hand and shook it. His palms were rough and just a little sweaty. It was a weird feeling. She didn't shake hands with females.

"Let's start the exercise routine," Malak suggested, running a hand over his shorn brown hair. Rhys winced.

"Listen, I'm not a wimp, but I don't know if I can participate. My shoulder is still pretty sore, and . . . you've been through the procedure?" Devon and Malak both nodded.

"What?" Scarlett asked, lowering her voice. "What is the procedure? Why did they cut into your shoulder?"

Malak and Devon both looked at her as though she were simply clueless. Then, their eyes fell as one to her green training uniform.

"You're a Green," Malak declared as though the fact had just hit him. "How can you be assigned to work in a City if you're a Green? No one can be sent to a City without the procedure."

"Why?" Scarlett asked.

Malak took a deep breath. "I have worked closely with Mr., and I should not share the information I have obtained."

Scarlett gave him an angry look. "I'll challenge you to it. An endurance challenge. If I win, you tell me what I want to know."

Malak scoffed at her challenge. "From a Green? I'll accept it, but what do I get if I win?"

Scarlett shrugged. "You get to keep your secret?"

"I already have the choice to do that," Malak informed her. "I need something better."

Scarlett shrugged again. She didn't have anything she could offer. She never had any knowledge to exchange . . . unless, she could make him think she did. She could make something up, and he would never be the wiser.

"I'll tell you about what happened in the females' dormitory last night."

"Why would I want to know that?" Malak asked. But Devon was leaning in, interested.

"Go for it, Malak. You don't have anything to lose."

"Rhys," Malak said. "You're fair. Call it. The Plank?"

Rhys nodded, and Malak and Scarlett positioned themselves. As other squadrons completed the approved exercises, Malak and Scarlett balanced on the balls of their feet and their forearms, bodies straight. Scarlett stared down at her hands, clenched into fists. "Relax," she told herself, slowing her breathing and focusing on the paleness of her skin against the fake grass that had been placed in the exercise ring. The longer her forearms spent pressed against its surface, the sharper the plastic blades felt.

She turned her head slightly to see how Malak was doing. He smiled at her, with no sense of strain on his face. Scarlett's stomach felt like it would die. Why had she tried to challenge him? She was only a Green and a female. But sometimes she couldn't help but challenge herself.

Scarlett gritted her teeth and let her neck relax, trying to distract her mind with other thoughts. She closed her eyes and breathed as methodically as possible. Then, her legs trembling, her knees collapsed to the ground. Her arms felt immediate relief. She looked over at Malak who held his position another thirty seconds to prove that he could. He sat up, stretched his legs, then stood. She looked up at Rhys, and he looked like he was enjoying her failure.

"Oh, stop," she told him, kind of mad. She swung out with her foot, but he dodged, before doubling over for a minute to cradle various parts of his body.

"So?" Devon asked, watching her from above. "Your part of the bargain?"

Scarlett took her time getting up, her brain scrambling for a lie to tell them. No use protesting at the unfairness of their bargain. She was the one who had suggested it.

Rhys lifted his eyebrows. They all three looked at her.

"You should stop playing around," a Blue male said as he jogged past, sweat trailing down his cheek.

Rhys shrugged. "He's right. We should really get started."

"Fine," Malak conceded. "But I do expect you to uphold your end of the bargain." Without another word, Malak and Devon began a series of burpees. A bit slower, Scarlett followed them in the exercise, glancing over at Rhys who was stretching slowly.

While her stomach burned, the exercises were not much different than what she did on a daily basis. The difference was these males seemed to have more endurance. Or perhaps, the Blues were only used to completing more of each exercise. Scarlett, her breath ragged, jogged off to the watering station, her green training uniform damp all along her back.

As she took her time drinking, Scarlett's heart stopped. She had been so surprised by this whole afternoon that she hadn't taken the chance to think through what it really meant. She and Rhys would be entering a City in rebellion. They would both be constantly armed. Accidents could happen . . .

Scarlett trudged back to the exercise ring where everyone was working hard. She joined in the exercises, determined to do her best, but she continued to glance at Rhys. He didn't seem worried about it at all, when just yesterday, he had acted as though they should never interact. She didn't understand.

A White came in and observed them briefly before alerting them to cease and proceed to the showers and prepare for dinner. Scarlett looked for the Blue females, assuming they would walk to the females' training center together. However, as several Blue females began splitting off in that direction, the White barked at them.

"Stay with the group. No free time tonight."

The females looked just as confused as Scarlett felt as they slowly grafted back with the group. The group was shepherded into the males' training center. Scarlett couldn't help looking around to capture the details as she was allowed into parts she had never before entered. The center was much the same as the females', except bigger. There were many more males' than females. That's the way it always had been, and the way she assumed it would continue to be.

The White stopped at the door to a room and used a keypad to unlock it. "Today's code is 452," he said. "You may use the code on this room and on the bathroom across the hall. Dinner will be in one hour. Prepare yourselves."

The Blues and Scarlett entered the room, not sure exactly what they were doing. Dinner wasn't usually for at least another two hours. Free hours should be starting around now, but, Scarlett realized, with their mission so soon, they wouldn't have the same freedoms as before.

Scarlett stopped just within the doorway. The room very much reflected the one she had slept in for the last three years since becoming a Green. The difference was the emptiness of the room. There was no chest of drawers under the lowest bed. There were no training uniforms littering the floor or personal objects on the bed.

A simple blue outfit, different from their training uniform lay across the covers. Scarlett looked around the room to see a green one. They were all Blue. Was she being promoted to a Blue? Wasn't there a whole process with that? And a procedure?

Scarlett looked for something familiar as she felt panic rising. Rhys was on one side of the room, examining the Blue outfit. Scarlett hurried to the bed next to him. There seemed to be no division between male and female, and if she would be sleeping in unfamiliar quarters, the least she could do was sleep near Rhys. It felt strange the mixing of males and females as Devon took a flying leap onto the bunk on top of Scarlett.

"Check out these suits!" Devon called, and several voices echoed his interest. Scarlett cautiously touched the blue fabric. The outfit was padded, not smooth and slick like the fabric they normally wore. The front and back were heavy. In fact, the whole suit must weigh at least five kilos. Why would they be wearing this?

As Scarlett watched two Blue males acting out a gun fight, she figured out why. These outfits were bulletproof. Because they were entering a City in rebellion. Because someone might shoot at her. She offered Rhys a weak smile as she held up the outfit. He nodded, his face serious.

"I want to talk," she said, sliding closer to him but not touching.

"Soon," he said. "Wait a bit." Why did he like putting her off when she wanted to talk? Scarlett turned away from him, feeling lost in this room of Blues. She looked down at the outfit. The sooner she became a Blue herself, the better. She headed to the bathroom. Except, the bathroom didn't match the female bathrooms. Scarlett examined the machines on the walls.

They were like toilets but without a seat. How could one sit comfortably on one of those? Scarlett looked at it for another moment, wondering if it was a sink. But no, there were already sinks at the front of the bathroom and toilets in the back. Well, whatever it was, Scarlett didn't have time to wait and figure it out. She wanted to shower and change before the bathroom crowded any further. She hurried into one of the tiny shower stalls, hanging her blue outfit just outside to avoid the water.

Once she had showered, Scarlett took a deep breath and donned the blue suit. She stepped in front of one of the mirrors as other Blues buzzed around her, laughing and joking. She looked strange in blue. She had never seen that color on herself before. But then, after a quick smile, she realized that nothing had really changed. She was still the same person. Being a Blue, if that's what she really was now, didn't make her automatically know everything, as she had always thought of the Blues.

Rhys came through the bathroom, his skin and hair damp. As Scarlett watched him, her stomach curled in a weird way. She wanted to go talk to him—or something. It was a strange feeling.

"Hey!" she called out a bit too loudly. A few heads turned her way as her face turned red. "Hey," she said again quietly, giving a little wave to her watchers. They turned around and continued to goof off as they waited for their turns in the showers. Scarlett wanted to run, but the suit seemed so heavy. This outfit would take adjusting.

Rhys was sitting on his bunk, the shoulder of his outfit down as he examined the mark on his shoulder. When he noticed Scarlett watching him, he quickly pulled the shoulder of his outfit back up. Scarlett opened her mouth, but a light started flashing on the wall. Red. White. Repeat. Scarlett hadn't been trained for this signal. What should they be doing? She went to the doorway of the room and saw a White leading the group of Blues down the hall.

"Come on!" she called to Rhys and another female in the dorm. They hurried after the group, just catching up as they turned the corner. They were led to a small room with a large table and chairs around. Instead of collecting a tray of food from a window, they sat down and were served food. The food looked different; someone had mashed it all up and mixed it together instead of having a meat serving in one space and a vegetable serving in another space. Scarlett looked strangely at the food before digging in. She wasn't about to turn her nose up at nutrition, even if it didn't look appetizing.

After the meal, they were shepherded into the screening room again. And as they sat there and listened to some Whites talk about their experiences in the field, something dawned on Scarlett. They hadn't had any contact with other Blues or Greens since they had been informed of their mission. Did Mr. and Mrs. not want other people to know where they were going? But why?

After an hour, they were allowed back in their room and told they were not to go anywhere other than the bathroom until lights out. Most of the Blues sat around on their beds talking, speculating about the mission. Somehow, someone had brought cards in, and a game started up on the far end of the dorm. Scarlett noticed Rhys being quiet.

Scarlett sat at the head of her bed, which backed up to the foot of Rhys's. He was leaning against the wall, staring at the card game on the other side of the room.

"Are you any good at cards?" Scarlett asked.

Rhys nodded. "Yeah, why do you think they didn't invite me to play? They don't like losing all the time."

Scarlett smiled. "I'm not so good, but I can usually give a pretty good run."

"Why don't you go play?"

"Because, I've been thinking. And . . . I don't know why I'm here."

Rhys pressed his lips together, rubbing them back and forth before looking at Scarlett clearly with his light brown eyes. "Because, it's fate."

"Fate?" Scarlett lowered her voice. "So, that old male—"

"If you didn't believe him before, it's kind of hard to ignore it now. What could be the reason you are included in a mission where only Blues are purposed and historically only Blues have been included?"

"But Rhys," Scarlett said. "I would never hurt you." She reached just over the metal bed railing and touched his hand, one of the only patches of skin she could see while he wore the blue suit.

Rhys shrugged and let out a long breath, turning his hand over so their palms touched. Scarlett's hand tingled as Rhys gave her hand a short squeeze before letting go. They both looked around the room quickly to see if anyone had noticed them. Scarlett sat on her hands, her mind on the tingling that had gone from their hands up and down her body. Why was touching prohibited? She liked the strange feeling, even if she didn't understand it.

Finally, Scarlett looked at Rhys again. He was watching her carefully. "I don't think you would on purpose," he responded. "But accidents happen."

"So you want to stay as far away as possible, huh?" Scarlett looked at the far corner of the room as though the card game had drawn her attention. Actually, she was blinking as rapidly as she could to avoid crying in front of Rhys. She wasn't a crier.

"I think fate's going to happen whether we try to stop it or not. I'd rather . . . be with you, be your friend these next few months than pretend we can avoid it."

"We can! I'm not going to shoot you," Scarlett demanded. "Never. I promise." She stared at Rhys, daring him to challenge her. He shook his head slowly, and Scarlett opened her mouth to protest further. But his eyebrows bounced up and down. Scarlett looked at him confused. Was this procedure causing him muscle spasms now?

Devon appeared, seemingly out of nowhere, causing Scarlett to lean back. What could he have heard?

"You all don't want in on a game of cards?" He held up a deck.

Scarlett had too much to think about to want to play. Besides, she and Rhys still had so much more to talk about. Did he really think she was capable of killing him?

"Sure," Rhys agreed. He slowly rose from the bed and followed Devon to another area where two males were already waiting. Scarlett stayed on her bed and looked around for the other Blue females. The only male she had ever really associated with was Rhys. And she probably wouldn't even have started talking with him if she hadn't almost shot his arm off that one time. Scarlett smiled at the memory of it. It had only been a bow and arrow, not a bullet. But still, at the speed it had been going, she could have done a lot of damage.

Rhys wanted to talk about the fate of what might or might not happen. That afternoon could definitely be chalked up to fate. The females' shooting range had been undergoing renovations, and Scarlett had not wanted to wait to practice. That was when she had met Rhys, and she hadn't returned to the females' shooting range since.

Scarlett watched the Blue females, comfortable with each other after having shared a dorm for so long, talking in a corner. Scarlett thought one of them looked familiar. She had been a Green less than a year ago, but even when she was a Green, Scarlett hadn't really talked with her.

So as the minutes ticked by to lights out, Scarlett watched everyone, these people she was now a part of. She watched Malak and Devon especially. They were part of her squadron, and she didn't know them at all. Malak was overly intelligent. He had checked out one of the screens and was reading so fast that Scarlett didn't know how his eyes could collect all of the words before he was flipping to the next page. Scarlett wanted to know what he knew, especially about the procedure, but anything else would be helpful, too. As she stared at him, Malak looked up, right at her, as though he could feel her look.

He stood and marched over to her, laying the screen to the side.

"You never upheld your end of the bargain," Malak insisted.

"Can we make a new bargain?" Scarlett asked, scared he would say no, but it'd be no worse off if he did.

"Why?" Malak asked.

"I just want to know," Scarlett told him, "what is done during the procedure. How can it hurt me to know?"

Malak studied her. "You will understand when we are in City 6. Though I have never traveled physically, I have visited through a virtual simulation. And perhaps, once we are there, I shall tell you."

Scarlett accepted his proposition as the best she could hope for.

"So?"

"Oh, right," Scarlett searched her mind for anything worth repeating, some juicy secret. It's not as though any of the Greens would ever see her again. Once you were sent to a City, it was rare to come back to a training center. Why would you? Her heart felt a little sad as she wondered what Jaylin and Miya were thinking after not seeing her for dinner or free hours or their last class together.

"Well," Scarlett finally said, landing on something that might be interesting. "Three nights ago, there was a really strange smell in our room. A bunch of us started sniffing everywhere, trying to find out where the smell was coming from."

Malak watched Scarlett with interest. "Had someone stashed food?" he asked.

Scarlett shook her head. "No, we thought maybe someone hadn't turned in their training uniforms. It smelled foul, like something gone wrong. Well, turns out it was a pile of tampons, bloody tampons."

Malak stared at Scarlett blankly.

"Used tampons," Scarlett clarified, waiting for him to nod—do anything.

"Oh, I've heard of those but never actually seen one," Malak responded.

Scarlett looked at him confused. "What do you mean? You've never seen one before? But . . ." Scarlett couldn't wrap her mind around it. "Don't males have monthly cleansings, too?"

Malak studied Scarlett for a minute. He just shrugged. Scarlett frowned and felt suddenly embarrassed, as this conversation had taken a very strange turn. They stared at each other for a moment, then Malak grabbed his screen and returned to his bunk. Scarlett watched him go. How could he not know what a tampon was? Didn't males have monthly cleansings? But Scarlett didn't want to ask for fear of appearing uneducated. Maybe this was something she was supposed to learn as a Blue, but she never had.

Chapter 6

The morning bell rang loud and clear the next morning. Scarlett rolled over and pulled the covers over her head for another minute, but the sheets didn't have their usual sweet smell. They smelled stale. Scarlett sat up, her stomach momentarily panicking as she saw so many unfamiliar faces.

Then, she remembered where she was. She fingered the blue suit she had slept in. She looked over at Rhys, and he was smiling at her, his brown hair ruffled.

"Good morning," he said.

"Morning," Scarlett smiled, rubbing the sleep from her eyes. "Today's the day."

Rhys nodded, yawning, before pulling down the shoulder of his suit to examine himself.

"Whoa! Look!" he said, leaning toward her. Scarlett crawled to the end of her bed to get a closer look at his shoulder. The thread had sunk into his skin. You could see the lines, but it wasn't as visible as the day before. The skin was still red but not as puffy.

"How does it feel?" Scarlett asked.

Rhys experimentally lifted his arm, wincing as he stretched upward. "Still sore, but not as bad as yesterday."

Scarlett nodded. Devon leaned down from the bed above Scarlett, his head hanging right next to hers. Scarlett scooted away a few inches.

"How are you both this morning?" Devon asked. "I can't believe it's finally the day," he continued without waiting for them to give more than a nod. "In a few months, we could all be Whites."

"Or we could die," Scarlett said, staring at Devon without humor.

"Oh, come on," Devon said, hopping out of his bed and turning to face them both. "We have guns. They don't. We won't die."

Scarlett shrugged, uncomfortable with the conversation. She didn't want to think about Rhys dying, but that's exactly where her thoughts went. "I'm getting ready for exercise."

* * *

After a vigorous round of exercises and a hearty breakfast, the group of Blues milled in the yard between the shooting range and the garage. It was time.

Two Whites came out and studied the Blues. "Attention!" the female White called. Everyone stood at attention, watching her carefully. "Squadrons One and Two in Jeep 8!" she shouted out, apparently not capable of speaking calmly. Scarlett panicked for a moment. She didn't know her squadron number. She just knew who was on her squadron. She looked over at Rhys and Devon, who was on the other side of him. Malak was some distance away.

Squadron Three was assigned and so was Squadron Four. Neither of the other three moved. When the female reached the last squadron, Squadron Ten, they were assigned to a Jeep. As they marched toward the Jeep, the White stared at Scarlett. She felt her palms get sweaty. She hadn't done anything wrong, had she? Did this female recognize her as the Green she had berated yesterday?

The four clambered into the back of the vehicle. They were the only squadron in this Jeep. A White, not the female, was driving.

"In four hours, we will stop for a short meal and bathroom break," the White announced, nodding to all four of them. "Welcome on board." Scarlett noticed that his uniform was decorated with various markings. She assumed they were meant to represent rank, but she didn't have enough time to get a good look at them.

Scarlett nodded her acceptance of his words. But she couldn't help it—she was excited to go somewhere, to see something new. She was leaving the training center walls behind.

Scarlett smiled at her squadron members. They all smiled back, the same Red-like excitement showing on their faces.

"Here we go!" Devon shouted as their Jeep pulled out of the garage and passed through the gate. The guard took each of their fingerprints before they left, assuring that the correct Blues were heading out of the gate.

Then, they started driving, leading the other vehicles. They headed toward the forest in the distance. Scarlett couldn't believe they were going to see the giant trees. She had always wondered what they would look like up close.

"Trees," she whispered to Rhys. Her whisper couldn't be heard over the sound of the vehicles, but he saw her lips move and nodded. Everyone was excited.

Four hours later, they still had not reached the edge of trees, but they were much closer. The squadrons were made to leave the vehicles and perform some basic exercises to keep their limbs from stiffening. They were given a small meal, but this meal was unlike anything Scarlett had ever seen before.

"How do we eat this?" she said, turning over the package in her hands. It felt smooth, but when she tested it with her tongue, it didn't taste like anything.

Malak laughed. "This is the packaging. You don't eat this." With expert movements, he ripped one side of the package so he could access the food inside. Scarlett peered in his. It appeared to be meat with . . . rice? But why was it in such a strange covering? Scarlett tried to open hers in the same way Malak had. She failed.

Malak took the package from her and ripped it open in a quick moment. "You open it like this."

"Oh, thanks, Malak." Malak beamed and offered to help Devon and Rhys. But Devon and Rhys continued to fight their packages, ignoring his offer. Scarlett laughed as Rhys finally used his teeth to rip the package open. Devon was last, but he did succeed. They finished eating quickly, the White telling them to get back in the Jeep. Their half-hour stop had concluded.

The movement of the Jeep rocked Scarlett, and her eyes continually drooped. It felt so nice. Despite her excitement, her head dropped time and time again.

"Tired?" Devon asked with a smile.

Scarlett shrugged, not having the energy to speak. Then, she saw it. Her first tree. She half rose with excitement, but Rhys pulled her back down. Devon and Malak watched where his hands had latched onto her arm. Rhys let go.

"What? I'm not going to let her fall out."

"I'm not going to fall out," Scarlett responded, pulling her arm from him angrily. She was a Blue now. They were equals. She wouldn't accept treatment as though she were a Red. She continued to stay seated, but she turned away from Rhys, watching the trees zip by. There was a path for the Jeeps, a space cleared between the trees. Her eyes gathered as many details as they could in the short time. The trees were tall, perhaps taller than the training centers. It was much darker and cooler under the trees, and the smell was different. Scarlett took a deep breath, and her stomach lurched. It smelled like the male, the old male who had surprised them on the Mound. It was something like freshly turned soil mixed with life.

Scarlett wanted to look at Rhys, to ask if he thought the same. But she wouldn't. She was mad at him for grabbing her. Why was he so flagrant about breaking the rules now when he had been so careful through all of their time as Greens? Did he think he was going to die anyway, so it didn't matter what he did?

A few hours later, Scarlett began to wonder when they would arrive in the City. She felt a burning need in her bladder and didn't see any sign of civilization. The Jeep's lights were illuminating the group in front of them. But the excitement of riding in a Jeep was wearing off. Her bottom hurt from sitting for so long.

Suddenly, the vehicles pulled off the path, into a clearing, and stopped. Scarlett rose, standing to see where they were. She didn't see anything. No building. No place to sleep.

"Where are we?" she asked, barely loud enough for her squadron to hear.

Malak looked around before answering. "This is a forest," he responded simply. Scarlett rolled her eyes but resisted a sarcastic answer.

The White who had been driving them stretched and turned around. "Grab a satchel," he said, serious as always. Scarlett looked toward a stack of four satchels that were in the footwells of the Jeep. Malak took the first one, hurrying to unzip it. Rhys handed one to Devon and one to Scarlett. She looked inside but didn't see anything, unless the inside of the bag counted. It was fluffy. As Scarlett pulled at what she thought was the lining, she realized it was something like a blanket, but slicker.

She continued to pull and found everyone else doing the same, in different stages of disgorging the satchels.

"Okay, what is this?" Scarlett asked.

Malak answered yet again. "These are sleep sacks," he responded. "I've never seen one before." He stepped out of the Jeep and held the sack against himself. It went up to his shoulders. Scarlett turned back to hers.

"So, we're sleeping here?" she asked.

"Looks like it," Devon said, hopping out of the Jeep and stretching his sleeping bag out to get a better look.

"How long do you think we'll be traveling in these Jeeps?" Scarlett asked Rhys.

He shrugged. "I don't know, but I know that I'm not quite ready to arrive in City 6 yet."

Scarlett nodded. "So, where do I use the bathroom?" That was really what she was worried about. That and the fact that she had always showered every day. It didn't look like they would be showering that night.

Rhys shrugged. "You could just go behind those trees."

Scarlett looked at him with shock. "Um, how? That won't really work."

Scarlett saw two Blue females heading into the trees, and she wondered if they were going to the bathroom as Rhys had suggested.

"Be back in a minute," Scarlett said, hurrying after them. They turned to see who was crashing through the forest after them. "Hi," Scarlett said, giving a little wave.

One of the females lifted her eyebrow as if to ask what Scarlett was doing.

"I'm just . . . would like to use the bathroom," she explained.

One of the Blues laughed. "You won't find a bathroom out here."

"So, how do I—?" Scarlett left her question unfinished.

"You . . ." the Blue stopped and gave her a strange look. "That's right. You're not really a Blue. You're the Greenie."

Scarlett frowned, even though everything they said was completely true.

"Well, if you *were* a Blue, you would have received our survival training. Things like using the bathroom in the forest are no big deal."

"You use a leaf," the other Blue said, laughing a little bit. "Now, come on. I don't have time to talk." She took off farther into the forest. It surprised Scarlett how just a few steps past the trees could quiet the sounds from the big group and make them impossible to see. She used the bathroom in the woods and hurried back as quickly as possible. She had never thought of herself as squeamish, and in comparison to Jaylin and Miya, she wasn't. But as a Blue, she had a lot to learn.

* * *

After another strange package dinner, Scarlett settled into her sleep sack. As it became dark, it got very cold in the forest. She burrowed her hands deep into the sack and listened to the light conversation around her. Most people were talking about City 6 and what they would see when they arrived. Scarlett wanted to listen, if only to soothe her fears, but she was so tired that her eyes drooped slowly closed.

The next morning, there was no morning bell to wake them. Instead a harsh whistle cut through their sleep.

"Good morning," Devon said, sitting up right next to Scarlett. Had he slept there the whole night? He certainly hadn't been there when Scarlett drifted off to sleep!

"Hey," Scarlett said, her eyes immediately scanning for Rhys. He was on the other side of the camp, next to another male. Scarlett frowned. Was he trying to stay away from her or not?

"What did you think of the sleep sack?" Devon asked.

Scarlett looked over at him, annoyed that he was interrupting her thoughts. "Yeah, it's fine."

"I heard that in the City, you always sleep in these."

"Really? I thought it would be a lot like the training center, except you know, smaller."

Devon shrugged. "Malak seems to know everything, and that's what he said."

"So, are we going to sleep on the floor?" Scarlett asked, not worried about the possibility, just trying to prepare herself.

Devon shrugged, stretching. "I don't know. We'll find out soon though."

As he stretched his arms upward, his body odor smacked Scarlett in the face, and she turned away in surprise. Could one day without a shower really affect them so much? Did she smell the same way?

Scarlett decided to find an appropriate place to use the bathroom, so she left Devon without further comment. When she was exiting the forest, she almost ran into Rhys.

"Oh, hey," he said. "How did you sleep?"

Scarlett shrugged. "It was strange, but I guess I was tired enough, it didn't matter." Rhys nodded, and they passed each other, continuing in their own directions.

* * *

After a midday stop, they emerged from the forest, and Scarlett could see buildings in front of them. They were still a distance away, and the dirt the Jeeps kicked up made it difficult to see, but she could make out shorter buildings than what the training center had. There was a familiar-looking fence around City 6, just like at their training centers. And there was a bright white building by the edge of the fence.

"Do you see it?" Scarlett asked, plopping back into her seat.

The boys nodded, craning their necks to get their own view. Malak's face was serious, but Devon and Rhys both looked just as excited as Scarlett felt. They had never left the training center, so even though their job was serious, they were all excited to see something new.

After another hour of traveling in the vehicle, they were reaching the edge of the City. The Jeeps stopped in a line, and their White driver turned around.

"Everyone get out. They will be carefully checking the vehicles, and you as well, to make sure we do not have any forbidden materials."

"Forbidden materials?" The driver didn't answer, but as Scarlett followed her squadron out of the Jeep, Malak explained.

"You can never be too careful. They check every vehicle and person exiting and entering the city so they can make sure nothing is going where it shouldn't be."

"Like what?"

Malak shook his head. "You really should have attended the Blue history classes. We learned so much about the inner workings of the Cities."

Scarlett rolled her eyes. She didn't need a lecture from Malak. Instead, she hopped out of the Jeep and walked a few steps away so she could see City 6, her new home, just a little better. The building built against the fence was made of whitewashed stone. A few windows farther out had bars on them, just as their training center windows did, to prevent any accidents when they were opened for the cool air.

Scarlett's eyes traveled down the building's two stories. She saw the walking paths, much wider than the ones typically around the training center. But the strange thing was that there were not multiple buildings, perhaps several for both males and females. Instead, there were small buildings, nestled under roofs of metal. The buildings could not hold more than one dormitory. Why was each dormitory in a separate building?

Scarlett took a few steps forward without realizing what she was doing.

"Back in line," a White from another Jeep shouted. Scarlett was startled and stepped back to her squadron, noticing that their driver was staring at her. Scarlett reddened as she realized she had already started committing errors before even entering the City.

"Why are they so small?" Scarlett asked Rhys in a lowered voice.

He was staring at the City with surprise as well. He shrugged. "I don't know, but I think this City isn't going to be anything like our training centers."

"You're right about that," Malak agreed, entering their conversation uninvited. "The small buildings are living spaces for families. Families generally consist of three to four members, and each family has a separate space."

"Families?" Scarlett asked. She might not like his delivery, but he sure had a lot of useful information.

Chapter 7

Scarlett's squadron finally reached the gate. The Whites began to search through the Jeep, moving seats and opening their sleep sacks. Scarlett watched with interest. A female White came over to her.

"Spread your arms out like this." Scarlett followed her demonstration. She hadn't been paying attention to the previous squadrons passing through the gate. She had been too busy gathering as much information as she could from Malak. Apparently, "families," as they were called, were units created to care for children. They consisted of a male and female and were similar to the training center but smaller.

Scarlett spread her arms and almost stepped back when the White began patting her down. Females were allowed to touch females, but the way she was patting was strange. Scarlett didn't ask questions, though. Back when she had been a Green, the Blues had always told her she should learn by listening and watching instead of talking. So, Scarlett watched as each of the three males on her squadron were patted down by a male White. She knew what Malak had said, but it didn't make any sense. What could they be bringing in that they shouldn't? Where would they even obtain something they weren't supposed to have?

"You may enter," one of the Whites said. Scarlett's squadron scrambled back into the vehicle before they rolled slowly behind the gate. The gate screeched into place behind them. All of the squadrons were in.

Scarlett waited for further instruction. Their driver motioned for them to get out of the Jeep. They got out, all looking at each other. Each of the other squadrons was motioned out of their vehicles, as well. The Jeeps were guided into a garage while one White led the group of Blues into the whitewashed building.

The sea of white uniforms before her surprised Scarlett. She had never seen so much white in one place before. "Wow," she said in a low voice. Some of the Whites turned to the Blues entering, surveying them.

One White stepped forward. "Welcome," the male White said. He reached forward to the first Blue's hand. He shook his hand and moved down the line. Scarlett's stomach turned over as he shook each person's hand, male and female alike. The White came to her. He said in a low voice. "Thank you for coming."

A few other Whites followed the first one's example, going down the line of new Blues. Scarlett's hand was shaken several times, the experience foreign to her. She turned to the other females to see how they were accepting the gestures. They didn't seem at all bothered.

"We'll show you around," the first White said. "My name is Irin. I'm sure you'll get to know us quite well in the next few days. Each of your squadrons will be assigned to a White squadron, and you will work together in an eight-hour shift. We rotate in three shifts per day."

Scarlett nodded, accepting the information. As Irin continued to speak, she peered around the heads of other Blues to see the entrance area more clearly. The walls were made of stones or cement. The floor was cement, and Scarlett saw a long hallway leading straight ahead of her and one to her right. The group began moving forward at a shuffle as Irin led them to the dining hall.

"This is where you will come three times a day to eat. Depending on what shift you have, your meal times will vary." Irin led the group of forty

Blues to a machine embedded in the wall. "Each of you will be given a number. This number will be used for various things, including leaving and entering the building. You will also use your number to get your meals."

Irin pointed to the keypad on the machine. Scarlett stood on her toes to get a better view, but she could hardly see. She wasn't short, but she certainly couldn't see over so many males, who tended to be taller and thicker than the females.

"You'll put your code in here, and your meal will come out. You're not to share your meal with anyone for any reason."

Scarlett wrinkled her nose. What a strange rule! Why would she want to share her meal with someone?

"You can sit anywhere to eat," Irin motioned to the empty dining hall. "Then, any waste will go in this deposit here." He indicated a hole in the wall. "Any questions about meals?"

After a brief two-second pause, he began walking quickly across the dining hall. Scarlett was able to get an up-close glance at the meal distributor as they hurried toward their next part of the tour. She was used to receiving her meal from a human. But this seemed so much more sophisticated.

"This place is so cool!" a Blue female squealed. Scarlett turned just enough to see it was Amirah. Scarlett didn't want to say that all the changes made her worried. How long would her code be? What if she forgot it? What if she did something wrong because there was a new rule that she didn't even know about?

"This room," Irin indicated, "is where we generally spend our time when not on duty. There are many forms of entertainment available, and both males and females are allowed in this room." Everyone poked their heads in the large room as they continued to walk past. There were chairs, but they were strange chairs. They looked plush, like pillows. There were different games, both cards and others that Scarlett didn't recognize. There was a giant screen on the wall, as well, with seats lined up in front of it.

"Next, we have the bathrooms," Irin pointed to the males' and females' separate bathrooms, one on each side of the hall. "These are the bathrooms for our Blues. We have very few Blues right now, so it will mostly be the lot of you."

Irin stopped in front of another two doors, one on each side of the hall. He pointed to their left. "This is the Blue males' dormitory. On the right, this is for the females." Irin nodded down the rest of the hall where a set of stairs turned upward.

"Upstairs are the accommodations for the Whites and a few offices and meeting rooms, as well as their entertainment room. You shouldn't have need to go upstairs until you become a White, if you reach that point. We don't appreciate snoopers, so stay where you belong," Irin moved his hand to indicate the area they had just come through.

"The exercise area is down the other hallway from the entrance. You'll go through the dining hall to reach it. Any questions?"

A Blue female lifted her hand shyly.

"Yes," Irin said, nodding in her direction.

"When will we know what shift we're on or what White squadron we'll be working with?"

Irin continued to stare at her as though she hadn't said anything. The Blue female broke his gaze and looked around at her fellow Blues to see if they understood what was happening.

"Sir," a Blue male whispered.

The Blue female repeated her question. "When will we know what shift we're on, Sir?"

Irin gave a tight smile. "You will be given assignments in the morning. This evening, you will be allowed to adjust to the facility. Tomorrow, you will begin working your eight-hour shift each day or night."

Everyone shuffled around quietly as they waited for some sort of signal or direction.

"You are free to go. For your next meal, you should be in the dining hall between nineteen and twenty hours."

With that, the group split, females investigating their dormitory while the males mostly headed toward the entertainment room. Scarlett couldn't think about anything else other than taking a hot shower.

She entered the dormitory but didn't see any sort of personal effects on the beds. In the bathroom, she found communal soap in the shower and clean towels folded on a rack. Scarlett grabbed one and hopped into the shower. There was only a single knob instead of two. Scarlett turned it on, standing out of the way so she could let it heat up. She stuck her hand under, feeling the water. Nothing. She turned the knob farther, but it didn't seem to make a difference in the water temperature. It just made the head spit out stronger streams.

Scarlett shivered, goosebumps scattering over her skin as she patiently flipped the knob back and forth, looking for a balance. A few minutes later, she still hadn't had success, and she could hear the other females in the showers screeching.

"It's actually cold!" one Blue said.

"You knew it would be!" another shouted back. "Don't be a baby about it."

"I knew it wouldn't be hot, but I didn't know that meant ice cream cold."

Scarlett smiled a little bit. So, it wasn't only her.

"Anyone getting hot water?" the same Blue called out.

Scarlett joined the chorus of *no*s.

"Great," the Blue said. Scarlett took a deep breath and dove under the waves of ice. When she stood in her towel after the shower, she could safely say that had been her fastest shower ever.

"That's one way to save water," Scarlett said with a smile to another shivering Blue.

The Blue laughed. "Yeah, that's right, though I hear Whites get hot water, like they just want to torture us. I'm Gayla. What's your name?"

"Scarlett," Scarlett said. They both nodded to each other; then they got dressed and moved around to warm up. Scarlett noticed a gash on Gayla's stomach, just under her belly button. Scarlett looked away, wondering what had happened but not wanting to ask. She wondered if it was similar to the brown mole on her upper stomach, a mark she had obtained through the birthing process.

Scarlett could still smell the soap on her skin as she decided to check out the exercise room. She'd never exercised inside before. There was no space big enough in the training center. She wondered what sort of machines they would have. Besides, the weather at the training centers was always the same—hot and hotter.

When Scarlett reached the exercise room, she was surprised to see it nearly as big as the dining room. Most of those in the exercise room were the Blues with whom she had just arrived. There were a few Whites scattered throughout, and clearly the Blues were giving them precedence at the best machines. Scarlett stood in the doorway for a few moments, observing those in the room.

Rhys wasn't among them but Devon was. He was lifting weights on a barbell. Scarlett watched as he strained to straighten his arms above his head. Another Blue male was spotting him. Devon lowered the bar and lifted it again. She couldn't see the numbers on the weights, but she knew it more than double what she could lift. She really just wanted to do some cardio. Those two days of sitting in a Jeep made her muscles feel weak.

Scarlett headed to a cycling machine and began working her legs as she stared at the wall, turning over everything she had learned in the last hour. One thing she did know was that her not being a Blue meant there was a lot she didn't know, which everyone else seemed to know. She had to find a way to make up for that knowledge. Scarlett's eyes fell on Devon. He wasn't a know-it-all like Malak. Maybe he could get her up-to-date, but the thing was, she didn't even know what questions to ask. Why was everything so different?

Devon turned and looked at Scarlett all of a sudden, as though he could feel her eyes burning a hole through him. He stood and shook hands with his spotting partner before going over to her cycling machine.

"What do you think?" he asked, nodding at the room.

Scarlett smiled. "It's neat. Very different from what we have at the training centers . . . or had. I guess that's not our home anymore."

"It'll take some adjusting," Devon replied.

Scarlett slowed her legs on the machine to a leisurely pace so she could talk without gasping between words. "So, what do I need to know?" she asked.

Devon shook his head. "About what?"

"About here, about the Cities, about City 6. I mean, as a Green, we mostly work on our physical preparation. We do regular classes, but we don't get any details on current situations or what to expect going into a City. Because, you don't go into a City as a Green."

"Ah," Devon nodded. "Yeah, they have a reason for that. There's a lot to learn."

"So, how much of today's information was a surprise to you?"

"Well, I've never been inside a City compound before. So, the tour was new."

"But did you know things like the number for food . . . and those *families* Malak said?"

Devon nodded. "Yeah, we had to take a City Society class where they explained all about what living in a City is like—duties, our job, etc."

"What do I need to know?" Scarlett asked.

Devon thought for a minute. "I'll tell you. Most of what we learned was pretty boring, so really, you went the best route. Skip the hours of classes and get the most important information in ten minutes."

Scarlett didn't respond as she cracked her neck and waited for Devon to get to the point.

"Basically, the people who live in the City have not been trained as we have. We were given the privilege of growing up in a training center, and we know exactly what the Government has done for us. But sometimes, Citizens get confused about that. They think that we are against them. We aren't. Our job is to keep order in the City. Let's say one Citizen steals food from another Citizen; it's our job to rectify that."

Scarlett nodded.

"But what does a shift look like? What do we do?"

"Your shift is mostly patrolling, seeing if anybody is breaking the rules, making sure the Citizens know we are always there for them to keep them safe. If there's an incident, we respond to it."

Scarlett nodded. This reflected some of what she had learned in her history classes. "So, why did they make us come out here all of a sudden?"

Devon shrugged. "That . . . is not something we learned in class. But, based on what I've heard, the Citizens aren't respecting the Government. They are working against us, trying to make their own decisions."

Scarlett nodded. That made sense. She remembered when she had tried to make her own decisions as a Red. It never ended well. Once, she had tried to go down the slide in the Reds' play area headfirst, even though she had been told not to. Well, it hadn't ended well. Rules were there for everyone to prosper. She thought about visiting the Mound while she had been at the training center. She wouldn't have run into the strange male if she had stayed in the dorms like she was supposed to. And just thinking of him made her feel nervous.

"And families? Why would they use small units instead of large units like we have?"

Devon shrugged. "Partly because there are so many adults, I suppose. Because we get sent out to work as adults, there are not enough adults to live as a family unit at training centers."

"I can't imagine living like that," Scarlett said. "I would be so lonely. Could you imagine not having any Blue males to socialize with, just a female and a Red or something?"

Devon laughed. "It wouldn't work as well either. How could you train a Red and complete your job at the same time?"

Scarlett shrugged, and there was silence for a moment as Scarlett continued working her legs at an even pace. "Thanks, Devon."

"No problem. I'm here to help you."

Scarlett started pedaling harder, her mind turning over the information she had received. She was ready to embrace her role in society, even if it included cold showers. As her mind turned over the idea of daily cold showers, she suddenly wondered. Had Citizens who grew up in a City never had a hot shower before? The idea was mind-boggling.

* * *

A speaker mounted in the corner of the ceiling began belching names and directing them to the office on the second floor. Scarlett idled on the machine, her legs moving in slow circles as her muscles radiated heat. She wanted her name to be called. She was more curious than ever about how things happened here, and she was hoping that whatever was happening when a name was called would help answer her questions.

A White approached Scarlett. "I'd like to use that machine now."

Scarlett nodded and hopped off so quickly that she lost her balance. She stumbled and righted herself, her face red. "Well, there you go," she said. She hurried out of the exercise room, looking for Rhys. She hadn't talked to him since they had arrived, and she wanted to see what he thought of the place. Even though he was a Blue, he hadn't had the training the rest of them had had. Surely he was just as surprised by the oddities as she was.

Scarlett walked slowly through the empty, well almost empty, dining hall. There were two White females in the back corner talking in low voices. Scarlett tried to wave so it wouldn't look like she was ignoring them, but they didn't give any indication of noticing her.

Scarlett stopped at the entertainment room. There was Rhys, trying out a machine. Apparently, the machine would shuffle the cards for you and spit them back out when you were ready to draw. Scarlett hurried over to inspect the machine and get a chance to talk to Rhys.

"How was your workout?" Rhys asked, pressing a button on the machine. The machine screeched at him, and they both leaned back.

Scarlett started laughing. "I don't think the machine likes you. And how did you know I was working out?"

"Because I saw you in the exercise room, and normally working out is the purpose for being there?"

Scarlett rolled her eyes at his sarcasm. "I didn't see you."

"You were talking to Devon," Rhys responded.

"Oh, well, yeah," Scarlett didn't know how to respond. "I asked him a bunch of questions about what he learned being a Blue."

"Yeah, we're really at a disadvantage here," Rhys agreed. "I know why they have the Blue society classes, and it makes me wonder why we were picked to come along on this mission if we weren't given the same preparation as everyone else?"

Scarlett sat in one of the chairs at the table as Rhys continued to fidget with the machine. "I don't know. I mean, you, you're top of your class. That's why you were promoted to Blue. But me? I don't think I'm supposed to be here."

They both thought as the machine finally spit the cards out. Rhys began dealing them both some cards, ignoring the Blue female that hovered at the corner of the table as though she might like to play. They continued their silence, conscious of the listening ears.

"What game are we playing?"

"Let's play 42," Rhys suggested as he placed the remaining cards back in the machine. "You up for losing?"

Scarlett smiled. "Hey, let's just wait and see your card skills before you get so confident."

"I'm telling you the truth," Rhys protested. "Why don't you believe me?"

Scarlett shrugged. "I tend to not believe it until I see it."

"Hold on a few minutes then," Rhys said, placing his first card in the middle. It was quickly followed by three more.

Scarlett gave him a disapproving look. "Okay, that doesn't count. You got a lucky first hand. Maybe what you're really good at is dealing."

"Are you suggesting I'm not honest?"

Scarlett shrugged as she hid her smile with her cards. She had never played a game like this with Rhys. Cards were only allowed in the dormitory during free hours. Normally, Rhys helped her with her shooting technique or they worked out together. This was very different.

"I see you chose not to answer."

"I think you're honest when it matters," Scarlett responded, laying down just one card. Rhys continued his streak of luck by laying down another two cards. Scarlett shook her head in disbelief.

She looked over her shoulder and saw that the Blue female had moved on. They were as alone as they were going to be.

"Be honest," Scarlett saw Rhys was about to interject with something humorous, and she waved her cards at him. "Seriously. Why am I here?"

Rhys was quiet for a few minutes, taking his turn and looking up at her to indicate it was her turn. He finally shook his head. "I don't know. Because the training centers thrive on policy and predictability. Sure, you don't know exactly when you'll become a Blue. It's usually a surprise, but there's a process. You're told. You're given a day to adjust to the uniform and schedule changes. You receive the procedure. You begin training, and still, it's usually at least a year before you can hope for an assignment."

Rhys was saying everything Scarlett already knew.

"Rhys," she said, lowering her voice. "I. . .feel a little bit scared. Because there's no good reason for me to be here. Except what that male said..."

Rhys shook his head and placed a few more cards down, frowned, and took one from the stack. "Just don't think about him," Rhys said.

"But I thought you said that . . ."

"Don't think about him," Rhys repeated, his words slow and even. "Look, I'm not going to sit here for two months and listen to you freaking out about this crap every day. I want to enjoy being a Blue, being here on assignment. Finally, we're going to do something important, the thing that we have been training for since we became Reds."

Scarlett nodded as she pursed her lips. It hurt, what he had said. Like, she should just shut up. But he was partly right; she shouldn't obsess over something completely crazy. She wished she could get an unbiased opinion, but Jaylin and Miya weren't here, and she didn't have anyone else she could confide in. Jaylin and Miya would never tell on her for breaking the rules, but these guys? Scarlett had a feeling they would turn her over faster than she could shoot a target.

Scarlett didn't say anything as the game continued. When Rhys won, Scarlett shook her head good-naturedly.

"I told you I would win," Rhys shrugged in fake modesty. "I tried to give you a fighting chance, but you know, I didn't want the game to last all day."

Scarlett heard her name over the speakers, and she stood automatically. "I guess I better go find that office," she said, heading out into the hallway and toward the stairs. Her stomach felt nervous. They had been told not to go upstairs unless they were required to do so. She was up there legally, but it still felt like she was doing something wrong. Breaking the rules here felt much more serious than the training center.

She passed similar doors to their dormitory and bathrooms. She passed some doors that didn't have windows until she reached an open door at the far end of the hallway. Scarlett paused in front of the door. The male sitting behind the desk was dressed all in black. Scarlett only knew of two Blacks- Mrs. and Mr.-. Once you became a Black, your name was considered sacred, and no one was allowed to use it. You had your own quarters, and disobedience to you would result in severe punishment.

Scarlett did an odd combination of curtseying and nodding her head. The Black nodded for her to come in. He studied her, his eyes a light color behind his bushy brows. "Scarlett," he spoke her name slowly.

Scarlett nodded. "Yes, Sir."

The Black studied her for another few moments, then he nodded toward the corner. Scarlett was surprised to see a White female standing there. She had been so worried about making a good impression or the Black finding something wrong with her, that she hadn't noticed much else.

Beside the White female was a scale.

"Please step on," the White requested.

Scarlett stepped on and looked at the number. She hadn't been weighed in at least eight months, since her last physical. 128. She looked to the White female to see if she would approve. The White female was marking on a screen. She pointed without looking up, and Scarlett found a measure against the wall to compute her height. She stood tall and waited for approval to move away from the wall.

Her eyes flicked back and forth from the White to the Black. The White showed the screen to the Black, and he pushed a few buttons. Scarlett was asked to press her fingers onto the screen. They took her picture and scanned her eyes. Then, they spent what felt like a long time hovering over the screen.

The Black finally looked up. "Your number is 1325."

Scarlett repeated the number in her head, desperate not to forget it.

"Do you have any questions?" the Black asked slowly as though she had better not.

"No, Sir," Scarlett responded, making eye contact with him. He held eye contact with her a few more moments until she looked down.

"You will be on second shift," he said. After another elongated pause, he added, "You may go."

Scarlett hurried out of the office, keeping herself from running as she reached the stairs. She reached the bottom floor and breathed more easily. She decided to stay in the dormitory for a few moments. She wanted to process what had happened.

Scarlett hadn't yet selected a bed as she had been more preoccupied about showering and exercising than where she would be sleeping that night. She walked slowly around the perimeter of the room, looking for an unoccupied bed. She found one on the far left. It was a top bunk. Scarlett frowned. She hated top bunks, but the only other one was a top bunk too. Oh well. She would just hope she didn't roll out of bed in the middle of the night and break something.

When it was dinner time, Scarlett followed the other Blues into the dining hall. A line formed beside the keypad as each person punched in their number and received their meal. Scarlett watched as person after person received a small tray with hot food. It looked much more appetizing than the food in a bag they had been consuming earlier.

Scarlett was in line in front of Rhys and punched in her number carefully 1-3-2-5.

She took her small platter of food and waited for Rhys to punch in his number. She watched his fingers move over the keyboard. 2-8-0-9. He took his plate, and they looked for an empty table.

"There's space by Devon," Scarlett pointed out. Rhys shrugged, and they walked over to where Devon was sitting with a few of the Blues who had been in City 6 before Scarlett's squadron arrived.

Scarlett picked up her fork and began to dig into her food, but as she did, she looked across the table at Rhys' platter. He had almost double the amount of food as Scarlett had. Her eyes quickly flicked to Devon's then the other platters at their table. All of them had larger plates. Scarlett looked back at her own.

Everyone had always gotten the same amount of food in the training centers. Of course, she had only ever eaten with females there. But on the road, they had all received the same packet of food, hadn't they? Scarlett took a bite of hers as she watched the males eat their plates of food. They were talking about something, and Scarlett knew she probably shouldn't miss any tidbit of information. One of the Blues she didn't know was laughing.

"No way! You've got it all wrong. They say you only work an eight hour shift every day, but that's a lie. You're just out of the compound eight hours a day. But when you get back, you have to complete the chores, which you get every week. I have washing this week, which sucks. So, then, once you finish those, you get free time. If you finish those."

Devon shook his head. "I thought there were specific Blues here just for washing or cooking, like at the training center."

"No way!" the same Blue explained, laughing like Devon was telling the funniest jokes ever. He clearly lacked real amusement in his daily life.

"What shift are you?" Scarlett asked, trying to figure out when she would be working, and if this fool would be covering her back.

"First," he responded as though just noticing her at their table. "You came in today too?"

Scarlett nodded, turning back to her food.

"Well, it's a pleasure to meet you. My name is Haman." He held his hand out as if he wanted to shake her hand. Scarlett looked at Rhys uncertainly.

Rhys stepped in. "Rhys, nice to make your acquaintance," he responded formally, shaking Haman's open hand.

Haman shook his hand, but his eyes flicked back to Scarlett. "What's your name?"

"Scarlett," she responded begrudgingly. She didn't like this male. She didn't like many males to be honest. Rhys was the only one she could stand for more than a few minutes time, though Devon was starting to reach a point where she didn't cringe when he started a conversation.

Haman nodded toward her, taking a giant bite of his food. The table floated in awkward silence while everyone chewed.

"You know," Haman said, having finished his large mouthful. "Touching isn't prohibited here."

Devon narrowed his eyebrows, Rhys looked confused, and Scarlett tipped her head to the side. What was he talking about?

Haman laughed like he was joking. He nudged his Blue buddy. "Right, Oliver?"

Oliver shrugged and nodded in a weird way that didn't confirm anything.

Devon shook his head. "No. We took a class about the Society of Cities, and it's true that in the Societies, among family units, touching isn't prohibited. But. . .that doesn't extend to us." Devon looked over his shoulder to where Malak was seated two tables over.

Haman shrugged. "Don't believe me then, but it's true."

Devon stood and retrieved Malak as though his knowledge were pertinent for the conversation. "Haman, here is telling us that touching is not prohibited. You're talking about between males and females, right?"

Haman nodded.

"So?" Devon asked Malak. Malak, already a tall individual, towered over them all as he screwed up his face in thought.

Malak leaned on the end of the table, his fingers splayed against the metallic surface. "There is no set rule against contact between males and females," Malak started. Before he could finish, Devon and Scarlett erupted in protest. Rhys was silent as he considered all the little pieces of the puzzle.

Haman cackled like a hyena as Devon and Scarlett continued to protest.

When it was quieter, except for an occasional chuckle from Haman, Malak continued. "However, there is no express permission either. The only course of action to be sure any contact is authorized would be to explicitly ask the Black." Devon was silent about that. No one was about to bring up such a question to the Black.

Haman laughed as they scratched their heads. "You're not in the training centers anymore."

Scarlett's eyes flicked to Rhys as she thought about how it felt the few times they had brushed hands when exchanging weapons, the tingles that reverated through her. If touching was prohibited, strangely, she felt a desire to explore those feelings more. Rhys rolled his eyes at Haman and got up, taking his tray with him. But, of course, Scarlett reminded herself. Rules were there for a reason. Just because there wasn't as much supervision here didn't mean they should go making their own. Scarlett highly doubted that such a serious rule would suddenly be taken away.

Chapter 8

The next day, Scarlett woke up to a scramble in her room. Females were pulling on their Blue suits and hurrying toward the door. Scarlett, half-asleep, pulled on her Blue suit and trailed after them, zipping and buttoning as she walked down the hallway. Some of the Blues were having a meal in the dining hall, while others congregated at the end. Scarlett didn't even notice the ones eating. She followed the Blues through bleary eyes.

They stopped by the entrance and began punching in their codes. Scarlett got in line, yawning, her eyes half-closed as she moved forward in a shuffle. She punched her code on the box, and the box beeped red. The entrance door locked in place, and all the Blues crowding around the area turned to look at her accusingly.

The alarm woke Scarlett up, and she looked around at the Blues. "What are you doing here?" a White asked. "You're second shift. Shift changes should be smooth. Now, we have to wait five minutes before the entrance door will open again."

Scarlett took a step backward toward the dining hall. "Sorry," she said.

"Rookie," the White muttered in a nasty tone.

Scarlett wandered, feeling a bit lost as she meandered back to the dorm. She looked over her shoulder but couldn't see the group of Blues she had thought was her group. Scarlett thumped back onto her bed, yawning. Amirah was getting dressed at a leisurely pace.

"I thought I saw you rush out of here," she said, her voice low but not in a whisper. That was something Scarlett had never done before. Because everyone was on the same schedule at the training center, they all woke up at the same time. They never had to be quiet while others slept later. Scarlett began to think about the pleasure of sleeping late, not having to wake before the sun.

"Yeah," Scarlett shrugged. "Years of getting in trouble if you're not ready for morning exercise."

Amirah nodded. "That's one thing that's great about being a Blue at the training center. We have to work a night shift one night per week, but other than that, our wake up call isn't until breakfast. We do exercise in the late morning and afternoon."

Scarlett nodded. She had heard about the luxury of "sleeping in" as it was called.

"Well, I'm awake now," Scarlett said, standing up from her bed and heading to the exercise room. Years of exercising first thing in the morning had conditioned her to feel strange without it.

There were a few Blues there, but most were Whites. There weren't any machines available, so Scarlett settled for lifting a few weights in the corner. Rhys came up behind her. He grabbed the weights out of her hands as she turned around.

"Hey!"

Rhys held them above his head, both in one hand as Scarlett frowned at him. "Why'd you do that?"

"I didn't want you to whack me in the face with them. I appreciate my perfect vision."

Scarlett rolled her eyes and held out her hand for them. "Please?" she said.

Instead of handing them back, Rhys danced his eyebrows at her.

"I heard about your . . . ahem, eventful morning."

Scarlett cocked her head. "How?"

"One of the males told me."

"What? Who?"

Rhys shrugged. "I don't remember. His name is . . . Barrel . . . no, that's not right. Barry? Barth? Something like that."

Scarlett covered her face. "Great! Now, everyone is going to tell everyone! I'm going to be the biggest idiot here."

"Hey, I don't think anyone else would have recognized you from his description. Let's be honest, there are a lot of Blue females who are on the short side. But when I saw you in here, early in the morning of your own volition, I knew it must have been you."

"Great, awesome. I get to be famous!" Scarlett said without any real enthusiasm. She wondered if this was the sort of story that would be told to the Black. Would he care? Or would he pass it off as first-day mistakes? Was she allowed the leeway of making mistakes?

"So, when do we start our first shift?"

"We're on the second shift," Rhys explained. "It's 16:00–24:00."

Scarlett gave a short nod. "Okay, so no early mornings?"

"Not unless there is a specific training." Rhys shrugged, "At least that's how I understood it."

"I can't wait until I know exactly what I'm supposed to do, and when I'm supposed to do it, so I can stop feeling confused."

"You've been here less than a day. You can't expect to know it all yet."

A White in the doorway of the exercise room summoned a group of the new Blues, all second shift, and led them toward the dining hall. He took them through a door at the back of the room and showed them where the dishes were cleaned. Scarlett plunged her hands into the hot water, cringing slightly. She had never washed a dish before. She had assumed the Blues did those chores around the training center, though she didn't know for sure.

She pulled her hands out and rubbed them on her blue suit, looking around to see if anyone had noticed her unprofessional move. Everyone was busy with their own jobs. Devon was sorting dishes from utensils. Rhys was drying cleaned dishes and placing them on a moving rack.

Scarlett took a deep breath and plunged her hands in again, grasping at one of the dirty dishes at the bottom. She found it and used the sponge to scrub it, rubbing the crusted food. Her stomach rolled over as the food flakes fell into the water, the smell pungent. Scarlett breathed through her mouth as she reached for another dish.

* * *

At half past fifteen, they were led into the dining hall for their second meal of the day. Scarlett's stomach was rumbling. They normally ate their second meal no later than thirteen hours. She punched in her number, received her meal, and sat down, eating it as quickly as possible. She finished her food too quickly and looked longingly at Rhys's half-full plate.

"I would give you some," he said, "but, I don't want to risk getting in trouble."

"I'm just thinking about the fact that we have our first eight-hour shift ahead of us, and I'm not sure I'm going to last, being so active this late and without much food."

"You'll make it work," Rhys promised. "I mean, if it seems like they aren't giving you enough food, we could always talk to someone about it."

Devon continued to shove food in his mouth. For once, Malak was sitting with them.

"Why do they give us different amounts?" Scarlett ventured to ask Malak, who was eating his food in a slow, measured way. "Because I'm a female?"

"They want you to lose weight," Malak said. "Based on the amount of food you have received, that is my best guess."

"Lose weight? Why? I wouldn't say I'm fat."

Scarlett rubbed a hand self-consciously over her stomach.

Rhys and Devon both looked at her closely. Devon shrugged, and Rhys shook his head. "Maybe because you're short?" Devon ventured.

Scarlett didn't want the conversation to continue. She had always excelled in the physical challenges. As a Green, she had been able to meet her goals and continue challenging herself further. She didn't like the thought that someone now thought her inadequate.

Ten minutes later, Irin demanded they deposit their dishes in the depository. "We must be out of the compound and ready to take the first shift's place at exactly 16:00."

Scarlett's heart began beating harder as they reached the machine near the door. She remembered punching in the numbers that morning, eight hours before, the way the machine had lit up and screamed at her for her error. She let Rhys slip in front of her and watched him punch in his number. Then, it was her turn. 1-3-2-5. Relief slipped over her as the machine turned green, and the door allowed her through.

She stood next to Rhys, waiting for the rest of their shift to sign out through the machine. Now that she was on the verge of really seeing the City, she felt more excited than before.

Irin stood in front of the group of Whites and Blues. "Squadron Scorpio, you will work with Squadron Ten. Squadron Cancer, you will work with Squadron Seven. Squadron Gemini, you will work with Squadron Two. Blues, stay with your squadron leader. Do everything they ask. We do not tolerate opinions or dissonance. It is important that we present a unified front when working with the Citizens."

Scarlett followed Devon and Rhys to the leader of Squadron Scorpio. They were released from the compound, and Scarlett matched her pace to the rapid pace of their leader's. They started down a walking path that led away from the gate where they had entered the evening before. Scarlett looked around quickly, her eyes scanning for more and more details as she tried to watch their leader for any clues. They passed many of the small units called houses.

Scarlett saw a small child, not old enough to be a Red, peeking from a doorway. The child's skin was light brown, and the child had slightly wavy hair. However, as the child swung the door just a little wider to peer at them more closely, Scarlett didn't see the customary Brown uniform of Tinies. The child was wearing a small cloth to cover his or her privacy. But his or her chest and legs were bare. The child lifted a hand in greeting. Scarlett waved back to the child. And as she watched, a female snatched the child away from the door, slamming the door closed.

Scarlett frowned. Had the child broken a rule? Were the rules here different? Why wouldn't they be? Everything else was different.

Scarlett looked at her squadron, and Devon was watching her. He must have seen the interaction because he looked just as confused.

Their squadron leader stopped as they reached the edge of the City. Scarlett could see the fence bordering the City. The White male looked at each one of them closely then surveyed the nearby area. Scarlett felt a start of recognition. He was the White who had driven them from the training center to the City. She tried to see if any of her squadron recognized him as well, but they either didn't notice or didn't care.

"My name is Phan," he said. Scarlett pressed her first three fingers over her heart as seemed appropriate at that moment. Devon, Rhys, and Malak slowly followed suit.

"We patrol Section Two of the City. Our job is to look for any subordinance, anyone breaking the rules. We are here to protect the Citizens, so if we see one Citizen harming another, we may step in."

Scarlett felt nervous, her palms clammy. How were they to step in? What were they to do? She had been given a pistol, but surely, they weren't supposed to pull that out and begin threatening everyone.

"Each of you Blues will be with two of us," Phan explained. "As Irin stated, you don't have time to ask questions in certain situations. You must take our orders and follow them immediately. Do you understand?"

Everyone nodded. "We'll take the female," Phan said, pointing to Scarlett. Scarlett stepped forward, as if pulled toward her new partners.

Phan's radio crackled. "Is second shift on the way? We could use some backup."

Phan cursed in a low voice, then he and another White male began striding toward the left, parallel to the fence several walkways over. Scarlett hurried after them, looking over her shoulder to see Rhys watching her hurry away. She felt scared. She had to prove herself. She had to prove that she was supposed to be here, and she would do anything to serve her country.

"I'm Marse," the other White male tossed over his shoulder. Scarlett nodded, her hand self-consciously on her pistol as she tried to take in as many details as she could. The walkways were not as loose as the sand she was used to. It was more like the dirt they had driven over on their way to City 6. Threads of grass grew around the edges of the walkway. Luscious plants could be seen through the fence.

The three suddenly pulled up to a stop at a place where several walkways crossed. Scarlett saw several Whites and Blues gathered in a circle around some Citizens. Other Citizens were outside of the circle, shouting raucously.

Scarlett whipped her head around, trying to assess the situation. One of the Whites from the first shift nodded toward Phan. He lifted a palm to Scarlett, indicating that she should stay where she was. Scarlett waited beside Marse, her heart beating out a rapid rhythm.

Two Whites had a male between them. But this male was very different from the males Scarlett knew. He had long facial hair. The dark-colored hair on his head was long as well. His face was shielded by his hair, and his head hung low, as though he didn't care what was happening around him.

One of the Citizens outside the circle shouted. "Let him go! He's causing you no harm! He has two children at home to feed!"

Another Citizen shouted, "Doesn't matter who he has to feed! We all have the same rations! And he has no right to help himself to anyone else's!"

Phan took a small stick from a hook on his belt and with a shake, lengthened it. He used the stick to push the people back. Marse followed his leader's example. Scarlett reached for the hooks on her belt, but she had no such weapon. She stood helplessly, not sure what she could do anyway. One Citizen was pushing toward the male who was held by the Whites. He was completely silent, crouched low as he moved forward, the crowd shifting out of his way softly as though allowing a small child to pass.

Scarlett's eyes darted back and forth between the male and the other Whites in the area, waiting for one of them to do something.

The Citizen moved stealthily toward the Whites, coming from behind them. As Scarlett watched, the Citizen pulled out a knife, a short blade no longer than eight centimeters. Scarlett's heart beat fast. Her eyes were glued on the Citizen, unable to look away. She had to do something!

Scarlett took a big step forward. Once she started moving her legs, she didn't have to think about it. They moved of their own accord, on her way to stop the male. How? She wasn't exactly sure.

"Hey! Stop!" Scarlett shouted, when she was just a step and a half away from the Citizen. He turned toward her, his eyes narrowed and hate strong in his eyes. He didn't say anything, but her shout had drawn attention. The Citizen and Scarlett knew that he wouldn't be able to reach his intended target in time. He settled on Scarlett. He lunged toward her, the knife aimed at her stomach.

Scarlett leaped to the side, her combat training causing her body to react without her thoughts having to catch up to the situation. The Citizen's knife cut through empty air. Then, Phan was tackling the Citizen, pulling his hands roughly into handcuffs as the knife clattered to the ground.

Scarlett watched as the Citizen was detained. She looked around at the other Citizens, a fear of them dawning on her. Did they really hate them? They were all there to serve the same purpose, to support the Government in creating a healthy, thriving society.

Phan handed the Citizen to Marse to contain, as he turned to Scarlett. He grabbed her roughly by one shoulder, his touch strange. Scarlett felt the urge to fight out of his grasp, but she had to remember that he was her superior. He wouldn't break rules or bring harm to her.

"A Citizen tried to hurt a member of the Government, a Blue here to protect you." Phan's voice was loud, and the crowd was suddenly very silent, all eyes focusing on Scarlett. Phan pointed toward the male who had been detained for stealing. "A Citizen tried to harm another one of you by robbing you of the rations given by the Government. Whose crime is worse?"

The crowd was silent. No one was willing to answer. Scarlett watched them and was surprised to see a few signs of fear from the females who watched silently.

"None of you can answer me?" Phan called again. "Are you all so uneducated?"

One child shouted out, a child who was no more than seven years old. "Both is so bad, because you can't never hurt another person."

Phan pointed toward the child as a nearby female Citizen pulled the child back, chastising the child. For what, Scarlett didn't know. The child's logic seemed sound. "This child knows more than all of you. Long live the teachers who have educated this child correctly."

"Any crime that causes harm to another member of our society shall be punished!" Phan waited a few moments. "It doesn't matter if the crime is against a plain Citizen, such as you, or a faithful servant, such as us. No one shall be harmed as long as we are here to stop it."

A White entered, pushing through the circle of Citizens. He carried a long leather rope in his hands. Scarlett's stomach curled as the White came closer. The whip had small pieces of glass embedded in it, and Scarlett could only imagine the pain it could cause. She had once dropped her glass as a Yellow, and she had been made to clean it up. Crawling on her hands and knees to make sure she got all the pieces, a few pieces had invariably pierced her skin.

"First crime receives the first punishment!" Phan announced. The Whites holding the long-haired male stripped him of his shirt. They threw it down and tied his handcuffs to a stake in the ground. Scarlett took a step back. She understood the concept of consequences for your actions, but she had never seen anyone punished in such a cruel way. One of the Whites positioned himself and nodded toward Phan.

"How many strikes?"

"Ten!" Phan commanded.

The White began, the whip whistling through the air. The crack thundered out as it hit the male. The skin on his back immediately broke. Blood trickled down in various streams. The whip whistled again and another crack. Scarlett heard crying, but it was not the male. A female in the crowd was covering her face as she weeped. She shepherded two small children away from the crowd, down one of the walkways as they constantly looked back, trying to see what was happening.

"Mommy, where's Daddy?" one of the children asked. The female didn't answer, but that one word—Mommy—echoed in Scarlett's brain. It was a foreign word, one she had never before used. But at the same time, it felt strangely familiar. It gave her this strange warm feeling in her stomach and elicited curiosity; she wondered about what it meant.

Scarlett took a deep breath to steady herself, finding other objects on which she could focus as the long-haired male received his punishment. Finally, the cracks stopped. The male was slumped over. He had not uttered a sound during the punishment. Scarlett wondered if he could have died. His back was bloody, the skin torn. Scarlett, who had merely watched, felt her hands shaking.

Phan nodded toward one of the other Whites, and the White undid the male's handcuffs. He kicked him, but the male didn't respond. Finally, two Whites bent down and carried the male to the edge of the square. They set him down with a thump, and he still didn't move.

Phan stepped toward Scarlett, extending the whip toward her, handle first. Scarlett looked at him, confused.

"This Citizen intended to harm you. You will establish your dominance, even as a Blue, by punishing him."

"Uh," Scarlett didn't know what to say. She couldn't whip this male. She couldn't be responsible for his pain, for making his back bloody like the other Citizen's. Scarlett looked past Phan and saw Marse readying the Citizen, chaining his handcuffs to the stake in the ground. The Citizen tugged on the chain, pulling to see if the stake was loose. It wasn't.

Phan's patience was coming toward an end as he wiggled the whip at Scarlett.

"Now. You will punish him. Ten strikes."

"I, okay," Scarlett shakily took the whip from him. She took a trembling breath. The whip was long, and it felt heavy in her hands. She couldn't make eye contact with any of the Citizens around her as she took the place of the White who had punished the other Citizen. Scarlett's breath was short as though she had just finished her daily laps around the exercise ring.

She raised the whip, paused, and pushed it forward, watching as the end slapped the male's back. His back arched, and Scarlett watched, mesmerized, as the blood dribbled, at first hesitant, then insistent, moving down his back more quickly.

Before Scarlett had quite absorbed the shock of the first blow, Phan was urging her in a low, insistent voice. "Continue. Nine more strikes." Scarlett raised her hands above her head. She slashed the whip through the air, the clout echoing through her head. As though something in Scarlett snapped, she delivered the next eight strikes directly, no pause between them. She didn't seem to see anything as her mind counted to ten. When she reached ten, she dropped the whip at her feet, her arms feeling empty of strength.

Scarlett forced herself to view the male. He was moving, not still like the other male had been. His back was raw, trails of blood combining to form a river on his back. His skin was torn and hung in strips. Scarlett's stomach felt weak. She took a step backward and another. Hearing a noise behind her, she turned to find angry Citizens narrowing their gazes at her.

Phan loosened the male, giving him a kick as he freed him. A brave Citizen rushed forward and helped the male to his feet. The male limped toward the crowd, which parted to let him through.

"You have no reason to continue gathering here," Phan announced. "Justice has been served. Return to your duties." The reaction was immediate. Citizens dispersed, heading down the various walkways. Scarlett looked around at the Whites. One White female broke from her group. She must have been part of the first shift. Scarlett couldn't even think about what time it was or her duties or what they would be doing next. The only thought crossing her mind was what she had done to that male.

The White female stood in front of Scarlett. She was tall and thin. "You have done it," she said, her voice stern. "The first administration of castigation is always the most difficult. It gets easier. Thank you for serving our Government."

Scarlett nodded, giving the customary salute of her fingers over her heart. The first shift marched wearily toward the compound, and Scarlett was left in the square with Marse and Phan. She looked at them, waiting for further commands, her body feeling exhausted even though their shift was just starting.

"We'll begin a patrol round of our section, but I doubt we'll see much trouble after this," Phan said, folding the pole into a concise stick and sticking it through his belt. Scarlett followed Phan and Marse, her steps stiff.

The next seven hours were spent with Scarlett following the Whites, looking over her shoulder, wondering if someone would try to avenge the male's punishment. She had never seen someone try to hurt a White or a Blue. High ranking meant respect. No matter how much you might dislike the rules, everyone at the training center knew they were for their own good. Punishments were earned not given.

Scarlett saw three Whites walking toward them through the dark; their uniforms seeming to glow. The lights in the small houses had long since gone out, and the streets were quiet. Scarlett had held back more than a dozen yawns.

Finally, she could retire. Phan and Marse joined with Rhys and the two Whites he had been accompanying. When Scarlett saw Rhys, her throat caught, as though he knew exactly what had happened to her, what she had done. She wanted him to tell her it was alright, that she had done the right thing. What other choice had there been?

As they joined with the other Blues and Whites, Rhys reached out and squeezed Scarlett's hand briefly. It was dark. The only lights came from Phan's and another White's light at the front of the group. Scarlett squeezed his hand back, trying to see his face through the dark. Had his first shift been just as difficult?

They saw the compound up front, and another squad was just entering. Scarlett watched as they were forced to look into a small box before being allowed to enter. Scarlett followed the actions of the others, and a red laser briefly lit up her face, surprising her into squeezing her eyes shut. Then, the door slammed behind them, and they were back in the compound.

Scarlett let out a deep breath. Rhys nodded toward the dining hall. Only the second shift was eating. The third shift was out, and the first shift was probably sleeping. Rhys guided Scarlett toward a table at the far end of the dining hall, and they set down their food. Scarlett stared at her food for a few minutes. Despite the hunger she had felt when consuming her last meal, she hadn't felt a return of that raging appetite.

"Okay, what happened?" Rhys asked. "I can tell something made you mad or something."

Scarlett told him what happened. "I punished a Citizen today."

Rhys nodded, no surprise showing on his face.

Scarlett continued. "He was trying to attack a White. I stopped him before he could. He had a knife! He was going to hurt a person . . . with a knife!" Scarlett pushed her fingers together one by one, until she had made a tent with her hands. She crushed the tent, then traced her thumb with her other. "I had to whip him."

When she looked up, Rhys's eyes looked angry . . . or maybe only firm. She shrugged. "I didn't want to, but I had to. Phan made me. And I know what the male Citizen did was wrong, but I still feel really bad, like it's all my fault."

Rhys chewed his lower lip. "My shift was pretty uneventful, I guess. We just walked around and watched some peaceful transactions. But you knew this was going to be different. I mean, do you think he was intending to kill someone?"

Scarlett shrugged. "I don't know. Maybe. At least hurt them pretty badly. I can't imagine what would happen if that knife was stuck in you. He almost stuck it in my stomach, but I was able to get out of the way in time."

"See?" Rhys reasoned. "This male was clearly someone who deserved punishment. Maybe if he hadn't tried to hurt you, he would have tried to hurt someone else. You were saving that other person from being hurt."

"He looked at me so angrily, like he might . . . try again or something. I kept looking over my shoulder the whole rest of my shift." Scarlett let out a long breath, ruffling her rice. "I thought coming here, it would be, like, helping people. But so far, it feels like . . . I don't know, hurting them."

"Tomorrow will be different," Rhys said, digging into his food. He glanced over Scarlett's shoulder and started talking. "Hey, want to sit with us?"

It was Devon, Scarlett realized when she turned to look over her shoulder. "Hi," she said, wanting to hear about his experience. "How was your shift?"

Devon shrugged, shoving food into his mouth. Scarlett took a moderate bite of her food and waited to see what he would say, but he didn't seem his normal, light-hearted self.

"I'm ready to sleep," Devon finally said around a mouthful of chicken. Scarlett and Rhys nodded. While Scarlett's body felt tired, her mind was running circles.

"What did you do on your shift?" Scarlett asked again. She had never been one to tiptoe around questions.

Devon shrugged. "We patrolled Section Two, just like everybody else."

"What did you think? Seeing the City up close?"

Devon took another large bite of rice. "It's nothing like I thought it would be. I thought, us being the ones who protect everybody, that we would be kind of like heroes to them, people they look up to and trust. But . . . it's like they're afraid of us."

"Like the child in one of the first houses we passed?" Scarlett said. Devon nodded, remembering that first child they had seen.

"Maybe I'm just crazy. I mean, we all knew we were coming here because those here were having trouble holding down the fort, per se. They needed backup because some Citizens aren't contributing. At least, that's what I heard."

"But," Rhys cut in, "it's bigger than just a week-long problem. It seems to be part of them, this dislike for us."

The three finished their dinners in silence. They mulled over their agreement that the Citizens were very different than they imagined. Scarlett stood, finishing her plate of food quickly. She didn't want to sit there and watch Devon and Rhys eat the rest of theirs.

"I'll see you both in the morning," Scarlett said, heading to the bathroom. She knew it was after midnight, but she wanted to wash the day out of her body and hair, even though the shower would be cold.

Chapter 9

The next morning, Scarlett woke up with a negative feeling in her stomach. Her thoughts immediately turned to the evening before, and she began dreading that afternoon's shift. She curled into a ball and turned to face the wall. There was a clock on the wall in their dormitory, but Scarlett couldn't quite see it without leaning halfway out of her warm bed. And she wasn't ready for acrobatics yet. She could see, though, that first shift wasn't in their beds. So it must be after eight o'clock. It wasn't as though she would sleep and miss her shift, though. No way she could sleep for sixteen hours straight.

When Scarlett woke up again, she still had the sickish feeling in her stomach, and she realized she wasn't going to escape it. Besides, she wasn't tired enough to drift off again.

Scarlett shuffled to the females' bathroom. When she came out, she saw Rhys, his hair wet, walking down the hall toward the dining hall.

"Good morning," he said, crossing the hall.

Scarlett grimaced as she remembered their last conversation. "How can you be so cheery?"

"Because I'm on my way to food?"

Scarlett knew he was trying to make light of the conversation. She played along. "Make sure to save some for me. I get little enough as it is."

"Will do. Hey, they're going to give us Blues radios today. We have to be in the exercise room at ten for a training on how to use them."

"What time is it?"

"I think almost nine thirty."

"Ah, I better get dressed and hurry up then." Scarlett rushed into her room and thought about warning the other slow risers. But as she looked around, she realized that the only ones sleeping were the ones who had crept in after their third shift, collapsing on the beds.

Scarlett hurried down the hall to the dining hall. There were only a few people finishing up their meals. She pushed her number into the machine. The machine beeped a red flash at her, and a message rolled across its machine.

Not a meal time.

"What?" Scarlett tried punching her number in the machine again, but it gave her the same message. Scarlett turned to look at those still in the dining hall. Were meals only served at a certain time? Rhys saw her struggling and came over to the machine.

"Is it not working?"

"Look, it just does this," Scarlett punched in her number to show its reaction.

"Huh, that's strange." Rhys ran his hand over the machine, but they both knew there was nothing he could do. "You can just have some of mine."

Scarlett looked over to where his plate sat at the table all by its lonely self. "Okay, really quickly. I don't want anyone to see."

She shoveled three bites of his food into her mouth and chewed it up, eating so quickly that her stomach turned over in disgust. "I shouldn't take any more," Scarlett said, taking a step away from the table where he was sitting by himself. "But seriously, if they have a specific time for eating, they should really let you know that ahead of time. But I guess the way around here is letting you find out the hard way. Seems I'm the one always finding out the hard way."

"I got mine at 9:28, according to the machine," Rhys said. "I guess breakfast is done at 9:30."

"Great. I'm going to the exercise room. I can at least be on time for learning how to use the radios."

"See you in a few."

Scarlett headed toward the exercise room, hoping to get in a few weight lifts before their training started. She was surprised at how crowded the room was. Some of the machines had been shifted out of the way. A table was set up with a few different models of radios. Scarlett slipped into the crowd and waited patiently as she saw Irin behind the table. He seemed to be a level above Whites. He had so much responsibility. Scarlett thought she should see what she could do to ingratiate herself with him. Maybe then she would receive important information, such as meal hours.

Irin looked at his watch twice. After the second look, Irin clasped his hands behind his back as he gazed at each person in turn.

"I assume everyone has signed in."

There was a rush as people who didn't know they needed to sign in, Scarlett included, hurried to the keypad placed on the table.

"Now, let's begin," Irin said as Rhys hurried into the room. Scarlett tried to subtly point to the keypad at the table. He could slide over and punch his number in. Scarlett wondered if she should have punched his number in. Of course that would be completely against the rules, but she thought she remembered it. The last thing she wanted was him getting in trouble.

She nodded toward the machine, but he wasn't looking at her. Irin had started speaking. Scarlett tried to move subtly toward Rhys, but everyone was stock still as they listened. Scarlett didn't want everyone turning to look at her.

Scarlett took a deep breath and let it out slowly. She *had* to stop getting so worried about every detail. No one had ever said anything about her silly mistake the day before. Nothing would be said about Rhys's mistake today.

"This button sends a constant beep across to all other radios in your squadron. That will let them know that, even if you can't communicate the details at that moment, something drastic is happening. They will track you down and be able to help you out. Each radio sends out a signal so that we can locate it by putting in the radio number."

Irin turned the radio over and indicated a knob. "This knob will allow you to change signals. Your leader at the time of your shift start will let you know your radio channel for the shift. Normally, we use channels five through eight as they have the best range. However, that may change depending on the day.

"We have two different styles of radios. These are the older model. Their reception is not as good. However, we don't have enough newer models for everyone at this point, so you should familiarize yourself with both." Irin set the radio down and took a step back. A couple of the Blues looked at each other. Were they supposed to "familiarize" themselves now? Once Amirah stepped forward and grabbed one off the table, others took one as well. Scarlett squeezed through the group until she was able to select one of the old radios. She clutched the plastic material tightly and backed away from the table, her eyes on the device.

They had used these as Yellows. It had been part of being able to graduate to a Green. They had played hide and seek and given each other clues about where they were hiding using the radio. Scarlett smiled down at the radio in remembrance.

Irin was giving further instructions. "You will never be alone. You should always be with at least one member of your squadron when you are on duty. However, both of you will have radios in the event one of them ceases to function. It is pertinent you learn to use the radio as your partner may not be an experienced White."

Irin wasn't saying anything important, so Scarlett began fiddling with the knobs and buttons. This old version was very similar to the one she had used before.

"You will check a radio out when you start your shift. You will do so using your code. Once you come back, you will check the radio in *before* going to the dining hall." Irin actually smiled slightly as though he was amusing himself. "However, I will allow you to use these radios around the building for the next half hour. You will practice the checking in procedure at twenty til eleven hours."

A few of the Blues took their radios out of the exercise room. Blues began speaking on the radio, and it crackled loudly at Scarlett. She used the knob on the side to change channels. Apparently, most of the Blues, content to play with the toy, were staying on the same channel.

"This is Veronica, over," a female Blue said in the exercise room. Scarlett showed an eight on her hands to Rhys then hurried out of the room, adjusting hers to channel eight. She went to the far end of the hall near the stairs that led up to the prestigious second floor.

"Rhys?" she said in a whisper while pressing the talk button.

"Here," his voice came back. Scarlett was quiet for a minute to see if anyone else would chime in and let them know they had found channel eight.

"Come find me," Scarlett giggled just a little, feeling ten years younger. She tucked herself further under the stairs.

"I already know you're not in the dining hall," Rhys radioed back. "You're still bitter about breakfast this morning."

"Or lack thereof," Scarlett responded.

"And I know you're not in the entertainment room because I would hear more background noise." Scarlett didn't like how quickly he was narrowing down her hiding spot. "I'm going to guess not the females' bathroom . . . and probably not the females' dormitory." Scarlett could hear footsteps out in the hall, and she turned her radio off. She didn't want him to hear his own voice echoing out from under the stairs.

She could hear him, sounding like he was talking to himself, as he continued down the hall. "I'll take a peek in the males' dormitory, but you're probably—"

Scarlett could hear ferocious hushing as he entered the dormitory talking. The third shift was probably trying to sleep a few hours. Rhys backed up and laughed a little. "Guess that wasn't a good idea. Can you give me a clue about where you are?"

Scarlett considered carefully. If she said something, he was close enough that he could hear her. She pressed the "help" button on her walkie talkie that sent a strong, beeping whine through on his. She was hoping the similarity of the two beeps on hers and his would echo enough that he wouldn't be able to tell where hers was coming from. It could make the annoyingly high-pitched beep even when the volume was turned down on hers.

"So, I'm close," Rhys whispered. "Good to know." He was silent for a few minutes, and Scarlett heard a random doorknob rattling. She tried to connect the noise to the doorknobs she knew. Maybe it was one of those doors along the way that had not been explained to them on the tour.

Then, Rhys was standing in the doorway of the stairs. He took a couple of steps closer and peered upward. "You didn't go upstairs, did you?" Rhys asked, his voice low. "Because I'm not that desperate to find you." Scarlett could see his shoes around the edge of the stairs. It would only be a matter of seconds before he found her.

Scarlett held her breath as Rhys tried talking in the radio again. "Scarlett—" he teased. He stepped out of the room with the stairs. She didn't dare look in his direction. Suddenly, his shoes slapped the floor. Scarlett looked up quickly to see why he had made such a noise. In looking up, she banged her head on the bottom of the stairs.

"Owwww," she groaned.

Rhys knelt down in front of her smiling. "Found you." Then, he saw she was rocking back and forth slowly in pain.

"What did you do?"

"My head," Scarlett said, her hands gripping it were apparently not a big enough clue as to what she was dealing with.

"Oh, sorry," Rhys said, as his smile disappeared. "Are you okay?"

Scarlett bit her lower lip as the first stabs of pain began to ebb into a constant throb. She let out a deep breath and looked up at Rhys. "Sorry."

Rhys shrugged, not sure why she was apologizing. They both stared at each other. Then, Rhys reached out his hand and touched the end of Scarlett's hair. Her eyes flew up to him, anxiety in her stomach. He fingered the strands of her hair between his fingers. He smiled just a little, then his hand traveled up to where she had bumped her head. He fingered the bump tenderly, intertwining his fingers with her hair and running them down to the ends again, his fingers sending tingles down her spine.

Scarlett held back a smile. It felt so strange, so forbidden, but Haman had insisted it wasn't against the rules. "What?" she said something to break the silence.

"I always wondered what your hair felt like," Rhys responded. "It's so soft."

"What do you mean it's soft?" Scarlett reached up and ruffled her own hair. "It feels like it always does."

"Feel mine," Rhys said, pointing to his own mesh of brown, tangled curls. Scarlett looked toward the hallway, but no one was there. No one could really see them or what they were doing anyway. Scarlett reached up hesitantly and touched Rhys's tight curls. His hair felt rougher, more like the protective material on their suits.

"You're right!" Scarlett agreed. She rubbed his curls more vigorously. "I didn't know hair could feel like that. I mean, Jaylin's hair is kind of like yours, but hers is so long, it's different."

Rhys nodded. "Told you."

Scarlett clasped her hands in her lap. She had a strange desire to touch his head again, to feel his curls until her fingers had memorized their pattern. But she didn't.

"I guess we should probably turn our radios back in now," Scarlett said. Rhys stood and held a hand protectively between Scarlett's head and the stairs as she crawled out and stood as well. They switched back to a busy channel and listened as they walked down the hall.

Once they had deposited their radios, they went to the washing up room to work on the dishes. Scarlett's hands stung at the thought of dipping them into the scalding water again. But she bit back her disagreement and dove in. She would do her job to the best of her ability, even as she wondered why there was hot water for the dishes but not for their showers.

"Hide and seek, huh?" Devon asked quietly as Scarlett scrubbed the remnants of breakfast off the plates. With how hungry she was, she had to admit she had been considering if anyone would notice if she took a few leftovers off a plate. It seemed such a waste just to throw them away.

"Huh?" Scarlett replied, startled.

"You and Rhys were playing hide and seek—"

Scarlett shrugged, not looking Devon in the eyes. What did it matter? It's not like they had done anything wrong.

"Seems like something a Red would play."

Scarlett screwed up her mouth and chose to keep it shut rather than responding to his insult.

"You should have joined the rest of us in capture the flag."

Scarlett's shoulders straightened. She had loved it when their physical training consisted of a game, and she was particularly good at capture the flag. "Next time," she said, not wanting to think that anyone could have been listening to their private game of hide and seek. Had they said anything else over the radio? Not that they had anything to hide. Having secrets meant you weren't backing the Government. But still . . . sometimes, she preferred to keep their conversations just between the two of them.

* * *

After their midday meal, they dumped their used dishes in the dispenser and lined up to receive their radios. Scarlett handled the old radio carefully as she hooked it onto her belt. Once everyone had been scanned out, she followed Phan as he led the group in the same direction as the day before.

They stopped in the same spot. Scarlett almost expected him to give the same safety speech he had the day before. But of course, he wouldn't. Instead, he said, "Different groups. Malak and Rhys. Devon and Scarlett. You can reach us by radio. You'll follow the same track as the day before. We'll be investigating a few complaints."

The Whites started off in two groups to investigate whatever complaints had come their way.

"So?" Rhys said. "I guess Malak and I can get a headstart on you two."

"Sure," Devon shrugged. Rhys and Malak started off in the direction of their circuit. Scarlett saw a few Blues and Whites from the first shift heading back to the compound.

They saluted the second shift.

"Good luck," one of them said. Scarlett looked at him strangely, his voice a grating reminder that she knew him. When she saw who it was, she tried to turn sideways and drop her gaze, but he noticed her too.

He laughed. "Hey, Scarlett! How are you liking it here in City 6?" Haman chuckled again. "Quite the heaven, isn't it?"

"That's bordering on traitorous speech," Scarlett responded tightly.

"Did you ask about that little rule change yet? Or are you not planning to ever ask?" Haman laughed, clapping his hands together as he did so. It reminded Scarlett of a video she had seen of an animal called a seal. Their noises were rougher, but the clapping was an exact imitation.

Scarlett frowned. She shrugged and diverted the question to Devon. He had been there when the whole subject was brought up. Maybe the question was really for him.

Devon shook his head. "You're crazy, male. We have no reason to question the rules. You're probably just trying to see what sort of consequence they would lay out for that one."

Haman laughed. "Ah, no, I wouldn't do that." He chuckled and crossed his arms. The first shift had gone on without him, and he looked toward them. "Well, I guess I should let you get to work. See ya."

Haman took off at a jog toward the rest of his shift. Scarlett rolled her eyes at Devon, and he laughed. She cocked her head at him as if to ask if he was going to start down the giggling path, too.

Devon shook his head. "Haman. I'm actually quite glad we don't have the same shift."

Scarlett nodded. It meant that they only rarely crossed paths, mostly at mealtimes. "Sometimes, you wonder how someone became a Blue," Scarlett said. "I mean, he's passed all the training that I didn't . . ." Devon looked at her. "Well, you know? I didn't exactly meet all the requirements for being a Blue. Or else, I would have been made one sooner, right?"

Devon shrugged. "I mean, I guess if you didn't have some skills you wouldn't be here right?" A Citizen stepped out of her house with a basket of clothes in her hands. She held the basket to the side of a large bump on her front that bulged conspicuously from under her dress. She looked curiously at the two Blues as she turned the opposite way and walked purposefully to another house. She knocked on the door and was let in promptly.

Scarlett stared after her then turned to Devon with horror. "What is wrong with her? Does she . . . was that an ulcer?"

Devon shook his head. "I've never actually seen a female like that, but they say that females here can grow babies in their bodies."

"They can? How? A baby in her body? But how would it come out?" Scarlett stared at the door where the female had gone.

Devon shrugged. "I don't know. They didn't give us a lot of details. They just warned us that if we saw a female with child we should be careful with her. They cannot do much physical labor as carrying a child is heavy work."

Scarlett blinked her eyes several times, trying to accept the information.

"We should probably start after Rhys and Malak, or they'll make the whole circuit and meet us back here."

"Yeah," Scarlett agreed, her feet moving mechanically. As they reached the door where the large female had entered, Scarlett stared at it in wonder. She knew they shouldn't have discussions with Citizens unless prompted or addressing a matter of safety. However, she wondered what would happen if she did. It wasn't exactly a rule, just a matter of guidance.

They marched past the house without Devon noticing Scarlett's rubbernecking. They continued to march the path they had followed the day before, their feet in sync. They had almost made the full circuit before their radios crackled.

"All good? Over." Rhys's voice was all that was needed to make Scarlett smile a little bit. She reached for her radio, but Devon got to his first.

"Nothing to report. Over."

Scarlett wondered where they were passing or what they were seeing on their route. She wondered if they had seen the large female, and if it was something they could talk about over the radio.

Scarlett pressed the talk button on her radio. "Rhys? Malak? Over." She only added Malak's name to be fair and not exclude him.

"Yessss," Rhys came back with an overly drawn out hissing sound.

Scarlett shook his head. He was so unprofessional. "We saw a female," she looked at Devon for confirmation, "with child."

"I've seen plenty of females with children. They are called families here, and instead of having Blues or Whites caring for the children, they have one female carrying for one to two children. That's very inefficient, if you ask me."

"Thanks for the history lesson," Scarlett responded. "However, Devon said this female had a child in her body."

Rhys laughed over the radio. "Was she that hungry?" Before he could end his side, Scarlett could hear Malak refuting his joke.

"Devon is speaking the truth. With child means—" Scarlett made a mental note to ask Malak for as many details as she could later. But at least that meant Devon had been telling the truth.

"Less talking. More completing your duties," Phan's harsh voice came over the radio. Scarlett reddened. Oops. She hadn't meant for anyone to overhear them, but the lack of privacy had grown even more obvious moving to this compound. At least at the training center, she could always find a quiet place to be by herself. Here, there was no extra room, nor private conversations.

A few rounds later, the light was starting to edge away. Scarlett now knew that meant their shift was nearly halfway done. She was already thinking about the meal they would have when they returned.

Several males tramped through the streets, tools on their shoulders from the work they had completed during the day. A few of the doors of the houses were open, and Scarlett could smell the preparations of a meal coming together. Gas lamps and candles flickered from inside. Scarlett tried to see what these "families" were doing without making it too obvious that she was trying to see what their lives were like.

Scarlett saw a small male, perhaps four or five years old, running around a table in the house. An older female was setting food on the table, and the male was singing a song about the food. Scarlett smiled. The female made eye contact with Scarlett, and Scarlett made the symbol of the Government over her heart. The woman echoed the symbol. A moment later, the door closed.

Scarlett saw the same large female carrying the same basket of clothes now from the house she had entered to the house she had left. Scarlett looked over her shoulder. No other soldiers were in sight, and Devon wouldn't report her, especially for something that wasn't technically against the rules.

"Hi," Scarlett said. The female stopped and shifted the basket to her hip, exposing her enlarged stomach area even more. "I'm Scarlett," she said, not knowing how she could politely ask all the questions she had.

Devon stood silently without comment.

The woman nodded to Scarlett but didn't seem inclined to speak.

"I have very much enjoyed seeing the City," Scarlett added.

The woman shifted the basket again. "I don't mean to be rude," she finally said, her voice a bit scratchy, "but unless you be needing something, I need to get home and prepare a meal for my husband."

Scarlett held out her hands for the basket. "I could help you with the basket."

The woman clutched it closer. "You been helping us enough," she said in a low voice. "Don't need anyone carrying my work for me," she said, her voice louder now.

"I don't mind," Scarlett said, still holding her hands out but not touching the basket. The female staunchly shook her head though she peered at Scarlett closely.

"I ain't seen you around here," she responded. "You new?"

"Yes," Scarlett responded. "I've only been here a couple of days. What about you? Have you always lived in City 6?"

"There's nowhere else to go, and if there were, there wouldn't be no way of getting there. Excuse me, I've got to prepare a meal now."

The large female bustled to her house, and Scarlett continued walking with Devon. She waited for Devon to say something, either condemning or applauding her for speaking with the woman. But he didn't say anything. He appeared to be in deep thought.

Chapter 10

The next day, as their shift was starting, Scarlett gravitated toward Devon, assuming they would follow the same routine as the day before. But apparently, Phan was nothing if not unpredictable.

"Today, let's do Rhys with Scarlett and Devon with Malak. Break up and work the perimeter of Section Two. First shift reported an incident. Be listening to your radios, channel six. We may call you in to observe."

And with that, Rhys and Scarlett started around the perimeter. They passed first shift heading toward the compound, and Haman sent a few chuckles their way but didn't dare stop to talk with Phan still so close by.

Finally, Rhys and Scarlett were alone—well, as alone as they could be in a City full of people. "I miss hanging out, just you and me," Rhys conceded after a few minutes of walking.

"Yeah, it feels different. It's like someone's always listening to our conversations."

"Well, because they are," Rhys said.

"I want to show you the female with child. I spoke with her yesterday."

"You spoke with a Citizen? Why?"

Scarlett shrugged. "I just wanted to be friendly. I know there is so much tension. But I feel like if they knew we are here to help them not hurt them, then perhaps everyone would get along a bit better."

"I'm pretty sure we should trust those who have been here longer," Rhys said. "Not try to improve upon the already successful strategies."

"Where's the Rhys who broke the rules to help me conquer my fear of heights?" Scarlett half-teased.

"I don't know what you're talking about, and by the way," Rhys looked around dramatically. "I don't even see any heights around here. I mean, I know we had no idea which City we would be sent to, but I guess heights is not a bad fear to have when you live in this City."

"I'm not afraid of heights anymore," Scarlett insisted. "That was the whole point of doing that." Scarlett was silent as they passed a few females and younger children in the street. Scarlett watched them carefully, curious about everything.

Rhys and she continued onward.

"I don't know why," Scarlett pondered. "I haven't really interacted with a child since our volunteering assignment as Yellows. But now, I see the children, and I feel like I want to care for them."

"You want a position as a Red nanny?"

Scarlett shook her head. "No, I don't think I could ever feel satisfied in that job. I've always wanted to be stationed in a City, not in the training center. I don't know. It's hard to explain. I guess I'm curious as to why a female in the City can have a child grow within her but no one at the training center ever has a child within them."

Rhys shrugged. "I'm not Malak. Wait until tomorrow, then you can ask him all your annoying little questions."

"Annoying?" Scarlett frowned at him.

"I didn't mean annoying," Rhys said. "Maybe repetitive is a better word."

"Maybe your unenthusiasm to learn about the Cities is annoying."

"I'm pretty sure unenthusiasm isn't a word."

Scarlett rolled her eyes, thinking Rhys was right. "It doesn't matter. I still don't appreciate it. Hey, wait. Are they supposed to do that?" Scarlett asked, pointing to two children pulling fruit off a fruit tree. The fruit tree had a small fence around its base, perhaps only four feet high. One of the children was standing on the other's shoulders, so he could reach over the fence to pluck the pinkish-red fruit.

"Hey!" Rhys shouted, moving toward them before Scarlett realized they were making a decision. They weren't playing at protecting the City. Now, they really were.

The two children turned to see Rhys coming toward them. The bottom child tried to step away without letting the top child leap down first. The top child came crashing down onto the fence while the other turned tail and ran. Rhys grabbed the child's arm and held him firmly.

"What are you doing?" Rhys asked the child who couldn't have been more than nine or ten years old. The child struggled against Rhys's hold, wiggling his body like a worm trying to escape the grip of a bird's beak. Rhys held on tightly. "I'm speaking to you. Answer."

Scarlett took a step back, surprised at the roughness in his voice. It reminded her of their conversation directly after the strange old male had predicted Rhys's demise.

The small male continued his attempt at freedom.

"What are you doing?" Rhys asked again, twisting the small male around so the two were facing each other.

The child slumped over as if recognizing defeat. "I'm sorry, Sir," he said, his eyes downward. Rhys relaxed his grip slowly, still hanging on loosely in case the small male tried to make a run for it. He stared longingly after his friend. Rhys looked at Scarlett, raising his eyebrow, asking her something. What? Scarlett tried to read his posture and look for clues, obviously a question he didn't want the Citizen overhearing.

Scarlett got closer to the small male and studied him. "Why were you stealing from the fruit tree? It is community property." She didn't think Rhys needed to play around and pretend he didn't know what crime the small male had been committing.

The small male shrugged and dug his toe into the dirt at their feet. Scarlett bent down, her hands on her knees so she was on eye level with him. There was no escaping her gaze now.

"Tell me why," she said, trying to make her voice firm. Rhys had moved his strong hand onto the small male's shoulder, but he was still prepared should anything happen.

"Because my sister's hungry," the small male said.

Scarlett opened her mouth to ask what a "sister" was but closed it again when she realized she probably shouldn't be asking a child for information she should have received in training. "That doesn't give you a right to touch community property. I understand they look delicious, but they will be divided among the Citizens when they are all ripe."

"They are ripe, and they're going to fall on the ground, and no one will eat them!" The small male protested, pointing through the fence to a few fruits laying on the ground. Part of them had turned brown, and they smelled a bit overripe. "We just get the ones that's about to fall."

Scarlett looked up at Rhys. It's not like he was really hurting anyone, was he?

"You still shouldn't be getting them," Scarlett responded in a half-scold.

The small male shrugged. "I know, but if I don't, my mama might die."

"Die? You won't die from having to wait a week or two to eat them."

"Cause we doesn't have enough. And my mama always gives her food to my sister. But if I got these for my sister, then my mama would eat."

Scarlett sighed. If his story was to be believed, then he hadn't even been stealing them for himself. Yeah, he shouldn't be climbing the fence and taking the almost rotten ones, but even Scarlett could see that they were almost too ripe to eat.

"Listen," Scarlett said, her voice low. "What's your name?"

"Arwic," he said softly.

"Arwic, you should never, never steal from a tree that is community property or take anything that belongs to the community. "But this time," Scarlett stood and looked to Rhys to see if he was thinking what she was thinking. For a small offense, and something that was probably no big deal anyway, they didn't have to administer consequences, did they?

Scarlett leaned closer to Rhys, so that her lips were almost touching his ear. "We should just let him go with a warning."

Rhys shook his head emphatically. "What are you talking about?"

"I'm talking about how it's a child, and he made a mistake. What he's doing isn't really that wrong. It's not like he's hurting someone else."

Rhys shook his head again. "It doesn't matter. If we let him get away with something little, then he'll break the law with bigger things later. You have to teach them when it's something small."

Scarlett took a deep breath. Though they were talking quietly, Scarlett knew he probably understood the gist of their conversation.

"We need to talk for a minute," Scarlett said. She indicated for Rhys to tie the small male to the fence surrounding the tree. Rhys sighed but did so, and they took a few steps away.

"I don't want to get him in trouble for something so small," Scarlett explained, watching the small male out of the corner of her eye. He didn't appear to be struggling with his bonds. Scarlett knew Malak and Devon could pass by in the next ten minutes since their route had been delayed. And they had to make a decision before then. There was no way she could convince Malak to do anything that might be considered breaking the rules.

"I don't even know why we're having this discussion. First of all, he broke the rules. Second, he knows he did. Why do you think his friend ran away? Why do you think he tried to run? If he knows he did something wrong, but he did it anyway, then there's no excuse for not reporting him."

"But, it's so small," Scarlett protested weakly. "Come on. We can just scare him into never thinking about doing it again. But if he gets a mark against him now, when he's young, won't that affect what kind of position he can have as an adult?"

Rhys shrugged. "I don't know how that works here. But I'm not willing to risk myself for him. If we don't report him, we'll have bigger consequences than he would have had. I'm done talking about this."

Rhys pulled out his radio. "Phan? This is Rhys. Over." Scarlett, so angry she wasn't thinking, reached for his radio. She tried to wrestle it from his hands. He pulled it out of her reach and marched purposely over to the kid.

Phan's voice crackled over the radio. "Phan here. Over."

"We have an offense to report, in the northwest corner of Section Two."

"Is the Citizen currently in custody?"

"Yes."

"Offense and Citizen number?"

"Stealing fruit, and I don't have a number. He said his name is Arwic."

"We will have two Whites out there soon. Please keep the Citizen in custody."

Rhys looked down the street for any approaching Whites. Scarlett was so mad she couldn't even look at Rhys. She took a few steps away from Rhys and the Citizen and found something else to look at. She took a few deep breaths. Rhys hadn't really done anything wrong, but at the same time, it seemed so cruel to turn in a child for an offense not even big enough to be considered a crime.

The Whites arrived at a steady pace, slowing when they saw the three standing at different distances. Their eyes fell on the child.

"This is the offender?" one White asked. Scarlett turned to watch their conversation from a short distance.

Rhys nodded. "This is him. There was another child with him, but that child ran away before we could get to him."

"A child ran faster than you?" the other White chuckled. They untied the child from the fence and half-walked and half-dragged him back in the direction from which they had come.

"What are they going to do to him?" Scarlett asked, still angry at Rhys.

He shrugged. "I don't know. I haven't exactly read a list of all the consequences for different offenses."

"They won't whip him like they did those males two days ago, will they?"

"How am I supposed to know?"

Scarlett let out an angry huff of breath. She marched ahead of Rhys to continue their route around Section Two. Rhys took a few hurried steps to catch up with her, but Scarlett ignored him. She didn't have anything to say to him.

When their shift was ending, Rhys and Scarlett met up with Devon and Malak. The four met with the Whites on their squad, and all of them walked with heavy steps back to the compound, the third shift taking their place.

Scarlett was tired, but that didn't make her any less angry with Rhys. She imagined the small male being beaten. Arwic didn't deserve that. Maybe this "sister" really was hungry. She didn't know. And if the fruit was just going to go bad after all, then who was she to reserve the bad fruit?

Scarlett stood in line behind Rhys, refusing to look at him or notice how curly his brown hair was. He got his meal and headed toward one of the two tables they normally occupied. Scarlett punched in her code, grabbed her small portion angrily, and marched toward the other side of the dining hall.

She stabbed her food mercilessly and shoved it into her mouth. As she tasted the warm food, she couldn't feel as angry as she had been before, but she still wasn't happy. Someone slid in across from her. Scarlett looked up briefly. It was Devon.

"Hey," he said, digging into his food.

Scarlett nodded and continued her eating.

"Did something happen during your shift?"

Scarlett shrugged. She wanted to talk about it, but Devon wasn't exactly like Jaylin and Miya. He didn't seem like a listener.

"Well, I'm here if you want to talk," Devon offered. Scarlett shrugged and took another bite as she considered his offer. Then, without her approval, the words started marching out of her mouth.

"Did you hear on the radio about the Citizen we found today?"

"Yeah, someone stealing something, you said?"

"I didn't say anything," Scarlett clarified. "Rhys is the one who reported it."

"Okay, you guys said it was a Citizen stealing something. What were they stealing?"

"It was a small male, a child," Scarlett clarified.

Devon still leaned forward, waiting for more details. "He was stealing fruit from one of the community trees."

Devon nodded understandingly.

"And I tried talking to him about it."

"You mean, convince him not to do it?" Devon asked, like she was crazy.

"No, I was just trying to understand why he did it. And, he mentioned a sister. What is that, by the way?"

"A sister is a female child that lives in one of the houses."

"Okay, well, he said he was stealing the fruit for her."

Devon looked surprised. "That's strange. Why would he want more food when every family is given the exact amount of food they need? That's not in the spirit of community."

Scarlett looked at her plate of food. The food was proportioned for her exactly. She thought the portions were small at first, but now she was accustomed to them. She felt full just as she was finishing. Why would Arwic think he had to steal if they were receiving just the right amount? That didn't mean that Scarlett didn't dream of the honey they would sometimes have for breakfast at the training center. But still, you think about it, but you don't actually do anything.

"I don't know. The way he explained it. It made me believe him, like his sister might really be hungry."

Devon nodded. "So? What did you do? And what did he say?"

"He told me they were only taking the ones that were about to go bad, or the ones that had fallen on the ground."

"Inside the fence or outside?"

"He didn't say," Scarlett responded.

"Because outside the fence is up for anyone to collect, but inside the fence is community property," Devon reminded.

Scarlett nodded. "I mean, I know when I saw them, they were taking ones off the tree."

"They?"

"There was another small male, too. He ran away. And I didn't want to report this male."

"Why not?"

"Because . . . he's just a child. It was not a big thing. It's not as though he was stealing food provisions from another Citizen's house. He couldn't really hurt anyone with what he was doing, right?"

Devon nodded. "I see your point."

"Yeah, and when I told Rhys that, he didn't understand me at all!" Scarlett looked across the dining room to where he was eating his meal. "I don't know. I don't even know what the consequence was. I just wish we had had more time to consider our options."

"You have to make a lot of your decisions quickly here," Devon said. "Everything is so different from the training center."

"No kidding!"

"But you guys reported him in the end . . . so—"

Scarlett shrugged. "Rhys called it in. I didn't have anything to do with it. I still don't know if it was the right decision."

"Well, it's done now," Devon confirmed.

Scarlett nodded and scooped the last of her food into her mouth. "I need to sleep."

"Night."

Scarlett trudged toward the female dormitory, not bothering with a cold shower before going to bed. That would only wake her up more.

Chapter 11

The next morning, Scarlett was woken as the first shift was getting ready. She had a sick feeling in her stomach, that feeling she used to get when she knew she was going to get in trouble for something as a Red. She had hated it when a Blue yelled at her for something. Like the whole glue incident that happened in her first class as a Red.

Scarlett watched each of the first shifts leave. Her eyes drifted closed again.

When she opened her eyes what felt like much later, there were two Whites standing beside her bed, watching her.

Scarlett sat up as an expression of surprise slipped out of her mouth.

"Uh, can I help you with something?" Scarlett asked. Two female Blues who also shared her second shift were watching her and the Whites curiously.

"Come with us," one of the Whites said. Scarlett slipped her shoes on and followed the two Whites down the hall. Her stomach was sinking. They knew. They knew that she had not wanted to report the small male. But how? Devon. It had to be. He had reported her!

Why would he do that? Scarlett was seething as she marched up the stairs to the office where she knew the Black would be. Scarlett clenched her jaw and clasped her hands behind her back, trying to control her anger. It certainly wasn't aimed at the Whites or the Black. No, she was mad at Devon and most of all, Rhys. If he hadn't reported the whole incident in the first place, then she wouldn't be here.

Scarlett saluted the Black and awaited his cue. Meanwhile, she was turning over everything she could remember from her conversation with Devon the night before. Had she mentioned anything about her and Rhys breaking the rules back at the training center?

"Scarlett," the Black said, his eyes piercing into her. "What did you do?"

Scarlett could feel her anger melting into fear. What would be the consequence for her actions? Would they consider her traitorous?

The Black was still waiting for her to speak. "I'm sorry," she offered, her words echoing the young male's from the day before.

"Tell me what you did," the Black said again, his words more forceful.

"I . . . I didn't want to report a young male's offense," Scarlett admitted, her cheeks echoing her shame. "I'm sorry. In the end, Rhys and I did report the incident. However, there were a few moments when we were unsure."

Scarlett winced at her words. They sounded so diplomatic, and really, she couldn't afford to be in trouble. But at the same time, she knew they were all lies.

"It seemed like more than insecurity. You did not, in fact, participate in the reporting of the incident. My understanding is that you were against the reporting and were still against it even after the report was made. Is this correct?"

Scarlett took a few deep breaths, but her silence was enough of an answer. The Black continued.

"You do not have a decision when you see an offense committed. Your job is to report it immediately. If you have trouble understanding that, then we will remove you from your squad." He was silent as the significance of his words sank into her head. She was being given a warning. The next offense would not be accepted.

"One day of isolation," the Black declared. Scarlett looked up in surprise. Isolation? Where?

The two Whites nodded for her to exit the room. With one behind and one in front, they marched further down the hallway until she assumed they must be above the exercise room. They took another set of stairs, a set of stairs Scarlett had never seen before. They went down, and even when it felt like they had taken enough steps to be on the first floor, they continued going. Scarlett's stomach was knotting up, reconsidering everything she had done in the last twenty-four hours. Maybe she shouldn't have tried to protect the child. After all, what was he to her? But then . . . Scarlett felt angry again as she remembered Devon's betrayal. He wouldn't get away with it. There was no way she could just pretend it didn't happen.

Without speaking, one of the Whites opened a heavy metal door. The inside of the room was dark. Scarlett hesitated, and the female White pushed Scarlett unceremoniously inside. The door closed behind her with a thump. Scarlett strained her ears for the noise of the two Whites ascending the stairs. Their footsteps faded away, and it was silent.

Scarlett closed her eyes and clutched her stomach. All she wanted in that moment was Jaylin or Miya to be there with her. Of course she didn't want them to be in trouble, but she didn't want to be by herself anymore. She hadn't connected with any of the other females. She hadn't really had an opportunity as the only other two females on the second shift were thick as thieves and didn't leave room for her.

Scarlett sighed, and her large breath made something rustle. But she didn't know what. It was pitch dark with no windows. Scarlett had seen a bench on one side of the cell when light had shone in from the hall. She crept forward, her hands in front of her, feeling for something. Her shins bumped into the bench, and she sat down. There, she had found the bench. Now what would she do for the rest of her time here?

He had said one day. Did that mean until her shift started that afternoon? Or would she miss her shift? What would everyone think?

Scarlett sighed again. The idea of hours before her with nothing to do except turn over in her head how angry she was did not sound appealing.

One hour.

Two hours.

Three hours.

Scarlett lost count of how many hours it had been. Her stomach was rumbling. Had they already changed shifts? Scarlett heard a loud thump from above. She had to be below the exercise room. But the walls were thick enough that she couldn't hear more than the occasional bump.

More hours.

The door opened, food was shoved in, and the door closed again. Scarlett saw only a painful flash of white before it was dark once more. Worried that she would step in the food, Scarlett crawled on her hands and knees toward the doorway. The floor was covered in a strange, moist grime. Scarlett touched the edge of the platter, wiped her hand on her uniform, and took the platter back to her bench. She felt her food gently, trying to guess what it was before it touched her tongue. She ate her food as slowly as she could. Was this the afternoon meal or the after-shift meal? It felt like it had been a long time, but she feared that it hadn't been long enough. Did she have to wait another two sets of that length? Scarlett sadly scooped the last handful of food into her mouth. She ran her hand over the platter, but it was truly the end of her meal.

Scarlett closed her eyes and opened them again, trying to see a difference in the darkness. She tapped her toes in a melody of a song from when she was a Red. She tried to remember as many words as she could. Scarlett next started counting backward from 1000, trying to estimate how many minutes 1000 seconds was.

She took off her shoes and massaged each one of her toes for sixty seconds, counting them as slowly as possible. Her fingers glided over her body to the scars and markings. The scar on the back of her hand from where another Red had stabbed her with scissors. The mole exactly five centimeters above her belly button. The scratch that was still healing on the back of her neck.

Finally, she fell asleep.

* * *

After consuming two more meals in the same slow fashion and spending what felt like many more hours occupying her mind with senseless thoughts, the door creaked open and stayed open.

Scarlett squinted against the brightness of the artificial light. After blinking several times, she stood, feeling just a little dizzy. She moved toward the two Whites who appeared to be glowing. Scarlett took the stairs upward slowly, moving in a haze at first. She felt as though she had been in isolation for weeks. As they reached the second floor landing, she began to feel more like herself. The Whites walked her to the top of the stairs that led down to the Blue hall and the entertainment room.

"You can go from here," one of the Whites said.

Scarlett descended the stairs slowly, trying to orient herself. What time was it? Would she go out on her shift soon? She really wanted a shower when she saw how dirty her uniform was.

She decided that a shower was the most important thing, then she would worry about . . . suddenly, she remembered her anger at Devon and Rhys, too. It seemed to take over her body like someone punching her in the gut.

Scarlett's feet found the energy to rush down the stairs.

They pounded on the hall's floor as she took hurried steps, yet not running, toward the exercise room. She didn't know why she was heading there, but for some reason it felt like the place Rhys and/or Devon would be.

Scarlett reached the door of the exercise room, and her eyes flew to the far wall. There was no hint of a stairway or that there could be anything beyond the thick wall. Scarlett surveyed the room. Neither Devon nor Rhys was there. What time was it? Were they out on their shift?

Scarlett marched with a little less anger in her steps back through the dining hall. She would talk to them eventually. Right now, she needed to take a shower.

Chapter 12

After a shower, Scarlett felt amazingly refreshed. While still angry, she knew it was better to have a quiet discussion rather than a shouting match in front of everyone.

"Hey? Where were you last night?" Malak asked as Scarlett walked from the bathroom to the female dormitory.

Scarlett took a deep breath to consider her answer. Surely, Rhys and Devon had figured out what happened. If they hadn't told Malak yet, that didn't mean they would hide it forever. She should just come clean, without all the details.

"I made a questionable decision when on my last shift."

Malak raised an eyebrow. "So what did they do? Torture you for the last twenty-four hours?"

"No," Scarlett shook her head. She didn't want to say it aloud. It felt degrading to announce that she had been punished like a child, put in timeout to think about what she had done. "It doesn't matter. But have you seen Rhys? Or Devon?"

Malak shook his head. "No, after we ate the morning meal, they kind of disappeared. I've just been in the entertainment room watching a film on the founding of the Americas."

Scarlett pressed her lips into a smile even though the thought of watching such a film didn't appeal to her much more than another few hours in isolation.

"Thanks anyway." Well, even if they were hiding out, she would find them soon enough when their shift started. Now, she was going to take a quick nap. Her sleep in the isolation cell hadn't exactly been the best, and she would need energy for her shift that evening.

* * *

At half past fifteen, Scarlett ate her meal in the dining hall gratefully. She saw Rhys and Devon sitting next to each other on the opposite side of the dining room. They were talking about something, and Devon laughed. Scarlett gritted her teeth to keep from throwing her platter across the room at them.

When her platter was emptied of its food, Scarlett stood and walked with poise across the room to deposit it.

"Hey!" Rhys said, hurrying up to her. "I didn't know you were back."

As though she had simply taken a leisurely stroll around the City. Scarlett turned to him, clenching her fists by her side. "We need to talk," she said.

"About what?"

"About the incident that got me in trouble in the first place," Scarlett said slowly as though she were helping a Red understand a simple math problem.

Rhys nodded. "Yeah, what did they do to you? We asked when we started our shift yesterday, but Phan just said you were occupied elsewhere. But I knew you must be in trouble or something because washing dishes would never trump your shift."

"Wow," Scarlett said, sarcasm blaring out clearly. "You are brilliant."

"Are you mad at me?" Rhys asked.

Scarlett let out a slow breath and turned away from him. "We will talk after our shift. I won't be late for you."

Scarlett marched toward the front entrance, grabbing a radio and punching in her number quickly. She was so mad that she almost didn't want to talk to Rhys, but she knew she had to. How could he be so clueless?

She stood in the holding area, waiting for everyone on her shift to punch in their numbers.

"Where were you yesterday?" another Blue female asked.

Scarlett turned to see the Blue female who had never said anything to her before now addressing her. Scarlett just shrugged. Maybe her story would get out. Maybe it wouldn't, but she didn't feel like she owed any explanation to the female who had never even spoken with her before.

The Blue female continued to study her as though she could figure out what Scarlett was hiding if she just stared long enough. Once everyone had arrived, the group was let out on the streets, and Scarlett followed Phan with purpose, ignoring the Blues on their squad. Phan divided them, and Scarlett was placed with Devon.

Malak suggested they go first that day, so Devon and Scarlett began striding forward, their feet on the familiar path.

"What happened to you yesterday?" Devon asked.

Scarlett ignored him, trying to get her anger under control.

"Hellooooo," Devon said, waving his hand in front of her as though she had zoned out. "Are you awake?"

"You're an idiot if you can't figure out what happened to me," Scarlett spit back. "It's all your fault. You're the one who basically spilled our conversation to someone. I'm not sure who, but whoever that was had the power to get me in trouble. The question was, were you just being stupid telling a private conversation to someone who had no business knowing it or were you purposely being cruel and reporting me? Honestly, though, it doesn't really matter because I still know I can't trust you."

Devon held up both his hands in a show of innocence as Scarlett took a deep breath. "Look, I didn't report you or tell anyone what we talked about. Well, I talked to Rhys about it. But that's it. I swear."

Scarlett shook her head. "Yeah, right. So the Black just figured out what happened without anyone telling him? He doesn't have time to worry about every detail of every shift. Someone told him!"

"It wasn't me, I swear." Devon shook his head. "I'm not that kind of friend."

Scarlett harrumphed at the word "friend." She definitely did not consider Devon a friend now. He was more like her worst enemy. "Why would you even bring it up to Rhys, though?" she persisted. "He already knew how I felt about it, so you didn't need to tell him again. You know what, if you are supposedly so innocent, someone probably overheard you running your big mouth to Rhys. Whatever it is, I know you're at fault."

"Hey, that's not fair," Devon protested. "I didn't do anything to report you. Honest."

Scarlett rolled her eyes, but Devon sounded so sincere. Had he really not reported her? But if he hadn't, her story didn't make sense.

"Whatever," Scarlett finally said.

"You have to believe me," Devon said.

"I don't. Get over it. Now, let's just focus on our shift and do what we're supposed to do."

Devon was quiet for a while as they marched along, patrolling the area. Every half hour, he would make some attempt at conversation, but Scarlett shut him down each time either with her silence or with a look that suggested he stop his attempt right there.

"I don't want to talk," Scarlett finally told him. "I don't know how to make that any clearer."

"Well, we're stuck on the same squad, which means we have to look out for each other. I'd rather not have you looking out for me if you would rather shoot me."

Scarlett rolled her eyes. "How do you think I felt when I realized the person I had confided in had turned around and gotten me in trouble?"

"I swear I didn't do it. Seriously."

"Whatever. Let's just work." They continued the same cycle of protests and accusations their whole shift. When their shift ended, Scarlett marched ahead of Devon to the compound. Rhys caught up to her just as she was turning in her radio.

"Hey, let's eat together. We need to talk," he said.

"I don't think that's a good idea," Scarlett responded quickly. The nosy Blue female was looking their way, her eyes flicking between their faces. "Later," Scarlett said.

"When?" Rhys persisted.

Scarlett leaned closer to him, feeling the same camaraderie she had always felt. "By my hiding spot after we eat."

Scarlett moved away from him to get in line at the food delivery machine. She didn't want to have a conversation in front of everyone. She didn't know if she should believe Devon or not. She felt conflicted, hurt, and betrayed all at once.

After their meal, most of her shift headed either for the showers or their dormitories. She tried to be discreet about heading for her spot under the stairs, hiding her nervousness as best she could. She didn't want to be mad at Rhys. He was her closest friend here, the only person she had really known before they left.

Scarlett sat under the stairs, her knees pulled up under her chin. The lights in the hallway had been dimmed. They always were when they got back from their shift. The lack of light reminded her of her time in isolation.

She heard rushed footsteps, and Rhys swung into their place under the stairs, nearly slamming into her. He stopped himself with one of the stairs above their head.

"I didn't know you were here yet," he said in a low voice.

Scarlett nodded. "Yeah," she sighed as she considered how to start.

"Are you okay? What happened?" Rhys sounded genuinely concerned for her. She wanted to be mad at him, but at the same time, she couldn't resist the invitation to talk.

"They put me in isolation," Scarlett admitted.

"What? For what?"

Scarlett gritted her teeth, disappointed that he couldn't figure anything out. "Because they somehow knew that I didn't want to report . . . the incident. Did Devon talk to you?"

Rhys nodded. "Yeah."

"About?"

"He was just asking what happened that day. He said you had told him some child was stealing fruit."

"But my question is how did anyone outside of our group even know that I didn't want to report the incident? It was only you, me, and Devon who knew."

"I didn't tell him you didn't want to report it."

"What did you say?" Scarlett persisted.

"I just told him that there was an incident, something silly, and maybe if we were partners next time, he would get in on the action."

Scarlett shrugged, feeling tears pricking at the corners of her eyes. "So who do I believe? I don't know what to do."

Rhys cautiously reached toward Scarlett. He touched the ends of her hair, just as he had before. "I don't know how to help you. I wouldn't tell anyone about anything that happened between us."

Scarlett sighed. "That's exactly what Devon said. He said 'I wouldn't tell on you, I swear.' So who do I believe?"

Rhys shrugged, his silence allowing her to make her own decision. They were quiet for a few minutes. "I guess, the point is, they aren't playing around," Rhys finally said. "However they found out, they wanted to make a point. We're here to serve the Government, and that means following all of the rules. The rules aren't there without a reason."

Scarlett bit the inside of her cheek softly. "So you are saying we should follow each of the rules to the letter?"

Rhys nodded.

"But you touched my hair just now." Scarlett pointed out.

Rhys sighed. "Okay, that doesn't count as rule-breaking."

"Why? Because you trust Haman out of all the people here?"

Rhys shrugged. "I've been hearing some rumors and not just from Haman. I don't know, but the point is that I'm not hurting anyone by doing this." Rhys reached out and touched her hair again. Scarlett felt goosebumps rise up on her skin as though she were in the cold.

"Yeah, like that," her voice was even lower.

Rhys smiled. "I don't know—"

"What?"

Rhys shrugged and looked away, clasping his hands in his lap. "We should get some sleep. Just remember, I'm here for you. I have your back."

Scarlett suddenly remembered the decrepit male, who had spoken to them back during that strange night on the mountain. Should she bring it up again? But Rhys was standing. Scarlett felt tired. She reached out to Rhys. He smiled and grabbed her hand, pulling her to her feet, a move she had done many times with her friends, complaining she was too weak to get up on her own. But with Rhys, it felt different. Maybe, she was just extra tired.

"Good night," Rhys said as they sneaked down the mostly empty hallway.

Scarlett slept fitfully. She kept having the same dream over and over and over. She was trying to walk back through the woods to the training center. Every time, she could see the light shining through the edge of the trees, but the mysterious male appeared and told her she would kill Rhys. Scarlett would wake up, then dream the same dream again when she fell back to sleep.

By the time the first shift began crawling out of their beds, Scarlett was wide awake. What could she do to stop thinking about what had happened? Scarlett decided a trip to the exercise room would be helpful. She got up and dressed slowly. As the first shift was eating their breakfast and the third shift had yet to return, the exercise room was empty. Scarlett grabbed a barbell and stacked weights on either side. She knew she should wait until someone was there to spot her, but she didn't have time for that. She wanted to get out some of her stress.

Scarlett bent down and hefted the bar up and above her head. The first lift was always the easiest. Just as she was completing her second lift, a White female entered. Scarlett recognized her from her shift, but she wasn't on the same squadron. She was just another of the faces that Scarlett could recognize but not name.

"Good morning," the White greeted cheerfully. She made her way over to a bike that was next to where Scarlett was lifting. The exercise room felt strangely occupied when the White took that space. Scarlett glanced over her shoulder at a machine for abs. Maybe she should work on her abs and give this White some space. Scarlett set the bar gently on the floor and wiped her hands on the pants of her uniform.

"I wanted to talk to you," the White said, her legs moving at a furious speed on the bike.

Scarlett looked at her, confused. Was this another of those nosy people who only wanted to know why she had missed her last shift? Because that was not the way it had been when they lived at the training center. They just assumed they had been needed for something or had gotten in trouble, but it wasn't the kind of thing that was mentioned.

"I don't even know your name. How could you have been wanting to talk to me?" Scarlett responded frankly.

"I'm Darlin," she responded. "I know you've met a lot of new people in the last few days. It can get confusing. I remember when I first arrived in the City."

"How long ago was that?" Scarlett asked.

"Almost nine years now."

Scarlett calculated. So that meant that this female, Darlin, would have been at least a Blue when Scarlett was only a Yellow. She didn't look so old.

Darlin continued. "I heard that you were in isolation recently."

How had she heard that? Were the Blues mocked by the Whites? Were their consequences common knowledge? And if she wasn't talking to her out of curiosity, what did she want?

"I'm here to offer you a chance at a higher position."

Scarlett screwed up her face. "Why?"

"A few of us have noticed your discipline and dedication in the few days you have been here. We believe you would be a great match for this, and . . . the person we want you to watch is on your squad."

Scarlett pulled her shoulders back. Her squad? As in her Blue squad or her White squad? Why would they want her to be watching someone, whatever that meant?

"I can see the confusion on your face," Darlin said. "I can't give you many details unless you accept the position. However, if you do, you can face rewards, such as extra food and a cushier position once your first year is up. I mean, no immediate promotions, of course. That would be too obvious."

"I'm still confused. You want me to report on someone? Basically, spy on them?"

Darlin tilted her head back and forth as though considering her response. "You could say it like that. We have noticed some holes in the team recently, dissonance in the way the squads are performing."

"Do you even know what I was in isolation for?"

Darlin smiled. "Yes, of course. It doesn't need to be spoken of."

"So you want someone whose behavior is already questioned to report on others with questionable behavior?"

"Think of it as a way to improve your status here. You've made a mistake, but that doesn't mean you lose all opportunities for higher positions."

Scarlett pressed her lips together, her eyes scanning the exercise machines as she thought. She would love any way to assure those higher ups that she was for the Government.

"How long do I have to decide?"

"I'm surprised you wouldn't immediately want the position," Darlin said. She didn't look impressed. "What reason would you have to turn it down?"

"I just . . . it's so unexpected. I like to think over decisions I make."

"Well, I'll give you about ten minutes," Darlin said. "Either you want the position or you're not interested. Whatever decision you make, you are not to mention our conversation to anyone."

Scarlett's mind flew to Rhys. What if she was supposed to be reporting on him? But of course, Darlin wouldn't tell her who the person of interest was until she accepted the position. Scarlett found herself nodding. If it was Rhys, then what better way to protect him than by being the person who was supposed to report his behavior?

"I'll do it then," Scarlett said.

Darlin nodded, her legs still moving at lightning speed. "Good choice. Keep your eyes on Phan. Report any traitorous behavior to me and me only."

Phan. Phan? He was the person they suspected of treason? He was her leader!

Chapter 13

That afternoon, as Scarlett took her radio to prepare for her shift, she kept her eyes open for Phan. What was she supposed to be watching? Did he know someone might be watching him? Phan seemed to be the strictest male on their squad, the person who upheld the rules the most. Scarlett felt nervous, and if she could have gone back to her conversation with Darlin, she might make a different decision. But really, what decision had she had? If she had turned down the offer, someone higher up might think she didn't really want what was best for the Government.

Scarlett scanned the area and found Darlin. Darlin was ignoring her just as she had before they had met.

"Keep moving," Devon urged from behind her. Scarlett moved forward, closer to the clump of people, people she didn't know if she could trust or not.

When they were outside the gate of the compound, Scarlett saw Phan. He was serious as usual, not smiling. Scarlett's eyes traveled over his White uniform. Everything was in place.

He turned and looked directly at her, and Scarlett's heart stopped. She would have to be subtle. Her mind was panicking. She caught Rhys's eye, and he smiled at her. His smile was so familiar that Scarlett had to smile back.

"Partner assignments," Phan announced. Everyone was quiet as they listened for him to instruct them further.

"Rhys with Devon. Scarlett with Malak. Don't hesitate to alert me of any offenses." He slowly looked at each one of them, meeting their eyes before moving to the next one. "By don't hesitate, I mean, don't have a fight in the middle of the street trying to decide if you should report it. If you aren't sure, report it." He looked directly at Scarlett. "We are presenting a unified front to the Citizens, and that means no arguing."

He watched them for another few moments.

"What are you waiting for? Start your rounds."

Scarlett looked at Malak, then Rhys and Devon.

"Let's go," Malak said, motioning to Scarlett. They marched forward, and Scarlett could feel Phan's eyes on them. How was she supposed to watch him when they never worked together on their shift?

She and Malak had taken a few rounds of their section, Scarlett picking Malak's brain for any important information she might need, when Phan's call came over the radio.

"Blues, Squad Ten, where are you? Over."

Malak answered for both of them. "Southwest corner of Section Two."

Scarlett heard Rhys's voice. "East of Section Two."

"There is a mandatory meeting for all Citizens this evening at 19:00. All Citizens should be gathered in one of the two squares. Once the meeting has started at 19:01, begin checking the houses of Citizens. Everyone must attend the meeting, even children, and anyone not in attendance is subject to a consequence. Rhys and Devon, you will take the east side of Section Two. Malak and Scarlett, you will take the west side. Report any infractions immediately. Radio back if you understood."

Malak immediately responded. "Understood, Sir."

Rhys responded likewise.

"Devon and Scarlett?" Phan responded.

Scarlett used her own radio to answer that she understood, rolling her eyes. Couldn't Malak's assurance count for both of them? Or was Phan keeping a special eye on her now? Scarlett looked at Malak for the time. Her timepiece needed a new battery. "We have half an hour," he said. "We can make a full circuit in that time, then begin checking the houses."

As they made their last circuit, Scarlett saw a considerable number of Citizens walking toward the eastern side of their section, toward the City center. She wondered what the meeting would be about, what every Citizen needed to know.

"Do they have meetings like this often?" Scarlett asked.

Malak shrugged. "They are held when needed. There is no specific schedule, other than the monthly meeting to pay respects to the Government."

Scarlett nodded. "Any idea why they are having a meeting now, then?"

Malak shrugged again. "No, I wish we could attend, but we have our duties to complete."

Scarlett smiled a little. Malak was so faithful to everything the law dictated, as though he were a robot with no ability to deviate in the slightest. Scarlett wondered how Malak would react if she reached out and poked him. She laughed as she imagined him jumping away in fear of being aberrant from the rules set before them.

"Why are you laughing?" Malak asked.

Now, it was Scarlett's turn to shrug. "Just thinking about something."

Malak eyed her for a moment before checking his timepiece again. The waves of people making their way to the City center had slowed considerably.

"Five minutes, and we'll begin checking the houses. We should reach the west side just on time." Scarlett accepted his report and watched as an older male used a cane to make his way to the square. He was much older than anyone she had ever seen at the training center, and one of his limbs was a bit turned, as though he had been assembled in the dark. Scarlett watched him until he turned and gave her a glare.

Scarlett looked away quickly.

"Alright, let's begin," Malak said, pointing to a row of houses in front of them.

"Do we just enter their houses and see if anyone is there?" Scarlett asked. She wasn't one to invade a space where she shouldn't be.

Malak considered her idea and reached for his radio.

Scarlett stopped him. "Don't ask Phan. Let's just figure it out ourselves."

Scarlett marched toward the nearest house and knocked firmly on the door. No one answered. She looked at Malak, and he shrugged. Scarlett turned the knob, and the door creaked open. The inside was dark as the light was beginning to fail outside.

"Turn on your torch," Scarlett suggested, taking charge. Malak clicked on his torch and shone it around the room. Scarlett hadn't ever really seen the inside of a house. She had only peeked at bits and pieces while passing by. There was a large bed in the corner of the room, the largest bed Scarlett had ever seen before. It was more square than rectangular. As Malak moved the torch toward the other side of the room, Scarlett saw a sink and a cabinet. A small stovetop with one burner was perched beside the sink.

"Do they cook there?" Scarlett asked.

Malak nodded. "Yes, each house has only one room. That room serves the purpose of a dormitory, kitchen, and entertainment room all in one."

He sounded as though he were reading something straight from an informational text. Scarlett nodded. There was a door in the corner, and even though there was obviously no one in the house, Scarlett couldn't help but be curious. She opened the door slowly and found the smallest bathroom ever. The lip of the toilet was practically against the wall. There was no sink, and the shower was just a tub with no faucet.

"How do they bathe?" Scarlett asked.

"They often fill a bucket with water from the public faucet or from their sink here and dump it over themselves as needed. This prevents waste of water rather than having a faucet head that spills out water for ten to twelve minutes at a time."

"Okay," Scarlett said, her mind whirling with the new information. "I don't think anyone is in here."

They stepped out of the house, and Scarlett closed the door firmly behind her. They continued down the row of houses, each one exactly like the next. The only difference was the state of organization of each one. Some were swept to perfection while a few looked as though they hadn't been dusted in years.

As they were exiting their ninth or tenth house, Scarlett heard a yell. She froze and turned to Malak. "Did you hear that?" Scarlett asked.

Malak nodded, making a shushing motion as they both listened. The screech came again. It sounded human, but they couldn't be sure. Scarlett and Malak both started rushing toward the sound, not knowing what it was but sure it needed their attention.

After passing another ten to twelve houses, they came to one that had a candle flickering in the window. The yell came again from inside, long and low, more groanlike this time.

Scarlett felt frightened as she reached for the door handle. Malak was pasty white. "You go first," Scarlett urged, backing down one step. Malak pulled out his pistol, poised at the door. Just as another scream was starting, Malak flung the door open, pointing his pistol indecisively into the room. Less than five seconds later, he was backing down the steps, bumping into Scarlett. Scarlett copied him, backing away without knowing why.

"What? What is it?" she said, looking fearfully at the open door.

"I believe it's the time for a child's arrival," Malak stated. Scarlett frowned. Wouldn't a child's arrival be a happy occasion? Scarlett looked around in the twilight. She knew this house. This was the house of the large female, the one with whom Scarlett had spoken. Devon had said she was with child. Was the child coming out? How could it possibly come out?

"I'll radio this in," Malak said, holstering his pistol and reaching for his radio with shaking fingers. Another angry shriek and some curses came from inside.

"Phan, sir?" Malak said. Scarlett waited for a response, a command of what she should do in this strange situation.

"This is Phan. What do you have to report?"

"We have found a Citizen in her house. It appears that she is bringing a child into this world."

There was a pause, then, "That's an acceptable reason to be absent," Phan responded.

"Sir, what should we do? Does she need a doctor?"

"The doctor is attending the meeting. She can wait until after the meeting, and the doctor will be sent to her house. What is the house number?"

"Twenty-four," Scarlett said, checking the door.

"Twenty-four," Malak passed the information on.

"Great. It has been noted. Continue checking houses."

The female screeched again just as Phan finished his order.

"We can't leave her," Scarlett protested. Malak nodded. Even he agreed that the female's needs were urgent.

"I shouldn't be present," Malak said. "However, I have read extensively about this process. I can walk you through it."

"You want *me* to help her?" Scarlett asked.

"I am a male," Malak explained as though she were unaware of that fact.

Scarlett entered the house and saw the female on the bed. She was wearing only a shirt, and Scarlett immediately felt her face burn. The bed was wet with a clear fluid, and the female looked at Scarlett through angry eyes.

"Get out! Get out!" she screeched. "I don't want you here!"

"I'm here to help," Scarlett explained. She felt scared and unwelcome, but she couldn't leave this female to face the pain alone.

"Wash your hands!" Malak called from just outside the doorway. His back was turned to them, his tall frame almost reaching the top of the doorway.

Scarlett turned toward the faucet and rubbed the soap on her hands obediently before turning on the flow of cold water.

"Get some water boiling in a pot. You will need it to clean the baby after. Once it's boiling, you can take it off the burner. It should be just warm when you use it."

Scarlett's mind felt scattered. Boil water?

"Under the sink!" the female shouted. Scarlett opened the cabinet and found a large pot. She filled it with water and used a match to light the cooktop.

"Okay," Scarlett said slowly.

"Put a cold compress on her head," Malak said.

Scarlett found a cloth, wet it with cool water, and placed it on the female's head. The female didn't look as angry anymore. She seemed as though she might be grateful for the help.

"It's coming," she said. "I feel it."

"What do I do?" Scarlett asked.

Malak answered. "Position yourself at the rear end with a blanket. The child should come out head first. You will need to catch the child. Prepare a sharp object to cut the umbilical cord."

"What? Cut the child? What's an umbilical cord?"

"Knife," the laboring female said, pointing toward the kitchen area again. Scarlett grabbed a knife that reminded her very much of the one the Citizen had used to try to attack her just a few days ago. In fact, it looked exactly the same.

"Okay, I've got a knife."

"Sanitize the knife in the boiling water," Malak demanded. "Is that done? You need to hurry. Citizen, how far apart are the contractions?"

The female responded. "There's no space between them. It's coming any minute."

"Scarlett, hurry," Malak demanded. "Put the knife near where the child will arrive, but not in any area where the child could land."

Scarlett placed the knife on a small box beside the bed. She grabbed a blanket from the side of the bed that had not yet been wet by the female's liquids.

"Where will the child come? How?" Scarlett asked the female, who seemed almost as knowledgeable as Malak.

The female spread her legs and lifted them up. Scarlett saw a bulbous circle pulsing its way out of the female.

"Is that the child?" Scarlett asked, her stomach turning in revulsion.

"Get over here," the female said with another horrendous scream. Scarlett held the blanket in her trembling hands, positioning herself to catch the child. With an even louder screech, the child was heaved out. Scarlett could see two tiny eyes, squeezed shut. She groaned low. What was happening?

Another push. More of the child emerged.

"What is happening?" Malak asked, his back still turned at the door.

"Um, I think it's coming," Scarlett responded, not taking her eyes off the new child. Another push, and the child slid into the waiting blanket. Scarlett's stomach felt queasy. This child was covered in a red and white liquid. Her surprise at the ugliness of the thing almost made her drop the child. The female Citizen had her eyes closed and was breathing slowly. A thick, red rope was hanging between the child and the female.

"Now?" Malak asked, desperate for an update.

"I'm . . . holding it," Scarlett responded.

"Cut the umbilical cord with the knife you found earlier."

Scarlett edged her way to the table, balancing the small human in the blanket. She clutched the child tightly and used the knife in a quick sweeping motion to cut the cord. Immediately, half of the cord came alive, spewing blood in all directions. The child started screaming just then as though it had realized that things were not going quite right.

"Blood! There's blood! What do I do?" Scarlett screamed her questions at Malak.

"Ah! The clamp! I forgot. You have to clamp the cord," Malak said.

"With what?" Scarlett yelled, trying to be heard over the squalling child.

The female was amazingly quiet. Her chest continued to rise and fall with her breathing, but her eyes were only half open. Scarlett grabbed the dancing cord with her hand, feeling the blood pulsing against her, but it slowed, and no more was spewing out. She looked around for something to clamp it with.

The woman lifted her hand. There was a red ribbon tied around it. Scarlett continued to balance the child in one hand as she worked the ribbon off the female's wrist and tied it on the cord. The flow of blood was only a drip.

"Now what?" Scarlett asked, taking a shuddering breath.

"You need to clean the child with the warm water. Test it on your arm to make sure it's not too hot. Use gentle cloths."

Scarlett winced. The child barely looked human, but as she cleaned off the gunk, she could see the beauty in the small nose and thin lips. The squawking continued at an annoyingly high pitch as both Malak's and Scarlett's radios sounded.

Phan's voice came over the radio. "Have you completed your check of the houses in the western side of Section Two?"

Malak hesitantly picked up his radio. "It seems as though the female in house twenty-four was not able to wait. She has just given birth to a baby."

The female reached toward Scarlett, and Scarlett handed her the naked baby, keeping the dirty blanket in her hands. The female kissed the small creature, and Scarlett watched in awe as she moved her shirt and pressed the child against her bare skin. The child's cacophony of cries slowed then stopped.

"Could you bring that diaper from there please?" the female asked softly, pointing in the direction of the shelf near the front door. Scarlett found a small diaper, like the ones she had changed on that terrible day she had had to help with the Minis, those too small to even have a color yet.

She handed the material to the female who immediately wrapped the child.

"What will you do with it now?" Scarlett asked.

Malak stood in the doorway. "Is it safe for me to turn around?"

Scarlett nodded then realized he couldn't see her nodding. "Yes, everything is done." Malak entered the small home.

"We need to finish checking the houses. Phan is not happy with us that we stopped so long here."

"We couldn't very well leave her on her own!" Scarlett protested. Then she remembered Phan's request from earlier that day. They shouldn't argue in front of Citizens. Scarlett took a deep breath. "We must go," she said to the female.

"Thank you," the female responded, half-smiling, but her eyes were only on her child.

Malak and Scarlett stepped back out into the night, which felt decidedly chillier with the wind hitting them in the face. They checked the rest of the rows in their section quickly, Malak taking one while Scarlett took another.

Scarlett's mind was turning over and over the experience she had witnessed, had been a part of. She had so many questions, but one was really bothering her. How had the child grown inside the woman? How had the child been placed there? And what frightened Scarlett most of all was if a child would be placed inside her? What could she do to prevent that? She couldn't imagine suffering through such pain.

Malak called in the emptiness of the other houses, and they continued a slow patrol of Section Two.

"You knew a lot about that," Scarlett said. "About having a child, I mean."

Malak nodded. "I took a few extra courses. And I have never been so grateful for the materials I studied as tonight."

"Can you tell me something, then? How did the child get inside her? Why?" Scarlett shook her head.

"The process of fertilization is a bit more complicated and only happens among Citizens."

"So, I couldn't have a child within me?" Scarlett asked, looking for reassurance.

"No, we have already done our duty serving the Government as Blues or Whites, either in a City or at the training center. The Citizens have the job of producing more Citizens."

Scarlett nodded. "I think I'm beginning to understand. Thanks, Malak. I couldn't have done that without you." Scarlett reached out as though he were Rhys, going to squeeze his hand, before she pulled her hand back at the last moment, her face turning red in the darkness. The thought of Rhys made Scarlett skip a little as she walked. He would *not* believe it when she told him that she had helped bring a child into the world.

As they continued yet another round of the section, Scarlett heard a rush of life in the streets. The meeting must have ended. What a long meeting! Scarlett checked Malak's timepiece and found it was after 21:00.

They stayed in the area, patrolling the returning Citizens to make sure no tomfoolery was started. Whites walked at a leisurely pace around the Citizens, keeping an open eye for anything. Scarlett's eye caught on Phan, and she remembered her mission. She watched him carefully. He didn't seem to even notice her and Malak as he patrolled the area.

He reached for his radio. "Squadron Ten, meet at the northernmost point of Section Two in ten minutes. Respond that you have received my message. Over."

Scarlett was too fascinated with watching Phan, a span of approximately five houses away, to respond. Malak answered for both of them. "We will be there, Sir."

Phan nodded as he heard the message on his radio.

"Let's walk there now," Malak said, pointing toward the north. Scarlett nodded toward Phan and his partner.

"They aren't going yet."

Malak smiled. "I didn't even see them over there." He looked ready to walk toward them.

"I'm surprised he hasn't seen us. For someone supposedly so observant, he doesn't seem very observant to me."

Malak shook his head. "You shouldn't say something like that."

"Why? Is expressing my opinion about his level of observation treasonous now?"

Malak shook his head again. "Sometimes your opinions are quite strange."

Scarlett continued to observe Phan. He didn't speak with his partner in a casual way, the way Scarlett did every shift she had. Instead, he studied each of the Citizens as though they were apt to start trouble at any moment.

"Come on. We need to go. I don't want to arrive after him."

Scarlett sighed and gave in to Malak's urging. They marched away from the thinning stream of Citizens toward the northernmost part of their section. This bordered the fence, and Scarlett looked through the fencing when they arrived. She could see the terrain beyond, full of trees and life, not like the desert land that surrounded their training center. Scarlett wanted to reach through the fence and touch the trees' greenness.

"Hey!" Rhys called, and Scarlett turned around with a jump of surprise.

"Hey!" Scarlett called back, taking a few steps toward him. "You'll never guess what we did today!"

"Whoa!" Rhys reacted. "Why . . . is that blood on you?"

Scarlett laughed but couldn't hold back her excitement, like a Red on Children's Day. "No! Malak and I helped a female bring a child into this world."

Rhys looked confused. "From where? Another world?"

Scarlett laughed. "No, from her stomach. Remember the large female we saw before? Well, I've seen her multiple times, and she had a child within her. Now, the child is out. Apparently, it's a painful process."

Malak nodded. "I had read all the steps that needed to be taken for a successful birth, but I have never experienced everything first hand. What a day!"

"What did you have to do?" Rhys asked as Devon made a face. Just then, Phan, without the rest of Squadron Scorpio, strode up.

"We should only take a few minutes, and then everyone can return to their posts." Phan took a deep breath and pressed his fingers together in a small tent before him. "We have a few Citizens who need special observation. These Citizens live in houses eighteen, forty-three, and forty-five. You will continue your rotations as normal, but I ask that you spend more time in the vicinity of those houses. Report anything out of the usual, even if it is not against the laws. Do you understand?"

Everyone bobbed their heads in agreement.

"I need your verbal assent."

"Yes, I understand," Scarlett said as Malak, Rhys, and Devon did the same. Phan nodded, meeting each of their eyes again.

"Continue your shifts now," he said.

Scarlett and Malak moved toward the east as Devon and Rhys moved westward. Scarlett shivered as the wind picked up. Her uniform covered her perfectly, but she still felt fear creeping up her spine.

"I wonder what those Citizens did to warrant extra attention," she said to Malak.

Malak didn't respond, and Scarlett hadn't really expected him to. What was scaring her was the number of secrets that seemed to abound in City 6. In the training center, everything was straightforward. The rules were set, and you didn't question authority. Everyone knew what would happen if you did.

"What would I have to do to warrant extra attention?" Scarlett said in a low voice, wanting Malak to say something. Did all of the secrets bother him?

Malak shook his head. "Don't talk that way. You're here for a reason, which means they identified you as a female who would do well serving in the City."

Malak had a way of putting words together to sound comforting, but when you really considered them, they didn't mean a whole lot.

"I already got in trouble here," Scarlett reminded him.

Malak performed an odd combination of nods and shrugs. "Yes, I am aware. However, adjusting to the new environment can take some time and cause some mistakes. That does not mean that your selection was incorrect."

Scarlett shook her head, ready to be done with the topic. The only problem was, her mind wouldn't shut off. A female Citizen almost brushed by them in a hurry. Scarlett watched her, then gazed at her timepiece. Wasn't it curfew time? What was the female doing out of her house?

Scarlett saw Malak turn to her in the darkness. She opened her mouth, but Malak just nodded before she could say anything else. Scarlett pointed her head toward the direction the female had gone. Malak nodded, and they followed after the female at a hurried clip. She didn't have a torch, so it was more a matter of following the shadows than an actual figure.

Scarlett's stomach turned over. It wasn't quite 22:00, but the way she had hurried made Scarlett feel as though she was doing something illicit. Scarlett and Malak continued until they reached the edge of Section Two. As they stood at the invisible border of Section Three, Malak reached for his radio as Scarlett's eyes scanned the darkness. Nothing. Nothing that she could see anyway.

"Malak, over," Malak said into the radio.

"Phan here," his low voice responded. Malak's eyes continued searching the darkness as he spoke into the radio, the crackling louder than the soft night noises of the City.

"We've just seen a female hurrying toward Section Three. We followed her to the edge of our Section, but I don't see any sign of her."

"Was she carrying anything with her?" Phan responded.

"Nothing that we saw. Our view of her was quick," Malak responded.

"What house did she come out of?"

Malak and Scarlett looked back over their shoulders. They couldn't remember where they had been standing when she had hurried by them, and they certainly had not seen the house she came out of. "Not sure, Sir," Malak responded.

"Thanks for the report," Phan responded. "Continue your regular patrol. I will take care of it." Scarlett looked over her shoulder. She knew they should stay in their Section at all times to maintain the balance of Blues and Whites and Citizens, but she was tempted to step over the line. She wondered if the female was doing something against the law, and if she was, why hadn't she been paying more attention when slipping out at night? Scarlett and Malak were not hard to see, even in the darkness.

Chapter 14

"And then I was holding the thing!" Scarlett recounted.

Rhys made a face. "That sounds disgusting."

"It was!" Scarlett agreed. "I thought I was going to be sick. The thing hardly looked like a human. But when I cleaned it off, it changed its appearance. It was still red . . . and rough, but it looked more . . . I don't know, like something I would want to help."

Devon exaggerated his gagging noises. "Glad I wasn't your partner tonight."

"Yeah, me too. What would you have told me to do if you had been in Malak's position? Run away!" Scarlett saw Devon's face spread into a smile, and she remembered she was supposed to be mad with him. But her anger was simmering down. He had sworn he didn't do anything anyway.

"I probably would have followed what Phan said and continued checking the houses," Devon responded, and Scarlett remembered how annoying he could be.

Scarlett rolled her eyes. "You're such a child. You have to do what you have to do when duty calls. Besides, I haven't seen any other large females like that one, so I don't think you'll have to be a doctor for some time yet."

Rhys shoveled the rest of his meal into his mouth, and Scarlett looked at her empty plate. Talking about the event of the night energized her. She didn't want to go to bed. "I think I'm going to get some exercise in before I sleep," she said.

Devon nodded, and Rhys looked toward the doorway that led toward the dormitories. "I am tired," he said. "My night wasn't as eventful as yours, and I had to keep myself from falling asleep while walking the last hour." Rhys stood, grabbing his tray. "I'll see you both tomorrow."

Scarlett headed toward the exercise room. The first shift was asleep, and the third shift had just started. Scarlett looked around and felt a creeping feeling slowly ascend her spine. She turned, and there was Darlin in the corner, lifting weights. There were only two other people in the exercise room, and Scarlett felt drawn to Darlin. Maybe it was the way Darlin watched her without blinking.

Scarlett subtly walked over and fiddled with the weights on another bar. Her arms were already protesting the thought of another workout, but she didn't care. Darlin set down her bar, and leaning forward, used it to stretch her legs.

"What do you have for me?" she asked, extending her arms until her chest was pressed against her leg.

Scarlett shook her head slightly as she slipped another five-pounder on the bar. "Nothing treasonous. And . . . I don't know if I'm the best person to keep an eye on him. I barely see him during my shift."

"You see enough," Darlin responded, switching the leg she was stretching. She stretched for a good minute as Scarlett squatted for her first lift. "What did you see? Even if it appears to be completely normal to you, it may have more meaning to the Government."

Scarlett grunted as she lifted the bar into the air. Her muscles complained about the exercise as she slowed the bar's descent. "We were told to keep a special eye on several houses, but not why."

"Which houses?"

Something in Scarlett's stomach felt wrong. She had no reason not to trust Darlin, but she didn't have any reason to trust her either. "I think it was twenty-four, forty, and forty-three, but I don't remember for sure. Malak is better at that sort of thing. He remembers everything."

Darlin didn't look pleased. "Tomorrow, make sure you have the right house numbers. You telling me the wrong number could have negative consequences for someone who didn't deserve them."

"Can you just be honest with me?" Scarlett asked in a voice louder than she meant. The other two exercising in the room looked their way. Scarlett ignored them, going back to lifting her bar. Darlin didn't say anything for a long time. Scarlett finally felt so uncomfortable with the silence that she left the room to head for the showers. Darlin didn't say anything about her quick exit.

* * *

As Scarlett rose the next morning, she avoided going to the exercise room for fear of another hushed conversation with Darlin, and she decided she had to tell Rhys what Darlin had said. As everyone lined up to receive their morning meal, Scarlett nodded toward Rhys. He nodded back good-naturedly.

Scarlett nodded toward a table in the back corner that was hardly ever used unless the dining hall was very full. Rhys continued to nod at her with a ridiculous smile on his face. Scarlett clenched her fists. Why was he so frustrating? Couldn't he understand what she was trying to say, or should she just shout everything at him?

Rhys burst out laughing, and Devon, who was standing between them, turned to him with a raised eyebrow. "You alright there?"

Rhys nodded some more, his lips pressed into a line to keep the giggles from escaping. Scarlett rolled her eyes. "Haman," she muttered.

They all grabbed their trays, and Devon started to head toward the cluster of tables where they normally sat.

"Hey, male, I'll catch you later," Rhys said, bumping Devon's arm.

"You too good to eat with me now?" Devon asked, feigning hurt.

"Now? Always have been," Rhys retorted. They both laughed, but Scarlett felt Devon watching them as they walked toward the more private table. It made her feel nervous, like she was doing something wrong, but really, she never knew if she was doing something wrong or not. It depended whose rules you followed.

"What's up?" Rhys asked as they sat down. "Getting tired of Devon?"

Scarlett smiled just slightly, but she couldn't help letting her eyes jump around the dining hall to see if they appeared to be drawing any attention. She remembered a conversation she had had with Devon just a few days ago at this very table. Her stomach suddenly clutched in fear. Everything she had said to Devon in this very spot had somehow gotten to the Black. What if the table was bugged? She had heard about devices that could record conversation.

"Nothing," Scarlett responded. "Just haven't talked to you in a little while." Scarlett's fingers pried at the edge of the table, working their way farther and farther under as her paranoia took hold of her.

Rhys looked at her strangely. He saw her arm creeping under the table, and he watched her carefully as he chewed slowly. "Yeah, it's been a while," he said when he finished his mouthful, still looking at her strangely. "A whole eight hours."

Scarlett pressed her lips together, but she didn't find any bumps under the table. Maybe there wasn't a bug; maybe she was just crazy. She took a deep breath and tried to use subtle signs to communicate. She pointed to her wrist where a timepiece would normally be, motioned a one with her finger, and made a climbing motion with her other hand. Meet her at the stairs in an hour?

Rhys shrugged and looked back over to where Devon was sitting with several others. "You're a very strange female," Rhys finally said.

Scarlett tried to respond lightly. "Thanks, I appreciate that. I would venture to say you're a strange human, encompassing both males and females."

"Ooh, now you've hurt me," Rhys said, faking a hit to the gut.

"Guess you should go see the nurse," Scarlett suggested innocently.

Rhys shook his head and stabbed another mouthful of rice and beans. "No way. Did you know I've never seen the nurse except for my yearly exam?"

Scarlett looked at him with disbelief. "You've never been sick? That's a lie. I remember just last year when you were like 'I think there's some germ having a party in my body.' And you said your whole body hurt when you moved? Yeah, I remember that."

Rhys laughed. "I didn't go to the nurse, though."

"Why?"

"Because I didn't need to. I've seen so many males get sick. The nurse gives them some pill, and they get better maybe two days later. I was doing my own experiment. How many days would it take me to get better without a pill?"

"And?"

"Three," Rhys held up three fingers proudly as though he had healed himself.

Scarlett shook her head but was appreciative of him for distracting her from what was on her mind. "I've always gone to the nurse, and yes, they give you a pill or a shot that fights the virus, but they also give you something for the pain. It helps you sleep, so you don't have to deal with all the sick feelings. That's why you should go."

"If I don't go through the pain, how can I appreciate it when I'm feeling well?"

"You're strange," Scarlett said, focusing on her food and checking her watch constantly. They finished their meal, and Scarlett nodded in the direction of the stairs and tapped her wrist to remind Rhys. He smiled and shook his head at the same time. Scarlett knew what he was thinking—that she was crazy.

But half an hour later, when they were under the stairs together, Scarlett felt much more comfortable telling him what she had spoken about with Darlin.

"There's a lot of secrets here," Scarlett said.

Rhys widened his eyes and faked surprise. Then, he turned serious. "Sure, there are. We're not ready or able to know everything. Just like when you're a Red, and they don't let you walk anywhere in the training center by yourself. It's not that they have something to hide; it's that you're not ready for that responsibility."

Scarlett frowned. She didn't like how accepting Rhys was of the authority, rules, and secrecy she was discovering. She had always been the kind of person who wanted to learn as much as she could, and she didn't tolerate information being held back. She wasn't as extreme as Malak, but she enjoyed learning and knowing exactly why everything was happening.

"Let me tell you what happened to me, and maybe you won't think the same thing anymore," Scarlett said. "Yesterday, some White female I've never contacted before started a conversation with me. She said that they needed my help, and she knew that I had been in isolation and why. It was like she knew everything about me."

"Maybe Whites are privy to more information than we are about the happenings in the compound," Rhys suggested, picking at a scab on his ankle. Scarlett didn't like how ready he was to wrap everything in a neat little explanation.

"She wanted me to watch Phan," Scarlett continued, "to see if he's doing anything traitorous. She said they need someone close to him to watch him, and I'm supposed to report anything I see to her."

"Which White is this?" Rhys looked confused. "That seems like an assignment you would be given from the Black, not a White in the exercise room."

"Yeah," Scarlett agreed softly. "I thought it was strange, too. It was a female. She said her name was Darlin. I can point her out when we go on our shift."

"So she wanted you to keep an eye on Phan? That's it? What did you say?"

"I just agreed. She didn't give me much time to make the decision, and I didn't want to turn it down. Because, what if I get an opportunity like this, but I turn it down? Then, they'll think I'm the traitorous one. Like, I'm not interested in helping the Government."

Rhys moved his head from side to side, cracking his neck as he considered Scarlett's point of view. "Okay, I can understand that. Accept any and all opportunities so you show how eager you are to serve." He used his hand to massage his neck as he thought, staring into the corner. Scarlett watched him eagerly for advice, something to tell her she was doing the right thing or how she could get on track to doing the right thing.

Rhys finally shrugged. "I think you did the right thing, given the situation. But it's still a bit suspicious. I would feel more comfortable if the Black had given you this assignment face to face. And, no offense, but why did Darlin, or whoever made the decision, pick you?"

Scarlett shook her head. "I have no idea. You can work on an explanation for that one. I guess, I'll just keep watching and gathering information. That's all I can do."

"Okay, what were you doing this morning?" Rhys asked suddenly, almost cutting off her last sentence.

"When?"

"At breakfast? You were acting like a mute."

Scarlett shrugged, feeling paranoid now for acting as she had. Still, she felt like she owed Rhys an explanation. "I know this is going to sound weird, but that conversation I had with Devon, about you and me and the child who was stealing fruit, we had that conversation there. And Devon and you insist you didn't tell anyone, and I just thought maybe that table was bugged . . . or somehow, the Whites could hear what we were saying."

Rhys's eyes widened in real surprise then. "I've never thought of that. If they bugged one table, why wouldn't they bug them all?"

Scarlett's mind scurried to remember what sorts of conversations she'd had over meals in the dining halls.

"Why stop with one table? And why just the tables? If you think there's one, there have to be multiples."

Scarlett shrugged. "I didn't actually find one. So I don't know. Maybe I'm just being paranoid. But it's a possibility, huh?"

"I don't like it," Rhys said, pounding his fist gently on the floor. "Because that means there is absolutely no trust here, and that's not the way we were raised in the training center. Sure, there was a whistleblowing system, but that's to be expected somewhat. I don't like the idea of every word I've spoken being recorded somewhere."

"Me neither," Scarlett said. She looked around the shadowy undercarriage of the stairs. "But from what I can tell, we've been safe here."

Rhys smiled. "From what you can tell are the key words there." They were both quiet for a moment. Scarlett felt an unwarranted desire to reach out and touch Rhys's hand. She struggled with herself as she watched him brush his fingers through his tight brown curls. His eyes locked with hers, and Scarlett's stomach flipped over. She wasn't sure why she was feeling this way, and she started talking to distract herself from her strange feelings.

"Well, anyway, it's not like we have anything to hide, except what I just told you. I wasn't supposed to tell anyone that, so if you could keep it a secret, that would be great. Because, I don't exactly want to get in trouble just for talking to you."

Rhys laughed a little. "Hey, you don't have to tell me twice. I'm not here to do anything to get you in trouble."

"Unless it involves a child stealing fruit?" she asked, cocking a knowing eyebrow.

Rhys shook his head. "That's different. I didn't know that would get you in trouble."

"I sort of wonder if I had never said anything to Devon, would I have gotten in trouble? I don't . . . trust Devon anymore, to be honest."

Rhys shrugged. "That's your decision. I think Devon's a great male, but he's a bit too eager for friends. I mean, he's been a Blue for I don't know how long before us, but he seems to hang out with us the most, like he doesn't have any friends. I don't know; it was just something I was thinking about yesterday."

They both heard something and hushed, listening in the hallway. A couple of Whites came down the stairs. Scarlett scooched farther into the opening, motioning for Rhys to move closer.

". . . in Section One," one of the Whites said, his feet pounding into the metal stairs above Scarlett's head. Rhys pressed into the opening, his head right by Scarlett's. His breath tickled her ear, and Scarlett held her body rigid. The Whites' feet tapped the bottom stair, and they headed down the hallway. If they had turned back and looked at just the right angle, they would have seen Rhys's Blue uniform shoe sticking out from under the stairs. But they didn't. Scarlett and Rhys held still for what felt like an hour before Rhys drew back.

Scarlett brushed her face with her hand. Why was she sweating?

"Maybe we shouldn't have any more secret meetings under here," Scarlett said, her voice a whisper.

Rhys nodded. "I don't think it's against the rules to be here, but it's better to be safe than sorry."

"You go first," Scarlett said. "I'll come out a few minutes after you, so no one sees us walking from the stairs together and asks what we were talking about."

Scarlett watched Rhys go, and she felt suddenly lonely, like the space below the stairs was much bigger than before.

As Scarlett emerged from under the stairs and began walking down the hallway, Darlin was striding toward her. She looked behind Scarlett, and Scarlett knew she was summing up her situation. There was nothing behind Scarlett that gave her a reason to be back there. The Blue dormitories and bathrooms were in front of her.

Scarlett pasted a smile on her face and tried to pretend as though she was where she belonged. "Hello," she said in a friendly voice.

Darlin gave another obvious look behind Scarlett but didn't seem to have time for an explanation anyway. "I didn't see you in the exercise room this morning," she stated as they met in the middle of the hall. Darlin kept her voice low.

Scarlett nodded and shrugged, her awkwardness reminding her of Malak. "I didn't know we had a set meeting time. Besides, all I did last night was sleep, so it's not as though I had time to discover any new information."

"That sounds like a lot of excuses," Darlin responded.

Scarlett let out a huff of breath, confused. Well, they were excuses and good ones, too. "I'm not very good at figuring stuff out," Scarlett said. "So if you expect something from me, you have to make it clear."

Darlin nodded and gave a slight nod. "I can see that. You should come every evening and every morning, even if you don't have anything to report. Don't you think it would look suspicious if something happens with Phan, and *then*, you and I are seen talking? However, if we always exercise together, no one will think anything of it."

Scarlett nodded. "Okay. I'll see you after our shift then." Darlin studied Scarlett for another few moments, her arms crossed over her chest.

"I'll see you then," Darlin said, effectively dismissing Scarlett. Scarlett hurried off to dish duty, her mind full. She wanted to spill everything to Rhys, but Scarlett realized that she couldn't rely on him to hold her secrets. She had to be strong enough to hold them herself. Besides, it's not as though this was anything overwhelming—other than the fact that Darlin seemed sure something would happen with Phan, something big.

That afternoon, Scarlett frowned when she was assigned to work with Devon. Her respect for him had slowly degraded since she had been put in isolation, but especially since her last conversation with Rhys; Scarlett was determined not to trust Devon. Not even a remark about Phan would be made in his presence.

"Nice to work with you again," Devon said amiably as they strode off to give a once over of Section Two. Scarlett gave a nod in response and pretended to be watching the houses carefully. They came upon the house where the child had been born. Had that only been the evening before? Scarlett desperately wanted to see the child, and the female as well. Was everyone doing well? Was the child healthy?

She gazed at house twenty-four as they strode past.

"Did you see something?" Devon asked.

Scarlett paused. "I know it's not exactly our duty, or even any of our business, but I would like to see the tiny child that came out of the female last night. You should see it, too. It's hard to believe something so small is alive."

Devon shrugged. "What do you want to do? Knock on their door?"

Scarlett shrugged. "I don't know. I suppose knocking couldn't hurt."

The door of the house was closed, while most were at least half-open to keep the houses from becoming stuffy in the afternoon heat. "I suppose it would be better now to visit than at night when everyone is preparing for bed."

"When we took the 'young children' class, we learned that children don't sleep at night."

Scarlett lifted her eyebrows. "Do they sleep during the day and stay awake at night?"

Devon shook his head. "It's like they sleep only for short periods of time, perhaps an hour or two. Then, they are awake for a few hours."

Scarlett frowned. "That's odd. Could you imagine waking up every two hours? I would feel tired, even after a night full of sleep."

Devon shrugged and held up his hands. "Hey, I've only ever read about it. I don't know if it's true or not."

"We should ask!" Scarlett concluded excitedly. Just as she was about to explain the brilliance of her plan to Devon, they saw Phan and his partner turning down the street. They both turned and continued down their route without a word. They wouldn't be caught conversing in the street when they were supposed to be patrolling. Scarlett looked back over her shoulder once, but she didn't see Phan and his partner. They had been there. She knew that. Devon had seen them, too.

Phan suddenly radioed them, both of their radios rustling in sync. "Scarlett and Malak, report to house twenty-four."

Scarlett looked over at Devon. Malak wasn't her partner now. Devon was. Did Phan want them to separate from their partners?"

Scarlett cautiously reached for her radio. "Reporting now to house twenty-four."

Malak's response was scratchy and hard to understand.

Phan gave one more instruction. "Devon and Rhys, continue patrolling your usual route. Your partners will join you soon."

Scarlett shrugged at Devon, her stomach twisting. Was she going to get in trouble for something else? But no, she couldn't imagine Malak having ever done anything slightly against the rules, so if she was getting called with him, then it couldn't be anything she had done.

Scarlett was close to house twenty-four. She knew it as soon as she arrived. It was the house she had been debating on entering just ten minutes before. Scarlett waited for a minute, her toes at the bottom of the first wooden stair. She saw Malak jogging toward her in the distance and decided to wait for him to catch up to her before entering. Even though Malak was not someone you would marvel at for physical strength, Scarlett felt much more confident about entering with him.

Malak nodded toward her and slowed his jog, not stopping to talk, just taking one giant step up the two wooden stairs and pushing the door open. Scarlett followed after him, her eyes taking in the scene as quickly as she could.

The female she had helped last night was sitting on the edge of the bed. Her hand was pressed against her abdomen, and her eyes were dancing around at their faces. Her eyes stopped on Scarlett's face for a moment before she turned away and bit her lip.

Scarlett saluted Phan with three fingers over her heart. "May the Government's wisdom and power live forever," she recited with Malak. Phan nodded to both of them.

"Stand down," he said. They relaxed, and Scarlett was allowed to look back to the female. The female still wasn't looking at her. Scarlett scanned the room. Where was the child? Shouldn't the child be with the female, so the female could care for it?

Phan spoke, not removing his eyes from the female.

"We received a report that a child was born here last night." Scarlett looked at the female, already starting to nod.

Why was the female shaking her head? She looked as though she might cry. Scarlett watched carefully. Where was the child? Didn't the children live with the females and males here? That's what Malak had told her, and Malak hadn't been wrong about anything yet. Scarlett looked to Malak to see how he was interpreting her expression.

"Can you please testify as to what you saw here last night?" Phan said, looking directly at Scarlett and Malak. Scarlett opened her mouth and had a few false starts, before Malak began speaking.

"Last night, we were checking houses to see that all Citizens had attended the mandatory meeting. Upon hearing a cry for help, Scarlett and I both hurried to this house, house twenty-four, in an attempt to see what was happening." Malak talked like a history book would about an important historical event. "We came upon this female in labor. I advised Scarlett of the process needed to safely help the child enter this world." Malak stopped, and Phan studied him before turning his harsh gaze on Scarlett.

"And?" Phan prompted.

"And I followed Malak's instructions," Scarlett said, not sure what he was looking for.

"Was the child born alive?" Phan asked.

"Oh, yes, the child was alive," Scarlett nodded rapidly. "It was crying." Phan looked at the female. "Where is the child now?"

"I told you," the female responded. "The child died a few hours later. My daughter is gone." Tears leaked down her cheeks. "My husband has buried her."

Phan shook his head and turned back to Scarlett, but she could see that he was barely controlling his anger. "Was the child healthy?" he asked Scarlett.

Her eyes widened. She knew nothing about such things. "I don't know," Scarlett said. "I didn't know what I was doing. I followed Malak's instructions, but after the child was cleaned, we both left to finish our rounds, checking the houses."

Phan looked between Scarlett and the female. "Search the house!" he declared. No one moved, and he turned his steely gaze on Scarlett, then Malak. Malak and Scarlett started moving around the small house. Scarlett opened cabinets and peered into them. What were they looking for? The child? The female had said the child died. Why shouldn't they believe her? But as Scarlett really accepted the fact that the child was gone, she began to feel sad. Everything she had done the night before was wasted. She had not helped the female. Perhaps she had done something wrong, something that had caused the child to die.

Scarlett sucked her cheeks in as she peered into a stack of shelves that was covered by a curtain. She felt like apologizing to the female for whatever she had done to hurt the child. She turned back to the rest of the room and found that Malak had already stopped his futile search. She was the only one still poking in odd corners.

Phan looked at the female hard for a long few minutes; she dropped her eyes and clutched her abdomen again. "I'm sorry for your loss," he said, his words slow, one at a time.

The female nodded. "Thank you."

"Let's go," Phan said. They stepped outside the house, and Phan motioned for Malak and Scarlett to follow him. Scarlett studied him quickly. Would anything she had said or done be considered treasonous?

Scarlett didn't know why they would want to see the child. Did the doctor want to make sure it was healthy? Scarlett knew nothing about babies.

Phan stopped suddenly, and Scarlett almost stepped on the back of his shoes. She stopped as he turned and took a step back so they weren't so close.

"Was she lying?" Scarlett asked.

Phan shook his head slowly and let out a long puff of air. "This does happen sometimes, especially if the female is not very healthy. It's a shame that they can't have healthy babies more often than they do." There was a pause as Scarlett wondered if she was expected to reply. "Do you remember which other houses you should watch?" Phan asked, studying both of them carefully.

"Yes," Scarlett nodded. "Forty, forty-three, and. . ."

"Eighteen," Malak finished. Phan gave Malak an approving nod.

"Correct. Now, return to your partners." Scarlett looked around, as if she would see Devon conveniently waiting on a corner for her.

"Use your radio," Phan said.

Scarlett nodded. Why hadn't she thought of that? She reached for her radio. "Devon. What's your location?" she asked.

Devon responded, then Malak used the radio to find Rhys. Scarlett started toward where Devon was, considering everything that had happened. Why did they want so desperately to find the child?

Chapter 15

After another evening and morning with nothing to report to Darlin, Scarlett began to feel as though she wasn't needed, as though Darlin had jumped the gun when asking her to report things about Phan. That evening on her shift, Scarlett was paired with Rhys, and she felt relief when she heard their names called together. She missed talking with him, and their shift would give them plenty of chances.

"So," Rhys said, taking off at a good pace. Scarlett matched his pace. "You were really busy today. Have you decided to bulk up or something? You're always in the exercise room."

Scarlett nodded. "Well, I want to keep up the routines we had in place at the training centers, even though we aren't assigned exercise times now."

Rhys agreed. "You're better than me. I always feel too tired after our shift, and when we wake up, I'm too eager to have the morning meal to consider exercising. I tend to only exercise before the midday meal if I exercise at all."

They were silent for a few minutes. "Phan wanted us to check those houses," Rhys finally added. "Do you want to go in now? We're near the first one." Rhys pointed to house number eighteen.

Scarlett nodded. "Sure, we can go in. Let's tell everyone, so they know they're being checked." Scarlett reached for her radio and informed those in Section Two that they were going to check out the two houses closest to them, eighteen and twenty-four.

"Report back anything unusual," Phan responded.

Scarlett and Rhys walked up two creaky steps to house number eighteen. "Should we knock?" Scarlett asked.

Rhys nodded thoughtfully. "That seems like a good idea. If they don't answer, we can go in."

Scarlett gave three loud knocks. The door flew open abruptly as though someone had been waiting for them. A female immediately made the sign of the Government over her heart. Scarlett saluted back as did Rhys, both of them slightly delayed. A small male of perhaps five years old waved at them. Scarlett smiled and wiggled her fingers back in a small wave.

"What can I do to help you?" the female asked, her tone brusque though not menacing.

"We want to take a look around your home," Rhys said. The female stepped aside and waited by the door as they completed a quick examination of the house. Nothing was unusual or out of place. Rhys made the sign of the Government again, and the two exited.

"She didn't seem to be acting suspicious at all," Scarlett commented. Rhys suddenly swerved in front of Scarlett and walked up the steps to house twenty. Scarlett crept up the steps behind him, listening for whatever had brought Rhys to the doorway. He rapped hard on the door.

Scarlett heard some sounds from inside but couldn't tell what they meant. "I'm coming!" a female called. "I just need to put on proper attire."

Scarlett and Rhys looked at each other and shrugged, both waiting in an awkward state of impatience. Less than a minute later, the door was opened before them. A female who looked much the same as other females in City 6 opened the door and studied them for a few moments.

"Can I help you?" she asked.

Scarlett nodded. "We are just coming in to do a check of your house and make sure everything complies with the regulations."

The female tilted her head. "Which regulations are you referring to? My house was just checked yesterday."

"I'm sorry. We're just doing our job, and we were told to check your house," Rhys said. Scarlett stopped herself just short of looking at him sideways. Nothing about house twenty had been mentioned as a suspicious house.

The female nodded. "Okay, come in. I must ask you to be quiet though, my child is sleeping. She has not been feeling well." The female lowered her voice as she stepped aside. Scarlett saw a small body curled up on the bed. The child looked to be about two years old.

"We'll be as quiet as possible," Scarlett responded.

"I appreciate it," the female said, going over to the bed and stroking the child's face gently. Scarlett looked around the one-room house again. There wasn't much to even see. Phan had listed potentially dangerous materials they could find that would be against regulations. The real question was why Rhys had become so interested in this house.

Scarlett looked in the closet, scanning the items grouped neatly on the shelves. There was nothing more than the bare necessities. It reminded Scarlett of her drawer at the training center.

Scarlett turned back to where the female was sitting beside the child on the bed. Scarlett leaned toward the bed, attempting to peer under it. But before she got a chance, she got a good look at the child. The child's hair was sweaty from sleep, and his skin was slightly tanned as most children seemed to be in this City. But his hand, if it could be called that, was twisted inward, the skin warped in strange patterns.

Scarlett's eyes flew up to the female. "What happened to the child?" she asked. She had never before seen a hand that seemed permanently locked in position.

The female shook her head slowly and pressed a finger to her lips, reminding Scarlett to speak in a whisper. "She was born with her hand like that. She can't use it," the female said.

Scarlett nodded as though she understood, but she really didn't. "Are many children born here with . . . hands like this?" Scarlett asked, still crouched by the bed.

The female shrugged. "It happens occasionally. We cannot control nature." Scarlett began to rise, before remembering that she was going to check under the bed.

"Excuse me, let me just look under the bed quickly," Scarlett said, bending down next to the female's legs.

The female spoke in a hush. "Sure, it's just a bin with some crackers and noodles. Then, if you wouldn't mind, I would like to take a rest with my child."

Scarlett didn't say anything as she bent down and squinted into the darkness beneath the bed. She saw a bin, as promised, and began to stand. Then, she saw something move in the bin, like the head of a snake readying to strike. Scarlett had seen plenty of those in her days at the training center. So while it surprised her, she wasn't so scared that she didn't know what to do.

"Hand me the broom," Scarlett said to Rhys. Rhys reached for it, looking at her strangely.

"What is it?" he asked, moving swiftly to grab the broom on the other side of the room.

"A snake. It was moving quickly, too. Let's get it out of here, and we can kill it outside." Scarlett looked up at the female who was looking on with fear. "Don't be scared. I'll get it out as quietly as possible. Do you often get snakes around here?"

"Uh, no, we don't get snakes. It's probably not a snake," the female said. "Maybe you shouldn't go sticking that broom under there. I'd rather not have . . . my noodles crushed."

Scarlett half-smiled. "I know what I saw. It was a snake. And I don't think you would want it biting your child while it's sleeping. I'll take care of it for you."

Scarlett got down on the ground again, using the broomstick to poke at the area where she had seen the snake. The female was suddenly on the ground, wrestling the stick from her. Rhys immediately got involved, grabbing the broomstick from both of them and throwing it across the house, ready to detain the female if necessary.

He stared at her, as she looked back and forth between them. The child on the bed woke and began crying in an odd mewing sort of noise. The sound seemed echoed as if its cries were bouncing off the walls. The female ignored her child and stared at both Rhys and Scarlett, feet and arms spread as if ready to attack.

"I think you should go now," she said. "My child can be hard to calm, and she does not understand disruptions to her normal schedule." Scarlett started to turn, used to following orders from her elders. But then she turned back. She *had* to find out what was under the bed.

Scarlett pulled the gloves from her belt and slipped them on her fingers with fast movements. Then, she dipped under the bed again, hoping Rhys would cover for her if the female acted crazy once more. Scarlett bravely reached for the bin. It didn't have a lid, and Scarlett slid it toward her and retracted her hand quickly to avoid a snake bite.

The cries seemed louder now. Scarlett tried to block her ears from the child's attention-grabbing technique and watched the bin. The female reached for Scarlett, but Rhys grabbed her wrist. With swift movements, he had both of her hands behind her back. He started saying something about how her actions weren't warranted, but Scarlett blocked him out as she leaned closer to the bin. Beside a few cartons of spaghetti, a child was squirming, echoing the cries of the older child. And Scarlett knew, looking at the child, that it was the same child she had helped deliver only two days ago.

Scarlett stared at the child a few moments, so surprised that she couldn't react. Then, she reached down and grabbed the child from the bin, its only covering a thin blanket. She was aware of a scuffle between

Rhys and the female, but the details didn't enter her mind. The child looked even smaller than before.

"Hello," Scarlett said to the child, holding it tightly as she looked up in shock. The child's mother had said she died. Yet, here she was. Alive. Why would she lie?

"We need to report this to Phan," Scarlett said to Rhys. Rhys nodded toward her radio. He was a bit occupied with holding the female.

"Please don't report the child," the female pleaded, her hands still restrained. "Please don't."

"But why would this child's mother have left the child here? Did you take the child from its mother?"

The female shook her head. "No, no, I didn't. I'm keeping her safe from your leaders. You don't know what they do to a child."

Scarlett frowned. "They would never hurt a child. They simply need a record of each child's birth and other pertinent information." She clutched the child closer and took a step away from the female.

"That child will never be returned to its mother. You will see!" the female cried, her child's wails piercing their conversation. "Your kind will take it away and destroy it."

Scarlett's mouth fell open. "That's treasonous talk. They wouldn't!"

"They will," the female said, looking directly into Scarlett's eyes. "This baby is a healthy one, and they always take the healthy ones. Why do you think I burned my child's hand?" The female laughed in a crazy way. "She's ruined, but at least she's mine!"

"Take them where?" Scarlett asked.

"I don't know!" the woman responded. "But we never see them again. They say it's for a checkup when they are born, but really they want to see if the child is worth having. In fact, you're probably a City-born Citizen, but they took you from your parents so young that you don't even remember."

Scarlett shook her head, not able to believe the information this woman was throwing at her. "That's not true," she said, reaching for her radio. With one hand, she pressed the button.

"We have a situation in house twenty. We have found a child, and I believe it is the child who was declared dead from house twenty-four. It . . . looks the same."

Phan responded almost before Scarlett was done talking. "Hold everyone there. We will be there immediately."

Scarlett stood there with the female, as she continued filling their ears with lies. Scarlett went over to the bed where the other child was still screaming. Scarlett balanced the baby in one arm and used her other to soothe the child, rubbing her hand gently in the child's hair. The child turned to her and snuggled against her, burrowing for warmth, even though her body was burning up.

She quieted quickly with Scarlett's hand brushing her hair, and Scarlett turned to the female who was still shouting.

"Your child is not hard to calm," she said. "You lied. And you continue to lie. Liars are not trusted." Her voice sounded cold, just like when she was reprimanded as a child.

Phan burst through the door with his partner. He looked around and immediately grabbed the female's wrists from Rhys. "I'll take her to the compound. Rawls, you and Rhys go to house twenty-four. Arrest the female from that household." Rawls and Rhys hurried out the door. The female knew better than to struggle against Phan's grip. He was much stronger, and she stood little chance of persuading him that what he was doing was wrong.

"Can you bring both children?" Phan asked. Scarlett looked at the older child. She wasn't very heavy. Scarlett thought so. And, the child seemed to have taken a liking to her.

"I can carry them both," Scarlett said. She hoisted the older child onto her hip, and the child curved onto her, clinging with her arms around Scarlett's neck and her legs around her waist. Scarlett moved slowly, Phan leading the female ahead of her.

"How did you know to look in this house?" Phan asked Scarlett.

She shrugged. "You would have to ask Rhys. He's the one who wanted to go in."

Scarlett's arms were aching by the time they reached the compound. This was the first time she had entered the compound in the middle of her shift, and everything seemed so busy. But instead of proceeding through the dining hall or exercise room, they took another door. Phan led them to a solidified room that had a metal table and several chairs. Phan handcuffed the female to the table.

"Where do I take the children?" Scarlett asked, her arms beginning to ache. The baby was beginning to whimper again.

Phan studied both children for a moment. "Take her to the medical center," he said, motioning to the older one. "I'll take care of this one." Scarlett, relieved of one of her burdens, turned away from the table as though she knew where that was. When she stepped outside of the door, she walked down the unfamiliar hallway until she found a clearly labeled door. It was locked. A few minutes later, a White appeared and punched in the code for her.

"Wait here. The doctor will arrive in a moment," the White said, closing the door firmly behind her. There was a strange bed-like structure but smaller. Scarlett set the two-year-old child on the structure, shaking her arm out as the muscle protested its use. The child reached for Scarlett again, her lower lip trembling. Her deformed hand once again caught Scarlett's attention. She touched it gently, and the child didn't seem to mind. She grunted and whined, waving her arms.

"What do you want?" Scarlett asked.

The child said, "Mama."

"I don't know what that means," Scarlett said.

The child just repeated herself. "Mama."

"Well, I'm sure the doctor will know what that is." Scarlett looked at the timepiece on the wall. It was nearly 19:00. Perhaps the child was hungry. Scarlett didn't have anything to give her. The door opened silently, and Scarlett watched a White enter. Though he was clearly a White, his uniform was different. He was wearing something to cover his face as though he was afraid of breathing in germs. He looked at the child and then at Scarlett.

"I've seen this one before," he said, nodding at the two-year-old. "She's useless. Why did you bring her back?"

Scarlett shrugged. "I'm just following orders. I was told to bring her here, so I brought her here."

"You can return that child. We have no use for her." Scarlett nodded toward the child who was still repeating the same word.

"Mama. Mama."

"What does she want?"

"She wants the female who lives in her house. From my understanding though, she won't be seeing her again."

"She won't? Why not?"

"You have a lot of questions," the doctor said. "Just do as you're told."

Scarlett hefted the two-year-old onto her hip and left the examining room. She passed by the room where they had left the child's female. Scarlett could see in through the window. She pointed to the female, so the two-year-old would look in that direction.

"There she is," Scarlett said. "Is that who you want?"

The child reached toward the window, making a grabbing motion with her hands. "Mama. Mama."

The female didn't react to them. Scarlett waved her arm in a wider arc to get the female's attention, but it was as though they were invisible. The female was soon joined by a female Scarlett recognized, the one she had helped just two nights before. This female moved slowly, shuffling toward the table where she was then handcuffed. Scarlett watched, apparently forgotten by everyone as she cradled the child.

Phan entered the room and stood rigidly between the two females. Scarlett could only see his back, but even she straightened a little as though her posture were under scrutiny.

She jumped back when Phan's voice came blaring out of a circle in the wall beside her. "You both are being charged with crimes against the Government."

Scarlett studied the circle for a moment, rubbing the child's back absentmindedly to keep her quiet. Her stomach turned over. Maybe she wasn't supposed to hear this conversation, but that only made her want to hear it even more.

He pointed to the larger female from house twenty-four. "You are charged with lying and obstructing the process of the Government. You," he pointed to the other female, "are charged with the same. In addition, you are charged with assaulting one of our soldiers." Scarlett frowned. Was he referring to when the female had fought against Rhys? She wouldn't consider it an assault. It was more like a desperate attempt to save her noodles and crackers.

Phan was silent for a moment. He lowered his voice, and Scarlett leaned forward to hear better. "I am willing to offer you both a deal. We will drop the lower charge and just charge you with obstructing the process of the Government if you have any information on the occupants of houses forty or forty-three." He was silent, letting his offer sink in. "The first one who offers to help will receive the deal. The other," Phan shrugged, "will be executed."

Scarlett's mouth dropped open. "Why?" she asked, her voice coming out in a scratchy whisper. How could he be so cruel? Had they done something else she didn't know about? Of course, they had both acted insubordinately by hiding a child, but why would they even hide a child? There was so much Scarlett didn't understand. And anyway, they had the child now. All's well that ends well, right?

"I'll give you a few hours to think it over," Phan said. He hefted the smaller female to her feet and undid her handcuffs. The larger female didn't even move as the other one was led toward the door. She thought she heard something else said, but Phan's voice was too low to catch the words. Besides, they were coming toward the door.

Scarlett's eyes widened, and she hurried back down the hall to the examining room. She tugged on the door, but the keypad just whined. Scarlett hurried to another door, tugged on it, and ducked inside, pulling it almost closed behind her. The room was pitch black, and Scarlett didn't know where she was. She continued to pat the child, desperate to keep her quiet. Her mind was scrambling.

She heard footsteps in the hall, and when everything was quiet, Scarlett ducked out of the room, shutting the door firmly behind her. She felt as though the compound were compressing in on her. Scarlett rushed to the front door, but she couldn't get out without punching in her code. Haman saw her as he was passing from the dining hall to the exercise room.

"What is that?" he asked with a nervous chuckle. He pointed at the small child.

"This is a child," Scarlett said, giving him an annoyed look.

Haman laughed heartily at that. "Clearly, but I mean, why do you have one?"

"I'm returning her to her house. She was . . . lost."

Scarlett turned to the keypad and punched in her number.

"Unauthorized exit" flashed on the screen, and the doors remained stubbornly closed. Scarlett frowned as Haman chuckled.

"Probably because you're trying to go out mid-shift." Haman stepped forward, a full smile on his face. He reached for the keypad. "All you have to do—" he laughed.

"Could you just stop laughing?" Scarlett said, angered. Here she was in a serious situation, and Haman was acting like everything was one big joke. How did this guy have any friends that could stand being around him for more than five minutes?

Haman stepped back, the smile barely on his lips. "Well, I was going to help you, but you don't have to be so grumpy about it."

"Oh, well, please, I can take any help I can get," Scarlett said, her voice lower as she tried to humbly back up from her rude question.

Haman's smile widened just a little. "Of course, I love to help anyone out. You just have to put in the code 387. That code indicates that you had a White excuse your strange exit or entrance. You are . . . cleared, right?"

"Yes," Scarlett nodded. "I've been cleared. Just had to come back to the compound in the middle of my shift to take care of a few things."

"Good, because it will send your info to someone, and they'll check to make sure you had all the right permissions."

"Oh, thanks. What was that code again?"

"387." Haman smiled, his face full of a toothy grin. "See you later, Scarlett."

Scarlett punched in the code, and the door opened. Scarlett slipped out into the night, surprised that it was fully dark already. The child clung to Scarlett, her deformed hand brushing Scarlett's bare neck. Scarlett winced but continued toward the child's house. She wasn't sure what she was going to do yet, but she thought that taking the child back to her house would be the first step.

Scarlett reached house number twenty and saw the door open. There was no light inside. Surely they wouldn't be sleeping already. Scarlett went up the stairs cautiously, but no one was inside.

The child recognized her house and reached to get down. Scarlett set the child on the floor. The child got up and began walking around the house, babbling strange syllables. Scarlett watched in wonder as she acted like a miniature female. Scarlett didn't know what to do. Should she leave the child there in the house? She couldn't very well finish her shift with the child on her hip.

Scarlett turned on her radio (it had to be turned off while in the compound, something about the signal) and radioed for Rhys. "Rhys? Rhys? I'm back in Section Two. Where are you?"

Rhys's voice crackled through. "I'm in the southernmost corner."

"Meet me—" Scarlett considered a way to respond without sounding urgent. "At the site of our earlier incident."

"R2," Rhys responded. Scarlett settled her radio onto her hip again and anxiously peered out the half-open door. Hopefully, Rhys would tell her what to do. He had to have at least one good idea, right?

The child went to the bed and patted it. She grabbed the blanket and used her knees to wiggle her way onto the bed. Once on the bed, she stood up and looked around. "Mama. Mama."

"Yes, I know. You've said that before," Scarlett said, peering out the front door.

"Papa," the child said.

"Well, that's new."

Scarlett leaned out the door and saw Rhys jogging toward the house. She gave a quick wave, and as she did so, the child fell from the bed. The child began screaming, wiggling on the floor like a worm that had been partially squished.

Scarlett hurried inside and scooped up the child as her screams grated on Scarlett's ears. She rocked the child back and forth, but still, the child cried. Rhys entered and saw her holding the child.

"She fell!" Scarlett shouted over the screams. "Now she won't stop crying!"

"Give her something to eat," Rhys suggested. "That usually makes small children happy." Scarlett nodded toward the kitchen. Rhys found a package of crackers and opened them. Scarlett grabbed one and dropped it into the child's mouth. The child coughed, leaned forward, and projected the cracker across the room. She continued to cry.

"That didn't work," Scarlett said.

"Ummm, maybe . . . is she bleeding?"

"No, I don't think so."

Just then the door slammed against the wall, and a male came in. A regular Citizen, not a Blue or White. Rhys pulled his pistol from the holster in smooth movement, but the male didn't seem to see him. He made a beeline for Scarlett. Scarlett turned her back to him to shield the child from whatever attack he might be planning.

"Citizen," Rhys said, his voice not sounding as commanding as he had perhaps planned, "Stand down. I have a gun trained on you, and I will use it."

The male reached for the child, and Scarlett was surprised to see the child reach for him and curl into his shoulder just the way she had curled into Scarlett that afternoon. Scarlett watched the male pat her back and make a hissing noise. Was that supposed to calm her?

"Who are you?"

"I live here," the male explained, showing the tattoo on his wrist that indicated his house number.

Rhys lowered his pistol and nodded when he saw the *20* engraved on his skin. The child's affection for the male was obvious. Scarlett had never seen a male with a child before. It was always females who worked with the children.

"Where was my child?" the male asked, now that she had quieted.

"We took her to the compound," Scarlett responded. Then, she realized maybe she wasn't supposed to give away information about what they were doing at the compound. Still, he should probably know that the female in this house had been arrested.

The male nodded. "Aleah?"

Scarlett looked at Rhys. What did he mean?

"The female who lives here?" the male asked.

"She has been arrested," Rhys said, his hand hovering near his pistol as the male's stance tensed. "Your child was taken to the compound for medical examination."

"She's been examined before," the male responded. "She was deemed useless."

Scarlett shrugged. The doctor had pretty much told her as much. Scarlett and Rhys looked at each other. They didn't have any other business in this house. They walked toward the door.

"When will I know what is happening to my wife?" Rhys and Scarlett turned. They didn't have answers.

"The female may be executed," Scarlett spoke frankly. Then, she regretted it. She couldn't tell what she knew unless she admitted that she had eavesdropped on a conversation.

The male clutched the child closer. "What can I do? Is there anything I can do to stop it? You must stop it!"

He reached for Scarlett, but she shied away. Rhys's hand was on his gun. "I don't think you want us to have to bring you in for assaulting one of us. I suggest you stay in your home. I'm sure . . . Phan will update you if necessary."

"Besides," Scarlett muttered as they safely exited the house. "It seems like punishments are pretty public here." They walked away from the house until they were far enough away that Scarlett didn't feel like she constantly had to look over her shoulder.

"We have to go back to the compound," she said, whispering furiously.

"Why?" Rhys didn't see any reason to lower his voice.

"Because, I saw something strange in the compound. And, they took the child from me, the small child, not her," Scarlett motioned over her shoulder to where the two-year-old child had been.

Rhys shrugged. "Well, they can't very well leave the child in the house alone. It is too young to care for itself."

Scarlett pressed her lips together. How could she explain the "feeling" she had about the child being taken? Everything she had seen in the past two days had really weighed on her. She wanted to see where the child was. "I understand that. But just as the child we left now has a male to care for her, perhaps the other child has a male as well. Malak said a male and female live in *every* house."

Rhys thought for a moment. "It's not our job to decide what should happen to the child. I'm sure we are not the only people who have come to that conclusion. The Whites—or someone—will figure out what to do."

Scarlett tightened her jaw. She didn't like Rhys's answer to sit back and let everything happen. She felt involved in this child's wellbeing. Perhaps because she had been such an integral part in the child's birth. Perhaps there was some other reason. Scarlett finally spoke again.

"Fine, that's your opinion. But I'm going to do something, and you better not say anything to stop me."

Rhys grabbed her arm, and they stopped in the middle of the street. His hand felt tight, not at all like when he gently stroked the ends of her hair.

"Scarlett, you can't do anything."

Scarlett wrenched her arm away from him—at least she tried. Rhys's grip was too tight. She fought against him, and he grabbed her other arm.

"Stop," he said, no laughter in his voice. "Look, you can't do anything against the Government. You don't want to do something that looks like you're working against them, do you?"

Scarlett let out a hefty sigh but didn't say anything. She just glared at Rhys with a furious look that said he had better let her go. A Citizen came out of his house, and Rhys quickly dropped Scarlett's arm. They watched the Citizen walk down the street. He hadn't even glanced in their direction. Rhys walked toward Scarlett, causing her to back up until they were sequestered between the two wooden walls of houses thirty-three and thirty-four.

"Listen," Rhys said, his voice low and urgent. "You can't do that here."

"Do what?" Scarlett whispered back furiously, arms crossed. She felt like stomping her foot too, but she held back.

"The Government has set up the system they have now for a reason. I don't think we should test them, draw attention to ourselves, and hurt others in the process."

"Oh yeah, that's my goal, hurt others!" The sarcasm rolled off her tongue easily. "Besides, I'm not asking you to do anything. I'm just saying it would be nice if you didn't go reporting me. You know, if you can manage that."

"Stop!" Rhys said, his voice louder. Scarlett glanced at the thin walls on either side of them.

"You stop," she said, keeping her voice low and hoping no one was listening through the walls. "Stop twisting things around. Just leave me alone!" Scarlett took a step backward. Rhys's jaw tightened. He didn't look like her friend, the one who had shared secrets with her as they climbed to the top of the Mound.

"I'm not twisting anything. I'm saying it like it is. You're choosing to work with the Government, or you're choosing to work against the Government. You can't have it both ways."

"I'm not working against anyone. I just have questions, and you would think someone could answer them. I mean, if the Government's all trustworthy and everything, then you would think they wouldn't be scared of answering my questions." Scarlett tightened her fingers into a fist, her anger burning through her. She felt like she could punch him, and it would make her feel better. "That female was saying some pretty strange things, and it got me thinking, where do the babies even come from? Mrs. has never been as large as that female. And if babies—"

Rhys moved faster than she had ever seen him. He was in front of her, his hand wrapping around her face in an awkward attempt to make her shut up. Scarlett wiggled out of his grasp, her body hot with anger. She stepped toward him and was shoving him as hard as she could before she even registered what was happening.

"Don't touch me!" she shouted. Rhys's hands were in fists at his side, but he didn't raise them to counteract Scarlett's push. His jaw twitched, and Scarlett saw the disappointment in his eyes. Scarlett's limbs slowly relaxed, the desire to fight completely leaving her. She looked around, anywhere except Rhys. Why had she done that? Rhys was her friend. She couldn't hurt him.

Rhys measured his words, pausing between each one. "Let's continue our circuit." Scarlett nodded, looking at the ground. Her arms were trembling as though she had been using a punching bag for hours on end.

She followed Rhys, a step or two behind, as they entered the street area once again. A few Citizens were meandering home from their jobs.

Scarlett could hear others having a meal. As they walked by, a male's raucous laugh sounded from inside a house. Scarlett felt suddenly sad. She wondered what it would have been like to grow up in a house with a male and female to take care of her.

As her thoughts continued circling through her mind, she couldn't go a minute without replaying the scene between Rhys and herself. He had been wrong, to try to make her act like he wanted, but that didn't mean she had made the best decisions either. Scarlett wondered if that was something she could get in trouble for. Would they send her to isolation for that?

"Rhys," Scarlett said, her voice like a mouse squeaking softly.

He grunted to show her he was listening.

"Don't tell anyone, okay?"

Rhys grunted again, but Scarlett didn't know what that meant. She ventured a look at Rhys through the darkness. Most of the houses were quiet now. Only a few still showed the flickering light of a candle.

"Please."

Rhys shook his head and sighed as though the last thing he wanted to do was talk to her. And he had every reason to be mad. Still, she couldn't get in trouble again. She didn't know what would happen if she did. Would she lose her place here? She didn't know of any Blues who worked in the training center and had lost their place. But then again, she had never known of any Blues to do something wrong either.

"I won't," Rhys said, causing relief to flow through her. They walked on. Scarlett checked her timepiece. It was just after 22:00. Their shift would be over in two hours. All she wanted to do was lift a few weights and get some of the pressure off her chest.

"It's late," Rhys said after ten minutes of silence. "Let's take that area by the fence and talk."

Scarlett nodded, but she was scared. What was Rhys going to say? She felt ashamed of her behavior and at the same time, justified. She was still going to the compound, and she *would* find out what had happened to the child. She just wouldn't do it while they were working their shift.

They arrived by the fence and started pacing up and down its length. Night noises floated through the fence.

"You're my best friend," Rhys said, keeping his head turned toward her and away from the interior of the City. "I'm here to protect you. And . . . my protecting you means I can't let you do something foolish like chasing down that child."

Scarlett's anger flared again. "I didn't ask for your 'protection,' and I don't need it. I am capable of making my own decisions, thank you very much." She felt her resentment from several hours before rising again. "I'm sorry. I'm really sorry about what happened, but you can't tell me what I can and can't do."

Rhys was silent as they turned and walked along the fence northward. "Fine." He said after a long silence. Scarlett rolled her eyes. Males were so difficult when conversing. Females were much better about explaining things. Males just let things run their course and didn't talk about their feelings.

* * *

When they arrived back at the compound, Scarlett pressed up against the door she had entered earlier that afternoon. She wiggled the knob with her hand behind her back as she waited for the entryway to clear. The knob was locked. As the entryway emptied, Scarlett headed for the dining hall as though she had just been waiting for space to pass through.

Scarlett didn't want to eat with Rhys. She didn't want to even look at him. Devon approached the small table where Scarlett had been eating by herself.

"So what happened after you radioed Phan about needing some back up?"

Scarlett shook her head and looked at Devon with a frown. "I don't want to talk about it."

Devon pounded a fist on the table in frustration. "Everyone's got their secrets. First Rhys, now you! What do you have to hide?"

His frustrations echoed Scarlett's earlier in the day. She gripped her tray tightly. "I'm not trying to hide anything," she said. "Believe me, I don't like secrets either. I'm just . . . not ready to talk about it." Scarlett was surprised to feel a ball forming in her throat.

"Oh, is it bad?" Devon asked. He seemed sympathetic, but then he cut a hand jokingly across his throat. "Are they—?"

Scarlett sighed heavily. "I don't know. Why don't you ask someone who actually knows what happens around here? Maybe a White, for example."

Devon shrugged, dropping the issue. "So, you and Rhys aren't on good terms?"

"Why do you say that?" Scarlett asked, searching for Rhys for the first time in the bustling dining hall.

"I don't know. Because you two aren't talking, and you always have something to say to him."

Scarlett shrugged. "Sometimes, we don't agree on things." Trying to lighten the situation, Scarlett pasted on a grin. "He hasn't yet realized that females are always right."

Devon rolled his eyes. "Clearly, you didn't pay attention in History class. Shall I bring up the story of Winda Graphins?"

"Don't," Scarlett said, shoveling the last of the food in her mouth. She hated History class because all of the stories made her feel so small. Winda Graphins was a great example. She had been alive over a hundred years ago. Back when presidents were chosen by the people, she had become president. She had ruined the country, and she had been part of the reason the Government was structured as it was now—a group of elites who had been chosen by elites who were intelligent enough to make those decisions, rather than the common Citizen who had no idea who was qualified to make important decisions.

"I'm going to exercise," Scarlett said as a farewell, taking her tray to the deposit before Devon had a chance to make her feel worse. Scarlett reached the exercise room and saw Darlin in the corner. Scarlett didn't want to talk to her today. She didn't want to tell her about what had happened with the females. She didn't want to relive giving the child up to Phan, and feeling like she was doing the wrong thing. She remembered the two-year-old sitting in her male's arms. She had seemed so content.

"Tell me," Darlin said quietly as she stretched. Scarlett sat on the floor and stretched her leg muscles slowly. With everything that had happened that day, she wasn't sure who she could trust anymore. Why was she even reporting to Darlin? The promise of a higher position felt so distant at the moment. But at the same time, she couldn't very well back out of the agreement.

Scarlett gave the briefest summary she could. "A female was hiding a child that had not yet been registered. I found the child on my shift, and we brought it here."

"And the female?"

"Phan brought her and the female who had claimed the child's death."

"What were the house numbers of both females?"

Scarlett bit her lower lip as she stretched over backwards and saw her thin body in the mirror. She always felt hungry now, and she didn't have the energy to exercise. She sighed. "I'm sure it will be in the official report," she said sweetly. Could she get in trouble for being rude to Darlin? It felt like everyone was above her, and she didn't know who she could trust or who could affect her in what way. It reminded her of the video she had seen of puppies. They were trampling over each other in the box, each trying to be the closest to the warm light. They didn't care if they stepped on each other.

Darlin was silent for several minutes. "What can you tell me about Phan's treatment of the females?"

Scarlett didn't want to reveal that she had overheard a conversation that wasn't meant for her ears. She still didn't know what to do with the information that the females could die. She wondered if they had already been executed. Surely not. It had only been a few hours, even though it felt like days.

"He took them to a private room," Scarlett said. "I didn't see what happened, because I was caring for the children."

"Children? I thought you said it was one child?"

"The one child we found, and the other belonged to the other female." Scarlett had only stretched, but she had no desire to exercise. She had nothing else to say anyway. "I'm tired, and I need to rest." She quickly left the exercise room, eager to have time to methodically figure everything out, as though with simply enough time to think, everything would make sense.

Chapter 16

The next morning, Scarlett awoke and stared at the ceiling. Her mind was immediately active, turning over the events from the previous day. Her stomach cringed when she thought of Rhys. She had to apologize to him. She didn't think she was wrong, but she should never have pushed him or yelled at him. She was acting like a Red who hadn't gotten her way.

Scarlett knew Darlin would expect her back in the exercise room, but she didn't want to go. Darlin would have to wait. How did she know Darlin wasn't just a manipulative White eager for gossip? Scarlett had no proof of Darlin being able to offer her anything except what she said.

Amirah tapped the side of Scarlett's bed. "Hey," she said in a whisper. "A male wants to see you." Scarlett sat up quickly, her throat catching.

"Who?" she whispered.

Amirah crinkled her nose as Scarlett's morning breath washed over her. "I don't remember his name. It's that one you are always with."

It had to be Rhys. Unless it was Devon. People who didn't really know her here might think that Devon was just as good a friend as Rhys. Scarlett started to ask Amirah something else, but she was already changing into her Blue suit. Scarlett started to turn to her own suit when she noticed something else. Amirah had the same scar on her lower abdomen that the Blue in the shower had had.

Scarlett hopped out of the bed and pulled on her suit, thinking about why that would be. Wasn't the surgery in their shoulder like Rhys's was? She knew her breath was bad, but she couldn't do anything about that until she was in the bathroom. Scarlett stepped out of the females' dormitory and saw Rhys leaning against the wall across the hall.

"Hey, good morning," Scarlett said.

Rhys nodded, but he didn't have his normally cheerful demeanor. "Going to the morning meal or to exercise?"

"To eat," Scarlett said.

"Okay, do you want to talk first?" Rhys made a motion with his hands that reminded Scarlett of their panicked conversation just a few days before about the bugs. They walked casually to their secret space under the stairs. Rhys stepped into the room that held the stairs, but there was a noise coming from the space. Scarlett looked up to see if a few Whites were coming down. Rhys stepped back into her, crushing her toes. Scarlett kept her yelp silent as Rhys pushed her back and hurried down the hall toward the dining hall without any other explanation.

"What? What was it?" Scarlett asked as she chased him down the hall.

"I . . . don't know," Rhys said. "But, I think our space was taken."

"Okay," Scarlett said. She had seen a flash of Blue, but that was all. Was someone else using their space to converse? She had sort of thought of it as a private space that no one else would think of. Obviously, she wasn't as original as she had presumed. They got their meals, and Devon waved them over to the table where he was. Rhys didn't even look to Scarlett for her opinion before heading in that direction. Scarlett slipped in at the table and dipped into her food.

"I see you two are back on speaking terms," Devon pronounced, taking another large bite of food.

Rhys shrugged. "We're always speaking. Just with different faces." He mimed a happy face then a sad face.

Devon laughed. Scarlett rolled her eyes at their immaturity and wondered what Rhys had been so desperate to tell her that morning that he had come to find her while she was still sleeping. He didn't seem bothered that he had to wait. As the males began their usual joking, Scarlett stood up and took her plate to the disposal. She knew she would see that plate again in an hour when she was washing dishes. She made a face as she thought about it. She had assumed she would be assigned a different chore each week, but that had been wrong.

Scarlett glanced longingly toward the exercise room, but she was still worried about finding Darlin there. And what she didn't understand, she wanted to avoid. Scarlett decided she might as well start washing dishes to get it over with. She descended into the room behind the wall, the room where everything was sanitized after eating.

The room was empty. They had never been told a specific time dishwashing was done, but whenever Scarlett had come down before, many other Blues and a few Whites had been there. Scarlett's stomach dropped as she scanned the empty kitchen. She would find something else to do. But then, her eyes landed on the closet in the corner of the kitchen. Scarlett slowly walked across the kitchen, looking over her shoulder as though someone else might be tempted to get an early headstart on his or her chore.

She reached out for the handle. It opened easily, and Scarlett's eyes scanned the shelves. There was no food, like noodles waiting to be cooked. It was only dishes, napkins, and cleaning materials. Something felt strange. Where was their food cooked? This kitchen only had sinks, towels, and other cleaning materials, no space for cooking.

Scarlett stepped further into the closet, keeping the door propped open with her foot as she reached forward and ran her hand over the shelves. She didn't know what she was looking for, and her stomach was flipping overtime. She stepped out of the closet and looked toward the other door in the room. This door was thicker. Scarlett stepped toward it and pushed it open. Once again, it wasn't locked.

As soon as she opened the door, she heard a bustle of noise. It was dark. The only light came from the kitchen, causing her shadow to be cast long in front of her. Scarlett felt exposed in the halo of light, but she could clearly see a long hall running to either side of her. Scarlett had to make a decision and quickly. Would she step inside and risk exposure, risk trouble? Or step back out and pretend she hadn't seen the hidden world?

Scarlett let the door close quietly behind her. After all, if the door wasn't locked, how was she supposed to know she couldn't be in there? She knew, but she didn't *know.* Scarlett stood in the alcove that was formed by the door entry. She tried to make sense of the passageway with the layout of the compound. How were there so many hidden spaces?

Distinct voices came from down the right hallway. Scarlett held her breath as she tried to listen to the conversation. ". . . lung capacity."

"How is the formula comparing to the control?"

Scarlett didn't understand the other male's answer. But then, she distinctly heard a crying, a mew almost. It picked up in strength, and Scarlett's heart stopped. It was the baby. It had to be. The baby she had delivered in house twenty-four. Was it four days ago now?

Scarlett took a deep breath. She wanted to go toward the cry. Her legs seemed to pull her in the direction, but Scarlett forced herself to exit. She couldn't. There were clearly several people near the child. They would question her. She would get in trouble. Still . . . to have a whole part of the compound not even mentioned in their welcome tour seemed a bit questionable.

Scarlett quickly took a step back and wrestled the door handle open in the dark. She stepped into the kitchen just as another Blue was entering the kitchen. It was Devon. They stared at each other as Devon pointed to the door that had just closed behind her.

"What are you doing? What's in there?" he pointed. There was no way that Scarlett could deny having entered. But she didn't trust Devon, despite his denials of telling anyone about their conversations. She tried to make light of it.

"I was looking for a mop," she said, as casually as she could, "but, I don't think that was the right door."

Devon looked behind her as though the door would reveal its contents. Scarlett heard more footsteps on the small set of stairs that led to the kitchen, and she stepped toward the closet, continuing her search for a mop even though she had no idea what she would do with it should she find one.

The next to enter was a pair of Blues, including Amirah. "Are we going to get started or not?" she asked, looking back and forth between Scarlett and Devon. "You guys don't look like you're getting anything done."

"We were waiting for you," Devon said, heading over to the rotating platform that constantly carried in more dirty dishes. But as he did so, he took one more look at Scarlett that made her feel like he didn't quite believe her answer. Scarlett sighed. Great. Someone else who didn't trust her. She would have to find a way to fix that. Meanwhile, she got the pleasure of plunging her hands in overly warm, soapy water. As she grimaced, she wondered why there always seemed to be a plethora of warm water for washing dishes but never warm water for showers. Maybe Malak would know.

* * *

When they were done washing the dishes, Scarlett made eye contact with Rhys and tried to signal that they should talk. But as she was performing a menagerie of nods and winks, Devon stepped in front of them and interrupted her line of sight. The other Blues, eager to enjoy their free hours, hurried up the narrow set of stairs to the dining hall. She, Devon, and Rhys were alone—well as alone as they could feel with the idea that someone was always watching them.

"What's back there?" Devon asked, pointing toward the door he had seen Scarlett enter from when he had stepped into the kitchen.

Scarlett looked over at the door, her stomach flipping over. She had entered by accident . . . kind of. If she told a lie, Devon could just flip the door open and see for himself. Then, he would never trust her again.

Rhys looked back and forth between them. "What are you talking about?"

"The door," Devon said, keeping his voice low but still above a whisper. "Scarlett was coming out of that door when I came down here."

Now Rhys cocked an eyebrow at her, clearly waiting for her confirmation before she believed it.

Scarlett nodded, still sticking to her story about the mop. "I was looking for a mop, and I thought I remembered someone saying there was a mop in the closet here. But apparently not."

"So?" Rhys questioned. "What was in it?" He looked fearful of touching the door himself.

"It was a hallway," Scarlett said frankly. "And I don't know what else because when I saw it wasn't a mop, I figured I didn't have any business walking down the hallway." She met both males with her eyes, daring them to challenge her.

Rhys looked at the door curiously.

"You just opened the door, and there was a hallway?"

"Yes, it was just there—"

Devon rolled his eyes at Scarlett, like he didn't believe her. He strode confidently over to the door and flung it open, barely stopping it before it banged into the wall. The hallway was flooded with yellow light from the kitchen. Scarlett's heart pounded hard.

"What are you doing?" she asked in a furious whisper.

"Exploring," Devon responded, not taking his eyes off the open hallway. "Come on." He stepped inside.

Scarlett looked at Rhys with a panicked expression. "We can't go in there. If it was a place we were supposed to be, then they would have shown us when we began living here," Scarlett protested, still not speaking at a normal level.

Rhys nodded his head in agreement.

Devon took another step into the darkness. "If we weren't supposed to be here, then it would be locked, wouldn't it?"

Rhys shook his head. "If you think you're supposed to be there, then why don't you go asking around about that space. Clearly, it's not meant for us."

Devon turned around to roll his eyes dramatically before facing the door again. "Whatever. Until someone tells me I can't do something, then I'm not breaking any rules." He turned and confidently took off down the hallway, toward the direction of the voices Scarlett had heard earlier. And now that Devon had made the decision, Scarlett didn't want to miss her opportunity to explore the area. Better to be caught down there with Devon than by herself.

"Wait!" she said in a harsh whisper. Devon paused but didn't turn. Scarlett looked over at Rhys, wanting him to stay behind as though she could protect him by having him stay in the kitchen. But Rhys had never been one to let her do anything by herself, as though he couldn't have a female showing him up.

He stepped in, almost pushing Scarlett forward in his haste. He shut the door firmly behind them. Scarlett panicked. What if they couldn't get back out? However, she squared her shoulders and stepped forward as confidently as she could. As soon as they were close to Devon, he continued moving forward as though he didn't want to allow them to see anything before he did. Scarlett shivered, feeling as though the temperature in this hallway had dropped ten degrees. Two doors on their left. Scarlett slowed as they started to reach them, but Devon continued his pace, his hand reaching out casually for the door handle.

Scarlett made a noise between a groan and a whimper as she worried about what would happen if they were caught. Devon whirled on her with an angry expression.

"Stop acting like a Red. It's like you want to get in trouble." Scarlett was surprised by the venom in his voice. It made her step back involuntarily. But Rhys stepped up.

"Leave her alone. She's a female."

Scarlett scoffed. Was that supposed to be an excuse? As though males didn't experience fear, but females could because they were the weaker gender?

"I'm fine," Scarlett said tightly. "I just think you should be a bit more cautious." She gritted her teeth to keep from saying anything else as she stepped closer to see in the slit of a window. She could only view a small slice of the room. There was a metal pole with a sack hanging from it. Just below it, in a small container similar to the shape of an egg, was a small face.

"It's the baby," Scarlett said. She reached toward the door as though she could reach through it and touch the child. Was it alive?

Devon pushed his head into the window to see then reached for the handle. He jiggled it a few times, but nothing happened. A keypad glowed beside the door. Scarlett tapped it gently to indicate that maybe males weren't the smartest gender after all. She wasn't about to begin pressing anything, but Devon pushed her hand away as though she had set off an alarm.

Scarlett let out a huff of air. "Stop!" she said, louder than she meant. Devon pushed her back against the wall with such force that Scarlett banged her head, unprepared to counter the force of the push. She felt her legs weaken under her, and the ground seemed to pull her down toward it. Scarlett pushed her hands against her skull. She tried to keep her eyes open, but it was hard as she watched two males wiggle on the ground like worms. What were they doing?

Chapter 17

When Scarlett woke up, Phan was standing over her. She was confused as to why she wasn't in her bed. Was it morning time? Why did her head hurt?

She moved her hands up to pat her head, and she felt a bandage wrapped around it. Phan's eyes never moved off her, and she felt very self-conscious.

She blinked several times. She couldn't turn her head without feeling dizzy again. "What . . . happened?" she asked again.

"You tell me," Phan said, crossing his arms. Scarlett suddenly knew how she recognized the room. It was where the doctor had examined the young child she had taken from the house. Now, here she was, lying on the examining table.

"I don't remember very well," Scarlett said. As she tried to think back, she remembered being in the kitchen and finding the door that opened to the hallway. They went in the hallway, and . . . she had seen something, something very important to her. Something that made her want to cry right now. But her head started throbbing with the beginnings of a headache.

"Tell me what you remember," Phan commanded, no sympathy in his voice.

"We found a door in the kitchen," Scarlett said. "And I remember walking down the hallway." She squeezed her eyes shut and opened them again. "Devon pushed me. But I don't remember why."

Phan nodded his head. "Why did you go in the hall?"

"I was curious," Scarlett said. "Devon was going, so I wanted to go, too."

"So you're a follower, incapable of making your own decisions?"

Scarlett was confused. She would never think of herself as a follower, but she didn't think he expected an answer anyway. Her stomach started hurting, but it wasn't a physical ailment. It was the fear that she was going to be in big trouble. She wasn't in handcuffs or isolation, but maybe that didn't mean anything yet. Apology seemed the best route.

"I'm sorry," Scarlett apologized, trying to sound as sincere as possible.

"For what?"

"For . . . causing trouble."

Phan made a noise. He continued to stare at her in such a way that Scarlett felt uncomfortable. "Did the doctor see me?" she finally asked to break the silence.

"Yes," Phan answered.

Scarlett waited for him to fill her in on the details. He didn't. So Scarlett found a spot on the wall to study and tried to pretend his silence didn't bother her.

Finally, Phan spoke again. "You seem such a trustworthy soldier. Apparently, we need to keep more of an eye on you." Scarlett squeezed and squinted her eyes before she looked at Phan again.

"I'm sorry," she said. "I wasn't trying to do something wrong. I was just curious."

"When you opened the door, did you think it was a place you should be or should not be?"

Scarlett shrugged.

"No!" Phan responded swiftly. "You thought one or the other. Choose. Are you brash or stupid?"

"I guess I thought we probably shouldn't be there, but then I thought if we really shouldn't, then the door would have been locked."

"So you went on, even though you knew you shouldn't?"

Scarlett gave the tiniest of nods.

Phan nodded. "I thought as much. Now, listen. You are *not* to go down that hallway. Do you hear me? You are expressly being told that if you have not been introduced to a space or an area then you shouldn't be there. Assent verbally."

"Yes, I understand."

"You'll be paired with me for our shift tonight," Phan said before turning toward the door. "You may go." He stepped out the door himself, giving Scarlett time to gather her thoughts and move slowly as thoughts of Rhys consumed her mind. What had happened to him?

Scarlett felt shaky as she sat up fully, examining herself. Other than the bandage on her head, she seemed to be whole. Still, as she stood, she felt a bit dizzy. She wasn't sure she was up for being on duty in just a few hours. Scarlett took a deep breath as she stared at the door in front of her. Was she really free to go? How would they guarantee she would go back to the main area and not explore the hidden areas more? Perhaps they were trying to test her.

Scarlett stepped out of the room and walked past the window where she had seen the females, the large female and the smaller one from house eighteen. She paused. The smaller female was in the room now. Scarlett had been so busy thinking about the child that she hadn't considered if the females were alive or not.

Scarlett stood at the window. There was no one with the female, but she was sure someone would return soon. Uneasy, Scarlett left the room behind her. She had already gotten into enough trouble today. As she stepped into the foyer that led to the exercise room or dining hall, she saw groups of males and females in the dining room. Her processing seemed very slow as she realized that her shift was eating. That meant that she had less than an hour until she would start. Scarlett didn't have much of a stomach for food, but she saw Rhys's tight curls from across the room. She felt relieved. He wasn't in isolation. Scarlett hurried over to him and paused mid-way into the seat.

Rhys's ear had dried blood under it. A large bruise peeked up from the neck of his Blue suit. One of his eyes had a colored ring around it.

"What happened?" she asked, finally sinking into her seat.

Rhys shook his head with a less than amused look as he continued to eat. He looked irritated with her, but she hadn't done anything. "Are you okay?" she tried again.

Rhys shrugged. Once again, the fact itched at her mind that he had wanted to tell her something that morning. What was it? Rhys nodded toward the bandage on her head.

"The doctor get that wrapped up for you?"

Scarlett nodded. "How long was I out for? It feels like I lost a lot of time."

"Several hours," Rhys said. Scarlett scanned the dining hall, but she didn't see Devon. She wasn't sure if she should ask Rhys in his present mood.

"I'm not sure if I'm ready to go out there," Scarlett said, nodding toward the front door.

"I wouldn't admit that," Rhys said. "We're lucky we didn't get in more trouble than we did. Just do as you're told." His voice was serious. Scarlett scrutinized him.

"If you remember, it wasn't my idea."

"No, but you sure didn't take a lot of encouragement to follow him."

"No one made you come," Scarlett responded.

"No one made me stand up for you either, but I did," Rhys said. "I would think you would appreciate that."

Scarlett pursed her lips. She had never asked anyone to do anything for her. She didn't think Devon would have pushed her again. He just had control issues in the moment. Rhys hadn't needed to step in.

As Scarlett strained to remember exactly what had happened, her head hurt. She rubbed her temple slowly, but the baby was in her mind again. She lowered her voice.

"Did we see a baby?"

Rhys nodded grimly. "That's what both of you said. I didn't see one."

Scarlett knew there had been a baby, and she knew the child had been alone, behind a locked door. Children that young couldn't care for themselves. But at the same time, what could Scarlett do about it?

"What . . . did you want to tell me about this morning?" Scarlett asked after a few minutes of silence.

"It doesn't matter," Rhys responded quickly, which only served to pique her interest. She stared at Rhys without flinching, knowing he could feel her gaze. He looked up and studied her for a moment, his face seeming to soften. "I'll talk to you about it later." He shook his head just slightly. "Just . . . stop trying to color outside the lines."

Scarlett scrunched up her brows as she tried to consider what he might mean by saying that. Coloring? She wasn't a Red. Scarlett hated the space she felt between herself and Rhys, like they were strangers dancing around subjects to avoid saying something that would hurt the other's feelings. She and Rhys had always been straightforward.

"We should punch in our numbers," Rhys said nodding toward the front door where the second shift was starting to gather. Scarlett stood up hurriedly, and her head swam. She closed her eyes for a moment and took a deep breath. Opening her eyes, she was able to move at a normal pace to the front door.

She punched her code in and waited for everyone else to do so. Devon rushed in at the last moment, and Scarlett's eyes opened wide in surprise. He looked just as bad as Rhys. Maybe if she couldn't get anything out of Rhys, Devon would be willing to spill the details. He was always more of a talker anyway.

Scarlett tried to shift closer to him in the crowd, but as she got closer, he turned a disgusted look her way. Scarlett stopped. Was he mad at her, too? What had she done?

As her squadron followed Phan, Scarlett tried to catch Malak's eye. Did he know what had happened?

Phan stopped abruptly, and Scarlett nearly ran up his heels. She stopped after just bumping into him slightly. He narrowed his eyes at all four of the Blues.

"You are all four under careful watch." Malak appeared surprised, but he was not one to speak a word of approach. He remained silent as he made eye contact with Scarlett. Scarlett tried to communicate that she would fill him in later, but he didn't understand her meaning as easily as Rhys did.

"You'll each be assigned to one of us," Phan said. He nodded toward his White companions. "Pick your own." His nod turned toward Scarlett. "You're with me."

Scarlett didn't allow herself a last look at her companions. She followed Phan straight away. He walked so quickly that it was hard to walk even with him, like he always wanted to be a step ahead of her. They were silent. Scarlett didn't know where they were going, but she didn't dare ask.

Finally, their pace slowed to a more leisurely one as they reached the northeastern quadrant. Phan's eyes were never still, darting everywhere. He directed his words toward Scarlett though.

"What did you see?" he asked.

Scarlett considered his question for a moment, not wanting to miss his meaning. But she didn't know what moment he was talking about. Surely, he didn't mean the hallway again. "I'm not sure what you mean, Sir."

"In the hall where you weren't supposed to be."

This topic again. Scarlett's head still throbbed gently as she thought back to the hallway. Her stomach dropped as she remembered the child.

Her eyes flickered to Phan to see if he had noticed her physical reaction to the memory. His eyes were fixed on her. He knew.

Scarlett wet her lips with her tongue before confessing. "A baby. The female's baby."

Phan nodded, though his eyes didn't move from her face. Scarlett anxiously awaited his punishment. "Why was it there?" he asked.

He was asking her? She had no idea. Was this some sort of trap?

Scarlett shrugged. "I don't know. Sir."

"Stop being so curious and stick to the rules. Don't bother with things that aren't your business." His tone was harsh, and Scarlett nodded. Did this mean he wasn't going to report her? She wouldn't get in trouble for being where she wasn't supposed to be? The thought gave her courage to ask Phan a question.

"What happened with the females in houses twenty-four and twenty?"

"The female in house twenty will be executed," Phan said. "The fate of the female from house twenty-four has not yet been decided."

Scarlett opened her mouth then closed it again. She didn't want Phan to know she had heard his discussion with the females, telling them that one would live if they gave information. He had answered so seriously, without an ounce of compassion. Phan's radio crackled. "Suspicious gathering near house twenty-eight. Do we have permission to break it up?"

"I'll be there in a moment," Phan said, striding off in the direction of the house. Scarlett rushed to keep up, her head feeling the slightest bit dizzy. She saw a group of Citizens between houses twenty-eight and twenty-nine. Shuffling noises emanated from between the houses. Phan jogged forward, pulling his pistol from his belt. He held it down but ready. Scarlett wondered if she should pull hers out, too. She did so, scared.

They entered the alleyway, and Scarlett assessed the situation quickly, even as Phan was acting. Two males and one female. They appeared to be in some sort of heated argument. The female's hands were clenched into fists. One of the males was amused by the whole situation, but his face quickly became serious when he saw Phan and her standing there.

"What's happening here?" Phan's voice boomed.

The Citizens became quiet, but Scarlett noticed that the female's position didn't relax. Phan studied each one, keeping his pistol conspicuously by his side.

"What's your work assignment?" Phan asked the male closest to him.

"I'm a chopper," the male responded, looking Phan in the eyes. Scarlett studied him from the side. He barely seemed to notice her. But she noticed him. His skin was tanned, not the natural dark that Rhys was, but a tan from working outside many hours. His dark hair fell straight across his forehead, not in the typical short cut that all Blues and Whites were required to wear. He stood confidently, even in the face of Phan's status.

"Why aren't you out with the other choppers, then?" Phan asked.

The male didn't waver in his confidence. "We were released early on good production." It was as though he was daring Phan to counter him.

Phan was stuck. If he called in to ask if it was true, it would show that he didn't even know what was happening within the Government. But if he didn't call in, and the Citizen was lying, then he would get away with a blatant lie and disrespect toward Phan. Phan took a step toward the male. They were approximately the same height, and Scarlett instantly gripped her pistol a bit tighter. The male didn't back down. He just stared into Phan's eyes.

Phan took another step until his chest was touching the male's. The male didn't move, other than shifting back and forth on the balls of his feet.

"Back away," Phan practically shouted in the male's face. He continued to stand there, not as though he was hesitating but as though he had absolutely no interest in the matter.

"One more chance," Phan said, his voice calmer and more even. Somehow, he sounded even more threatening than when he shouted.

Scarlett's stomach flipped over, silently willing the male to get on his knees, even though she had no idea what crime he had committed. "Get on your knees."

The male continued to stand there. "Sir," he responded, his voice void of respect, spitting the word out in almost a mockery. "Could you state the charges you are bringing against me? I haven't touched you or said anything untrue. It's your own fear of the fragility of the Government that has you so touchy."

"You won't speak to *us* like that," Phan said, his voice still level. "You have one more chance to avoid being brought in. On your knees." Once again, the man didn't move. Scarlett screamed at him inside her head.

Scarlett's eyes fell to where Phan had his hand on his pistol. Would he shoot this Citizen? Scarlett was so confused. She pressed a hand to her head to push away the fuzziness, her palm pressing against the bandage. Her movement caused Phan to whirl on her, pointing his pistol at her as though she were a threat to him.

Scarlett held her hands up, her pistol hanging loosely from one finger. The tanned male laughed at their interaction, throwing his head back to the sky and letting loose a guffaw. Just as Phan was turning toward the tanned male, the other male, who had been so still during the whole interaction that Scarlett had almost forgotten he was there, rushed Phan. Scarlett, always reacting slowly, fumbled to straighten her hold on the pistol.

The male slammed into Phan, knocking him over. Scarlett pointed her pistol at the attacking male then whirled on the other two. The female was watching, her face full of surprise. The tanned male was clearly not about to do anything, so Scarlett turned back to the action. Phan was still under the attacking male, his pistol close to his hand. Phan grasped for the gun, moving swiftly out from under the attacking male. He aimed his gun at the male and shot. The sound echoed, making them all freeze. But as Scarlett looked up, she saw the tanned male crumple to the ground. The other male must have jumped out of the way just in time.

After a moment frozen, Phan went into action, jumping on the male who had attacked him and quickly securing him in a pair of handcuffs. He had control of the situation once again. The hurt male's painful groan, a guttural growl, broke the silence.

"Get back to work," Phan commanded the female. "None of this gathering between houses. If you have business to take care of, do it in the street."

The female nodded and backed away slowly, entering the street in a roundabout way to avoid getting too close to either Scarlett or Phan. Phan holstered his pistol after looking at the crumpled male. Phan let out another of his long, low sighs as he handcuffed the male who had attacked him. He then led the male out of the alley, tossing a comment over his shoulder.

"We will take him to the detainment facility."

Scarlett couldn't just leave the injured male there. She battled with herself over whether to even attempt to help him. She shouldn't do anything. Phan wouldn't help the male, and she already knew from his set face that he wouldn't allow her to do anything.

She followed Phan slowly as Phan spoke into the radio. "The gathering between houses twenty-eight and twenty-nine has been disbanded. Continue to report any such gatherings. Marse and Rhys, meet me at house twenty-eight now." Various voices chimed in with their understanding of the message.

"I may need to sit down for a minute," Scarlett said to Phan, who was striding in front of her. Her head was swimming with the sudden movement. Scarlett didn't know if it was related to her head or something else, but she was having trouble keeping her footing.

Phan frowned at her. "Your stupidity of going where you should not have does not earn you time to rest. You are expected to fulfill your duties as much as anyone else."

Scarlett nodded, blinking her eyes several times as a headache began on the right side. It felt as though someone was drilling a hole through her skull. She followed Phan but could not properly register where they were going or all of the details in the City around her. She saw Rhys and a White distinctly coming toward them, but all she could think was that she needed to rest.

And with that, her legs made the decision for her. She met the ground as she had that morning. But she didn't pass out. It felt as though she was outside her body, watching the scene around her unfold. Phan took at least five more steps before he noticed she was not behind him. He came over toward her and nudged her with his foot. Scarlett tried to say that she just needed a minute, but the words were stuck in her head. She watched Phan but couldn't seem to respond to his command.

"Get up! I don't have the patience for this."

Scarlett told her brain to move her legs, but it didn't work. Then, she saw Rhys's face appear in her vision. He squatted next to her, his hands on his knees.

"Are you okay?"

Scarlett tried to nod, but it seemed as though she had no control over her body anymore. That frustrated her, but she couldn't even control the features on her face.

"I think her sugar's dropped," Rhys said, standing. "She needs something sweet."

Phan studied Rhys with an angry look. "Everyone gets the same food at mealtimes. We don't have food sitting around for you to have whenever you need."

Scarlett tried to communicate that she wasn't the dramatic type, but once again, her body failed to serve her. She felt her eyes seeming to drift closed, but she strained to hear Rhys's voice. She needed him to help her. This had happened to her once before, and he had carried her to the nurse, who had instantly pumped her with sugar. It had cleared her head quickly.

"This happened before," Rhys said. "I can go get her something. Honestly, it's—"

"I refuse to believe they sent us a faulty Blue who can't be in the sun for a few hours without needing *sugar* of all things." Phan scoffed. He nudged Scarlett again with the toe of his boot as though she were a dead slug that he didn't dare touch.

He evaluated the situation silently for a moment. The streets were mostly empty. But there were still a few people going about evening chores and last-minute visits with the neighbors.

Scarlett was suddenly aware of a scream from the alley they had left, the alley where the male had been shot. Scarlett concentrated. Maybe if she just thought hard enough, she could get up and keep going. Scarlett's legs moved. She got her knees under her, each movement feeling momentous. She started to get up from her knees, but she fell forward, clumsily catching herself.

She breathed heavily, pebbles from the walkway cutting into her palms.

"Please," Rhys begged. "She needs something sweet. It can come out of my ration. There's got to be something."

Phan growled. "Fine," he said. Scarlett heard more than saw Rhys take off down the street at a jog. Scarlett stayed where she was, her arms trembling with the effort of staying up. She didn't want to hit the rocks. Her arms gave way with no warning, and she crashed into the ground. The pebbles cut into her face, pressing into the bandage on her forehead. Scarlett rolled onto her back and felt her eyes slowly close. She could still hear them, but she couldn't move.

Suddenly, a hand came and was lifting her head up at a slight angle. A bottle was being pressed to her lips. Scarlett wasn't prepared to drink the liquid. Only half of it stayed in her mouth as Rhys forced the liquid on her too quickly. The sour/sweet taste of a soda burned down her throat. Scarlett took another long sip and felt its coolness enter her stomach, spreading coolness throughout her body.

Scarlett took a deep breath, pushing the bottle away when Rhys tried to get her to drink more. Suddenly, she felt very self-conscious of everyone staring at her. She stood up slowly, Rhys hovering close by the whole time.

"You sure you feel okay?" Rhys asked, his hand jerking out as though to touch her then pulling back. Scarlett's face stung as though a dozen fire ants had bitten her. She reached up and was surprised to touch a few dots of blood. She sighed but had never been vain about her appearance. It was what it was.

"I'm fine," Scarlett said. She could see Malak and his White partner coming down the walkway to them at a normal pace.

"We've wasted enough time," Phan announced, turning to march in the direction he had been going. Scarlett noticed that neither Rhys's partner nor the arrested male were there. Rhys pressed the small bottle of soda into Scarlett's hand, and she took it before trying to match Phan's rapid pace. She continued to sip from the soda bottle over the next half hour, feeling sick. Phan must hate her now. She always seemed to do everything wrong. The only thing that comforted her was the thought of speaking with Darlin that night. She didn't know why Darlin wanted an informant on Phan, but boy did Scarlett have something to tell her now.

Chapter 18

Scarlett examined herself carefully in one of the mirrors in the exercise room. Her face appeared to have zits speckling it, but they were small spots of blood where the pebbles had cut into her. Her bandage was dirty from her dance on the ground, and she wasn't sure how much good it was doing at that point. Scarlett peeled the bandage off slowly and touched the back of her head gently. It was sensitive, and she could feel where she had cut it open. But it wasn't bad.

Turning away from the mirror, Scarlett saw Darlin watching her from the corner. Scarlett strolled over casually and used a machine for her legs. She had peered in the alley as they had walked away, but the male hadn't been there anymore. What had happened to him?

"Hey," Scarlett said, not slowing her movement any.

"Anything happen today?" Darlin asked, adjusting the weights on her barbell. The exercise room was empty except for one other person. Not a lot of second shifters wanted to exercise after midnight. But Scarlett was grateful for the movement today. The leg machine allowed her to get out her frustration without making her dizzy.

"I think Phan killed someone," Scarlett said, her stomach turning over as she said the words.

Darlin's eyebrows shot up, but Scarlett took a moment to gather her thoughts before spilling the information. "A Citizen?" Darlin asked.

"Of course!" Scarlett responded a bit too loudly. "He wouldn't hurt one of us."

Darlin pressed her lips together as she lifted the bar above her head, lowering it slowly. Scarlett didn't like the feeling of disbelief oozing off her.

"Well, Phan shot the male, and I didn't see where. But he fell to the ground, and I could see the blood coming out . . . and we didn't stay long enough to find out the end result."

"What was his infraction?" Darlin asked.

"It was the one male who was attacking Phan. But the shot accidentally hit the other male." Scarlett wasn't sure of herself anymore. Who was she to be spreading this information? She was the only one who had been there, so by her giving this information away, Phan would know it was her. And it seemed as though he didn't like her very much as it was due to her low blood sugar that afternoon.

Darlin waited for more.

"The Citizen was very disrespectful. There was some sort of gathering going on between the houses. It was suspicious, but we never found out why they were gathering or what they were doing. Then, I had an episode, well, has it ever happened to you? Where your blood sugar drops, and it's like suddenly, you have no control over your body?"

Darlin frowned and shook her head. "I have no idea what that is."

Scarlett bit her lower lip, still unsure about detailing the incident. Everything that had happened when she was on the ground seemed a bit unreal. "Well, it has happened to me before. But every time I talk to someone about it, it's never happened to them. But the nurse back at the training center knew what to do."

"The point is—" Darlin urged.

"Well, it happened to me. I couldn't move, but Phan had no sympathy." Scarlett's legs burned. She let them come slowly together as the sides of the machine pressed her in. "That's all. Now, I really should get some rest. This head wound of mine is making me a little dizzy."

"How did you get that?" Darlin asked.

Scarlett frowned. Usually all of her bugheaded mistakes were freely known among those at the compound. "I . . . Devon . . . pushed me. I hit my head. It was a stupid thing."

"Has nothing to do with Phan?"

"No." Scarlett stood. She remembered Phan being there when she woke up, but he was her squadron's leader, it made sense that he would be there to talk to her about it.

"So, I checked into that story you told me about the baby. There *was* a baby. But, it's dead now. You said it was alive."

Scarlett's stomach dropped. The baby was dead? She shook her head. "I didn't know that. I mean, it was alive yesterday, but it was so fragile." Scarlett was surprised at the sadness welling up in her. "That's disappointing."

"You didn't know?"

"No, people don't tend to tell me a lot," she responded, still turning over the idea that the baby she had seen just that day had been dead. Had it been dead already? Or was that something that had happened after they had seen it? Phan hadn't acted like it was dead. Was Darlin lying to her? Scarlett's head started to hurt as she tried to connect all of the pieces.

* * *

The next morning, Scarlett woke up slowly as though her brain wasn't ready for the day. As soon as she blinked and looked around, evaluating which shift was in their beds to tell the time, she remembered the child. She felt angry. There shouldn't be secrets here. They were all supposed to be working together. And if they were working together, then she had every right to know why there was a child in that room. Why wasn't the child with the male from its house or with someone who could take care of it?

Scarlett sat up slowly, determined that today would be the day she would get answers. She slowly dressed and made her way to the dining hall. Surely she had talked with Darlin enough the night before that she wouldn't be expecting her in the exercise room.

Scarlett saw Rhys waiting in line to punch in his number, and she rushed over to him.

"Hey, good morning," she said.

"Good morning. How are you doing?" he asked. "No more fainting?"

"No, I'm fine," Scarlett replied. "Let's talk. Maybe, we should go wash dishes a bit early?"

"No," Rhys responded.

Scarlett's heart dropped. So he really wouldn't be willing to go down the hallway again with her. Scarlett didn't know if she could do it on her own, but maybe she would have to. She shrugged like it wasn't a big deal and punched in her number. Rhys waited until she had her tray, then they moved toward the table where Malak was sitting. He had one of the books from the entertainment room library in front of him. Rhys and Scarlett sat side by side across from him. He looked up, marked his page, and closed the book reluctantly.

"Good morning," he said.

"Hi, Malak," Scarlett greeted, her brain turning over questions. Malak could have the answers. She glanced at the title of the book. *The History of the Cities.* She frowned. That was something she had heard so many times, she could probably quote the book word for word.

"How's the reading?" she asked instead.

Malak shrugged. "I didn't think the book would contain any new information, but I always like to review what I know to prevent forgetting it."

Scarlett prepared her next question, but Malak beat her to the punch.

"To what was Phan referring when he mentioned not trusting us last shift? Has someone on our squadron done something?"

Scarlett sighed. Malak might as well be included, and this would be the perfect opportunity to bring up the child. "Yes, actually." Rhys jumped in, cutting Scarlett off and only telling half the story.

"Before our chore time yesterday, we discovered a hidden passage behind the kitchen. We started walking down there, and Devon got too cocky. We ended up getting in a fight of sorts," Rhys pointed to his bruises.

Malak nodded, looking over to Scarlett as though he could tell that she wanted to add more. Scarlett just shrugged, knowing Rhys would be mad if she brought up the baby thing again. But at the same time, she couldn't pretend it hadn't happened. Scarlett purposely ignored Rhys.

"We saw a baby down there, the baby that you helped me deliver," Scarlett declared.

Malak raised his eyebrows as he continued chewing at the same pace. "Was it alive?" he asked matter-of-factly.

Scarlett blinked. She didn't know. She didn't know who to believe. A disgusting thought crossed her mind of using the baby's meat to supplement their meal, and Scarlett lost her appetite.

"Um, yes?" she asked. "It looked alive." The only way she could get her questions answered was if she entertained the idea that the baby was still living and breathing. And as soon as she could find out, she would.

Malak nodded and looked thoughtful.

"So, why was it there?" Scarlett asked.

Malak tilted his head as though considering her question very carefully. "I don't know. That's an excellent query."

Scarlett pressed her lips together, staring hard into Malak's eyes. "You're not telling me everything."

Rhys kept his eyes fixed on Malak as well. Malak shrugged. "I know some things that perhaps I should not. But I assure you, if you are worried for the health of the child, the child will be most well cared for."

"And if it's . . . dead, why would it be down there?"

"Perhaps, they want to know why it died, and they shall investigate."

Scarlett pushed her tray away. She noticed that Rhys had stopped eating as well.

"Okay," she finally said. But it wasn't. She knew that she should always follow the rules, that she should never question. But she couldn't help it. Her stomach hurt as she thought about the small bundle of child bawling.

The image of the child haunted her throughout her dish duties. Every time she put a wet stack of dishes in front of Malak for drying, Scarlett glanced at the door. It looked the same. No lock had been placed on it. She could still enter the hallway, and there was no way anyone would know, not if Devon wasn't there to mess everything up.

She went back and forth, toying with the idea of Phan's anger versus leaving her curiosity unsatiated. She *had* to know what was going on, and no one seemed upfront about answering her questions. Scarlett offered to be the one to mop up the sudsy floor after the dishes had been cleaned. No one fought her for that right. But Rhys hung back, not hurrying up the stairs like everyone else. He was watching her, and Scarlett hated that. She was slow about her work, but Rhys seemed in no hurry. Scarlett took a deep breath and tried to appear as casual as possible.

"So what will you do with the rest of your free hours?" Scarlett asked.

Rhys shrugged. "I'm not sure. I was thinking of challenging you to another round of cards, unless you're not up for losing."

Scarlett smiled just a little, her mind rushing to think of some plausible excuse. "I didn't exercise like I normally do in the morning," she said, before a large yawn overtook her. "Or maybe I'll just sleep a little."

"You're not interested in hanging out with me," Rhys concluded. "That's alright. I can take a hint." But he still didn't move.

Scarlett had mopped the whole floor, so she removed the mopping cloths and placed them in the pile of dirty linens. She slowly placed the now-empty mop handle in the corner. Scarlett followed Rhys out of the kitchen, wondering if she would have a chance to come back later.

"So which is it?" Rhys asked when they reached the top of the stairs. "Exercise or a nap?"

"I'll exercise," Scarlett responded, needing some way to get rid of her stress.

"I need to work my legs," Rhys said, following her amiably to the exercise room. Scarlett had never wanted to get rid of Rhys's company before, but now, she felt as though he suspected what she wanted to do and wasn't about to give her the chance to do it. She smiled fakely at him, trying to pass along her irritation. He didn't seem to understand.

Rhys managed to stay by her side the whole day, giving her no time to follow up on her suspicions. Scarlett was irritated, but she would find a way to investigate. She would never let on that Rhys was bothering her though. She just hoped they wouldn't be assigned as partners today. She'd had enough contact with him to make her wish they weren't friends.

Phan stood at the front of their squadron. His eyes passed over Scarlett as he announced that Whites would be picking a Blue partner again. Phan selected Devon, and Scarlett was selected by a White whom she didn't even know. She followed him. He took confident steps like Phan, but he had always remained mostly quiet, letting Phan take charge when they were together. Scarlett remembered him being the target of the Citizen's knife on that first shift. Scarlett had distracted the Citizen just enough to almost get stabbed herself.

"What was your name?" Scarlett finally asked.

"Marse," he responded.

Scarlett nodded. "Thanks, I just couldn't . . . yeah, remember. I don't remember if I heard it before or not." She stopped herself from babbling as she saw where they were heading—house twenty-four.

"Where are we going?" Scarlett asked, even though Marse's steps made it obvious. He pointed instead of answering. Scarlett didn't have time to ask why and what they were doing before they reached the door.

Marse marched in without a cursory knock. Scarlett followed him quickly, her hand reaching for her pistol, even though she didn't know why. Scarlett saw the male on the bed. His body looked frail, as though he never got enough to eat. Scarlett stepped closer, coming even with Marse. The male didn't move.

Marse extracted his stick and lengthened it, using it to poke the male.

"Get up!" Marse commanded. Scarlett quickly understood the situation. If someone didn't report to work that day, someone from second shift had to check on them and see if their excuse was warranted or not. This male had clearly not been working that day. Scarlett wondered if he had enough muscle to even work. He didn't look like the tanned male she had seen the day before. Scarlett's mind went to the dark-haired male who had been shot. She wondered if he was still alive and if he was suffering much.

Marse repeated his command with a harder poke. The male didn't so much as flinch.

"Is he alive?" Scarlett asked as Marse shortened his stick and leaned forward. He took off his glove and placed a finger under the male's nose.

"No, he's dead." Marse pushed the male much harder as though expecting a reaction even after declaring him dead. Marse sighed and looked around the house. Scarlett followed his line of sight. Everything looked just as it had when she had delivered the baby. Was that less than a week ago? It felt as though it had been months.

"How?" Scarlett asked. She had never seen a dead person before. She had only seen pictures. In pictures, they always looked strangely peaceful. This male looked anything but peaceful. The skin was stretched tight across his features as though his bones were too big for his body. He looked stressed. Scarlett kept glancing over at him nervously, as though he would sit up at any moment and reprimand them for poking about his house.

Marse shook his head. "It was probably suicide."

"Suicide," Scarlett repeated the word in a whisper. She didn't know what that was, but it sounded like a nasty disease, especially if it made his skin as drawn as a stretched-out climbing cord. Scarlett suddenly wondered if they could catch the suicide. Maybe they should stay away from the male. Scarlett glanced uneasily over at Marse. He didn't seem worried at all. In fact, he was moving closer to the body.

"Um," Scarlett put a hand to her stomach. "I've never seen . . . a dead person," she said, fumbling through her excuse. "I just need a minute."

Marse smiled and nodded toward the door, releasing her.

Scarlett stepped out into the fresh air. She paced in the road, the familiar movement comforting her just a little. Was this disease going to spread around the City? Scarlett remembered one time when one student had gotten a virus. It had passed to all the Yellows before they could stop it. Every one of the twenty-two girls in her dormitory had been vomiting. The memory made her shudder.

Scarlett kept an eye on the walking path, but her mind was consumed with the picture of the immobile male laying on the bed. What would happen to him? Would he just stay there forever? The female was still imprisoned as far as Scarlett knew.

Scarlett's breath caught in her throat as a lone figure started down the street. What caught her eye was the uneasy way in which he moved. His leg was stiff; it didn't bend the right way at all. Scarlett's eyes traveled up to the male's face. His dark hair was familiar. She had met him just yesterday; well, not met in the common sense of the word. But they had come in contact.

Scarlett took a few steps to meet him in front of house twenty-three.

"Are you okay?" she asked, feeling relieved that he wasn't dead.

The male scoffed. "Why? Did you want to shoot my other leg?"

"No," Scarlett shook her head. "I don't—" How could she explain that she felt like his pain was her fault? Phan had shot him, but Scarlett felt as though she could have done something to change the outcome. Scarlett took a deep breath as the male crossed his arms and studied her.

"You're new here," he said.

Scarlett nodded.

The male's eyebrows rose. "Not hard to tell."

"I just, I thought you might be dead," Scarlett scrunched her face up. That didn't sound like she had thought it would. "I'm glad to see that you're not."

"No, but I might as well be. I can't work now. No way to bring in an income. Do you think I'm going to get a wife like this?" The male rolled his eyes. "No, so I'll be living with my parents the rest of my life, until they die, then, you know I'll be at the mercy of the City."

"You can't work?" Scarlett asked.

"Yeah, that's probably what your friend wanted too. He knew it would be too easy for me to die." The male looked around, as though realizing how strange their conversation was. "Where's your partner?"

"He's in house twenty-four," Scarlett pointed over her shoulder. The male made a chin-up gesture at the house.

"Why?"

"The male is dead," Scarlett pronounced. "Marse thinks it's suicide. Do you know if that's . . . contagious?"

The male burst into heavy laughter. He laughed so loud and long that he leaned over to catch his breath on his knees, one of which didn't function in the normal manner. He groaned and moved his injured leg slowly, his laugh ending suddenly.

"Wow! Are you sure they educated you well?"

Scarlett decided not to mention the fact that she was really only a Green.

Scarlett shrugged. "The training center is a lot different than here," she said.

The male nodded, his eyes lighting with interest. "No kidding. I'm Kendrick. What's your name?"

"Scarlett," she said, staring at his outstretched hand uncertainly. He drew his hand back after a moment, but he didn't seem offended in the slightest.

He just laughed a little. "I'd like to learn about the training centers," Kendrick said. "Do you think you could tell me about them, and I'd tell you about life in the City? I can tell you all about suicide, and whatever else you want to know."

"Sure," Scarlett shrugged. She heard the door to house twenty-four swing open, and she looked over her shoulder. Marse held up a container. A clear liquid splashed inside. He noticed Kendrick and stared at him with piercing eyes.

Kendrick saluted with a relatively respectful stance. "I'm just on my way to the market to pick up some things for my ma."

Marse nodded and continued to watch as Kendrick made his way slowly down the street. He motioned Scarlett over and shoved the container into her hand. "Take this back to the compound. I'll make sure the body gets properly taken care of."

Clutching the strange vial of liquid, Scarlett followed orders, her mind on Kendrick. What information would he tell her?

Chapter 19

Scarlett marched directly back to the compound with the liquid, but her thoughts were on Kendrick. Had that one bullet ruined his life? Would it be so hard for him to work? Surely, there could be a place for him somewhere, perhaps, sitting.

Scarlett punched her number to get into the compound and stood uncertainly in the entrance. Where exactly was she supposed to take this? Just find a responsible-looking White to pawn it off on? First shift was enjoying a meal as they unwound. Haman, as if sensing Scarlett was there, stood up and moseyed over.

Haman's chuckling started when he was five steps away. "You seem to have a way of slipping out of work. I haven't been in the compound as much as you have during a shift, and I've been here for two years."

Scarlett smiled politely, purposely keeping her temper down at his apparent amusement. "I'm supposed to bring this here, but I have no idea who I should give it to."

Haman reached for the container, but Scarlett moved it away from him. "I don't think you're the person who is supposed to receive it."

Haman gave a loud guffaw at that. "No, not me," he laughed. "I can help you ask around. I would suppose the doctor would know what to do with it, since it appears to be some sort of drug."

Scarlett looked at it again. It wasn't as clear as water, but it certainly didn't look like something she wanted to put in her body. "Anyway, I'll go look for him." Scarlett started toward the door in the entryway where she had taken the two small children. It was locked. She looked back at Haman. "Do you know how to get this one open?"

"Never been back there," Haman said. "I haven't been sick in the two years I've been here. Kind of a superpower of mine." Haman laughed and slapped his knee for good measure. He reached over to a White who was on his way to the exercise room.

"Do you know where she could find the doctor?"

The White studied them both, Scarlett's hand still on the knob. "She already looked in there?"

"No," Haman answered for Scarlett, infuriating her. "It wouldn't open." He laughed a little, like a goat choking on a mouthful of grass.

The White strode over and tried the handle. He shrugged. "It's usually open. I'd take it to the Black if you don't know what to do with it, if it's important, that is."

Scarlett nodded, knowing she would do no such thing. An idea had suddenly popped into her head. And she wasn't about to let go of it.

"Thanks," she said suddenly. "I just remembered something the doctor told me when I took him—" She didn't want to mention the children. "Last time I saw him. So, thanks," Scarlett nodded and waited for the two to disband. The White continued on to the exercise room, but Haman hung out.

"So, you're on close terms with the doctor, huh?" he laughed.

"I'd love to talk," Scarlett said. "But I really have to deliver this and get back to my partner."

Haman nodded and stepped aside, back toward the dining hall. With one final wave and chuckle, he turned away. Scarlett slipped down the stairs to the kitchen. It was empty, but she saw the large pile of dishes balanced below the depository. A group would be down here soon enough to clean them up.

205

Without a moment more to think about what she was doing, Scarlett opened the door in the corner and slipped into the dark passageway. She paused, closing the door quietly behind her. The hallway was completely silent. Scarlett hurried toward the right, to the doorway they had first peered in. Anxiously glancing over her shoulder, Scarlett stepped up to the slit of the window. The tiny window had been papered over as though the baby wanted its privacy. Was the child even still in the room?

Scarlett took a deep breath and turned her attention to the keypad. What would happen if she put in the wrong code? Would it beep as it had when she had tried to leave the compound?

As much as she didn't want to, Scarlett hurried further down the hallway. There were three more doorways along it. She peered quickly into each one. She could only see a bit into the rooms, but she could see enough to know there wasn't anyone inside them, baby or otherwise. She went back to the baby door, her stomach turning over.

Slowly, she punched in the exit code Haman had given her that day she couldn't get out of the compound on her own. The keypad hesitated then lit up. Scarlett pushed against the door, and it opened. She was so surprised that it almost swung shut again before she got moving and entered the room.

Scarlett studied the baby, who didn't seem to notice she was there. The child had a cloth wrapped carefully around it, so that only its fragile head peeked out of the top. A clear tube ran into the folds of the blanket. Scarlett couldn't see where it was attached. The child's eyes were closed, but if Scarlett was still enough, she could see the bundle gently moving up and down with the baby's breath. Scarlett heaved a sigh of relief. The baby was alive.

Curious, Scarlett edged forward. She peeled back the edge of the blanket, moving another and another layer until she saw the soft, pink baby skin. The child stirred. Scarlett jumped back a little. The baby had opened its eyes and was staring fixedly at Scarlett. She didn't show any sign of recognition or happiness.

Scarlett pulled back the blanket a little more. She found what she had been looking for- where the tube was going. It buried itself in the child's belly button. Scarlett touched just the tip of the tube, where it merged with the child's skin, wondering what it could be for. Was the child receiving nutrients through a tube? Wouldn't the child need to eat food as she did?

The child's continued stare unnerved Scarlett, as though the child were somehow older and wiser than she was. Scarlett's fingers reached out of their own volition. She stroked the child's soft cheek. The child jerked in response, her baby hands free of the blanket.

"Did you not like that blanket restraining you?" Scarlett asked in a whisper. "I couldn't imagine sleeping like that." The child's arms moved sporadically as though she didn't know what to do with them. "You're so small," Scarlett said. The child didn't look as though she had grown at all; in fact as though she might even have lost some weight.

Scarlett scooped up the child, cradling the small body next to hers but being careful of the tube. "Hey," she said, down into the small face. The mouth moved, opening and closing as Scarlett stroked a few wisps of her hair away from her face. The hair was a dusty brown color like the male's. They had similar features, and once the thought had entered her brain, Scarlett couldn't stop thinking of the male's face.

"Do you remember him?" Scarlett asked. While the baby certainly appeared intelligent, she didn't think the baby could really understand what she was saying. "He's dead," Scarlett said. The baby didn't even blink, so Scarlett knew for sure that she didn't understand. The child felt warm in Scarlett's arms, but the baby's skin quickly covered with goosebumps as the cold air hit her.

"I guess the blanket is on you for good reason," Scarlett decided, wrapping it back as best she could. She held the child and noticed the child's eyes starting to droop. Was she falling asleep? Scarlett set the child on the table once again, but the child protested, her eyes opening again and a strange squawk exiting her mouth. Scarlett quickly scooped up the child again and held her securely, looking around to see if someone had heard and would be coming, but the room felt very self-contained, as though they were in their own little world.

Scarlett rocked the baby to sleep, watching in amazement at how a being so tiny could function. Finally, the child was snoring softly, and Scarlett laid her down on the table. She adjusted the blanket one more time and grabbed the vial of liquid she had set down upon entering. Who knew how long she had been down here? Would Marse be missing her already?

Scarlett slipped out of the hallway into the kitchen. As she shut the door behind her, a Blue from first shift stepped off the bottom stair into the kitchen. He stared at Scarlett, and Scarlett looked back. She cleared her throat and continued on up the stairs. Maybe if she looked like she knew what she was doing, no one would assume anything. After all, that Blue was a newbie like her. Scarlett hoped nothing would come from it.

Scarlett tried the door again to the doctor's room and the interrogation space, but it was still locked. Scarlett left the vial on a shelf by the door with specific instructions, already constructing a story that would explain her long absence to Marse. Hopefully, he wouldn't question it.

Chapter 20

"Good morning, Malak," Scarlett greeted cheerily as soon as she saw Malak sitting at a corner table by himself. Not surprisingly, he had a book by his elbow. He looked up a bit confused then smiled when he saw Scarlett.

"Good morning. Sorry. I was reading."

"Yes," Scarlett nodded as though she hadn't been able to figure that out on her own. "Sorry to interrupt."

"No, it's no problem at all," Malak responded, giving the book one last glance before pushing it to the side. Scarlett sat down and took a bite of food, eyeing the others in the dining hall to see if they were thinking of approaching. She self-consciously pressed her fingers under the edge of the table. There weren't any bugs or anything that she could detect, but she still felt worried.

"Anything particular on your mind?" Malak finally asked after they had eaten in silence for a few moments.

"Yes," Scarlett nodded. "I just want to ask about the baby. Look," she could see Malak starting to protest, but Scarlett didn't want to be interrupted. She just wanted Malak to answer her questions without asking for anything in return. "I know maybe you're not supposed to answer questions, but you know a lot more than the rest of us. So please, just tell me this, will the baby be taken back to her family, so she's not lonely all the time?"

Malak let out a huge puff of air. "I have studied a lot, but that does not mean I can tell the future," Malak responded.

Scarlett sighed as she felt the frustration rising within her. "I understand. However, I would appreciate it if you were able to tell me anything you know." Scarlett stirred the rice and beans around on her plate. "You were there. You helped me help the female. I helped that child. I was the first one that child saw when she was born. And . . . I feel some sort of connection to her, like I'm responsible for her wellbeing. I just want to know that she's well taken care of, that someone will take her back to the male or, I don't know, someone who cares about her."

Malak nodded, seemingly moved by her speech. "I do understand. That's the natural instinct females have to nurture the young. However, I really don't know. I know, well, I'm sure you've figured out by now, now that you've been part of the process. But, the child, if proven strong and capable, will probably be taken to our training center and grow up there."

The theory had ruminated inside Scarlett's head for a long time, but to have Malak admit it, that it was possible, it meant that she had been born in one of these Cities. Her throat felt dry, and she grasped for her water glass. She took a few sips, almost choking on them as a sudden sense of loss overwhelmed her.

"I . . . I wasn't born in the training center? I had a . . . family?" Scarlett questioned, her thoughts full of gaps as though it hurt to put the pieces together. Of course, everyone was curious at one time or another where the Tinies came from. However, a Blue or Green (who back then had seemed so old) had always told them that the Government provided Tinies when we needed more. Scarlett hadn't questioned past that. But being here, seeing the baby and the process of being born, she had begun to suspect something. Now, she felt sickened. The female who had put forth such effort to birth the child had been separated from her soon after. But, of course, if it was for the good of the Government, it must be okay, right?

Malak was shaking his head. "We all had to come from somewhere. However, I wouldn't say you had a family. Each one of us was chosen within a few days of our births. We were selected to serve the Government." Malak sounded almost proud, but Scarlett was still shaken.

"I just . . . I didn't know. But the baby, this baby. If she's going to the training center, why isn't she already there?"

Malak shrugged. "I can only theorize on that. Perhaps, they need to gather more things before they send a Jeep to the training center. Perhaps they are observing the baby; they don't know if she will be an adequate guard or not." Malak shrugged again. "I'm not privy to this information. I didn't even know a baby was here until you told me."

Scarlett felt her heart beating hard, and her scalp prickled. She had seen the baby just the evening before, but already, it felt like a long time. She wanted to see the child again, make sure it was okay. Most of all, she wanted to know the fate of the child. She tried not to let her worry show.

"Yeah, there's just a lot of surprises here," she said, pasting her lips into a semblance of a smile.

* * *

That afternoon, Phan divided them into pairs quickly. Scarlett's stomach turned over, when he selected her to be his partner again. If he hated her so much, why would he pick her to be his partner? Was he trying to keep a close eye on her, like she was supposed to be keeping a close eye on him?

They walked in silence, with no particular destination, as far as Scarlett knew. She tried to keep pace with Phan, though he didn't look back to check on her. They made a full round of their quadrant, then Phan found a place where two walkways met and stood by the corner. Scarlett placed herself next to him, trying to stay as alert as possible, while her body told her a nap would feel nice.

"You visited the baby again," Phan said, his voice matter-of-fact.

Scarlett froze, unable to process all that his statement meant. He was somehow watching everything she did. He hadn't stopped her in the middle of the visit. He hadn't reported her. He wanted to talk to her about it. Scarlett finally nodded shakily.

"Why?" His voice was firm but not deadly.

"I was worried for her," Scarlett responded softly. "I'm sorry. I know you said not to go back, and . . ." she couldn't think of an excuse to make up for going against a direct order, one received less than forty-eight hours before.

"You don't trust the Government," Phan declared.

"I do!" Scarlett rushed to reassure him. "This has nothing to do with that. Sir."

Phan studied Scarlett with his sharp eyes. She felt as though he could see all her thoughts. "You question the Government."

Scarlett couldn't admit to any such thing, even questioning the rights or abilities of the Government was grounds for treason. Scarlett readied herself for another round of denials, when Phan surprised her.

"You don't like how babies are separated from their families and sent to training centers."

Scarlett simply shrugged. He wasn't believing her denials, and she certainly couldn't agree with it.

"I do not either," Phan continued as though she had responded.

"You . . . don't?"

Phan shook his head.

"But you . . ." she was about to say he was the biggest supporter the Government had, at least as far as she knew. He shot Kendrick! How could he be against the Government?

Phan made the sign of the Government to a passing Citizen, who hurried to do the same. Phan followed the Citizen's path with a critical eye. Scarlett's brain couldn't process this. Phan wasn't a loyal follower of the Government?

When the Citizen was a good distance ahead, Phan continued to peruse the streets with his eyes as he waited for Scarlett to come to terms with what he had said.

"So why are you telling me this?" Scarlett asked.

"Because I can see how stupid you are," Phan responded quickly. "You have questions, but you don't try to answer them the right way. No one knows that the baby is there except you and your friends and one other trusted White."

So, Phan had put the baby in that room?

"If you go around making trouble and asking so many questions, you are going to make that baby lose her opportunity."

"Her opportunity?"

"Her opportunity to get out."

Scarlett waited for further explanation.

"I can get her the opportunity to get out of going to the training center. But, I won't have that opportunity for another few days. You need to stop asking questions and bringing the baby up to other people, or you will take that opportunity away from her."

Scarlett didn't completely understand, but she didn't know how many questions she was allowed. Still, the thought of taking away the baby's opportunity . . . no way could she do that. What was this opportunity? It was either the training center or the City, wasn't it?

Scarlett was just forming her next question when Phan's radio crackled with a report on the other side of the quadrant. Phan barked his response and started hurrying in the direction of the issue, his face a mask of seriousness.

"So—"

"The conversation is over," Phan responded in his normal gruff tone. No trace of the humanity she had detected before was there. But the conversation had happened. There was no doubting that. Now Scarlett knew that Phan wasn't the devoted follower he played.

Chapter 21

That evening, Scarlett went to the exercise room, knowing that Darlin would be waiting for her. Scarlett's mouth felt dry, even as she grabbed an extra bottle of water. She took a slow sip, her mind desperately searching for an answer. Should she tell Darlin what Phan had told her? Clearly, Phan had something to hide. But if she did report Phan, then what would happen to the baby? Did she trust Darlin more than Phan?

Scarlett felt Darlin's eyes on her, so she set down her water bottle and busied herself with one of the barbells, taking off a weight or two before beginning to use it. "Will you spot me?" she asked Darlin.

Darlin nodded and stood over Scarlett as she lifted the barbell again and again. Scarlett's arms were burning, and she felt sweat trickling down her face. No way Darlin could tell how nervous she actually was.

"Today?" Darlin asked.

Scarlett grunted as she lifted the barbell again, and Darlin stopped her from doing another repetition by placing the barbell on its' supports. She was waiting for an answer.

Scarlett wiped away some sweat, mumbling out her answer as she dried her face. "Just checked out some reports but nothing serious."

"You were with him the whole shift. He didn't say anything?"

How did Darlin know they had been paired? The other squadrons didn't see each other during shifts. Was someone else reporting on Phan, too? The idea that Darlin also met with someone else crossed Scarlett's mind. But why should the thought surprise her? If they suspected Phan of something, and clearly they had a reason to, then why would she be the only eyes out? But who else could be reporting? Not Rhys. He would have told her if Darlin had given him the same speech. Would Malak agree to something like this? He was such a rule follower. Devon seemed the most likely candidate, which made Scarlett even warier of him.

"No," Scarlett responded. "He's not really much of a talker." She reached for the barbell again, so she could avoid making eye contact with Darlin. No one had heard their conversation. No one could know what Phan said. But now that Scarlett had lied for him, she couldn't go back. She was siding with Phan, if there were even sides here.

* * *

For the next day's shift, Scarlett was paired with Devon. After her conversation with Darlin the night before, Scarlett wasn't sure if she could trust Devon. If he had had the same conversation with Phan, would he tell Darlin what Phan had said? Would Phan know that Devon might report him? Had Phan even known that Scarlett was supposed to be reporting on him? The number of questions caused Scarlett to march silently beside Devon, ignoring most of his conversation attempts.

Shortly into their shift, Scarlett spotted Kendrick coming toward them at a slow pace. She could see the way he dragged his leg. She was surprised that he was so determined to walk and always seemed to have an errand to complete.

Kendrick was looking down until he neared them. His face a stoic mask of indifference, he looked up and was halfway through completing the sign of the Government over his heart when he recognized Scarlett.

She saw the change come over him. It was the same change that came over her after a long day of training and classes.

He turned toward them. "Good evening!" he greeted, somewhere between formal and informal. Devon stopped and eyed him, his eyes stopping on Kendrick's stiff leg.

"What's your business?" Devon asked.

Kendrick's eyes flitted back and forth between the two Blues. His eyes lingered on Scarlett for a moment, but she looked away, down the street as though this conversation disinterested her. She was just mentally sending Kendrick messages that he shouldn't disrespect Devon because she didn't want him to get his other leg injured.

Kendrick cleared his throat and held up the basket that each house had. It was used for storing food. "Getting our rations for this week."

Devon looked over his shoulder, where the supply station had a line in front of it. He nodded. "Continue on."

Kendrick nodded to them both and started moving on in a pained fashion. Scarlett avoided eye contact with Devon. "He seemed especially friendly," Devon commented a few moments later.

Scarlett responded with a grunt. If Devon was reporting on Phan, then maybe he would report on Kendrick if he thought him too friendly. Best just to pretend like nothing was a big deal.

"We have work to do," she finally said, taking off with a steady gate. But meanwhile, she was thinking about Kendrick and when she would ever have an opportunity to speak to him. She was always with her partner, and clearly, none of her possible partners would approve of her actually having a friendly conversation with a Citizen, as if they weren't enemies.

* * *

"I think Devon might be supposed to report on Phan, too," she said softly. Rhys fumbled with the weight for a moment before setting it on the brace to rest.

"Don't tell me that while I'm holding weights that could easily smash my face in. Any other surprising things you want to tell me this morning?"

Scarlett half-smiled. "No, I don't think so. I mean, maybe I'm wrong, but . . . I don't know. Couldn't you see Devon as being the type to be bought out as a sort of spy?"

Rhys shrugged. "I don't need to worry about that because I'm not sneaking around breaking any rules." He gave her a pointed look.

"Well, I mean, after everything that happened with Phan shooting the Citizen and—"

"What?" Rhys had been in the process of lifting the bar off the brace again, but he set it back with a clatter. Scarlett looked around. A couple of exercisers were looking at them.

"How about I take a turn?" Scarlett suggested, nudging Rhys with the toe of her shoe. Rhys rolled off the bench and began taking off weights as though he already knew how much she could lift. Scarlett took one extra off, focusing more on talking to Rhys than strengthening her upper body. She lifted the bar as she continued to explain what had happened.

"Phan shot a Citizen on our shift. One Citizen attacked Phan, and while that was happening, Phan tried to shoot him but missed and shot a different Citizen instead. And I thought he was dead, but I saw him yesterday. He isn't." Scarlett stopped suddenly, short of telling Rhys about the conversation she had had with the male. She had learned that his name was Kendrick, and he had seemed so . . . normal. Not less intelligent as she had always thought.

Rhys shook his head. "I heard something, but I didn't know what was true and what wasn't. So what does that have to do with Devon?"

"I don't know," Scarlett puffed out. "I . . . I just don't feel like I can trust him."

"Then don't," Rhys said, heaving the weight onto the bar and leaning down close to Scarlett. "Malak told me that the Citizens are trying to learn as much about the Government as they can because they want to get rid of us."

"What do you mean? Get rid of us?"

"The Citizens want to be in charge."

Scarlett frowned. "But we already tried that. That's why the Government is set up as it is now. Haven't they ever taken a history class—or a thousand—like we had to?"

Rhys shrugged. "I'm just telling you what I know. And if I got it from Malak, it's pretty reliable." Scarlett had to agree with his assessment. Malak's information tended to be accurate. But at the same time, Kendrick's request had seemed to be genuinely curious. Did he actually have nefarious motives?

Scarlett didn't want to continue their conversation. "Let's go eat," she suggested, ducking out from under the bar. Rhys heartily agreed.

Scarlett nodded, her mind going to the time. No one would wash dishes until the morning. The kitchen should be empty. Now would be the best time to check on the baby. But should she just leave it alone? If she was careful that no one saw her, and she didn't tell anyone about it, what would be the harm? Scarlett excused herself from the gym, citing a shower as her need to go. Rhys nodded as he walked her down the hallway to the female dorm.

She doubled back and slipped down the stairs and into the kitchen. She didn't even have a vial of mysterious liquid this time to count as an excuse. Scarlett eased the door open and listened carefully before stepping inside the hallway.

Hurriedly, she entered the code on the keypad, before even looking in the room. But as soon as she started opening the newly unlocked door, she froze. The child was screaming. The walls were so thick and her heartbeat so loud that she hadn't heard it outside the room. She quickly closed the door behind herself and went to the child. The child's face was red and droplets of tears had formed a puddle on either side of her head. Scarlett looked to see what was wrong, but she couldn't find anything. She peeled back the blankets, exposing the child to the cold. The tube was firmly fixed in her stomach, unmoved from the previous day.

The cold air seemed to startle the child. But what startled Scarlett was the smell. As soon as the blankets were pulled back, she could see that the child had soiled herself. Scarlett nearly gagged as she stared at the mess. It had leaked out of the nappy and onto the blanket. The child tried to fix her eyes on Scarlett, and Scarlett reached up and stroked her cheek. The child calmed and waved her arms, newly freed from the bundle. Scarlett gagged as fragments of the nasty smelling substance flew off the child's fingers and splattered both Scarlett and a few pieces of equipment around. The child didn't seem to notice, but Scarlett began to freak out.

If she left the child as she had been, she would begin crying again, besides the fact that she had made a mess everywhere. But if she were to try to clean the child, she might vomit, plus the fact that in such an orderly room like this, a soiled blanket in the corner would not go unnoticed.

Scarlett looked around frantically, constantly glancing back at the child. She saw a stack of blankets on a shelf. Beside the stack of blankets was a box and then more nappies. Scarlett cautiously stepped toward them. They were organized, but surely they weren't accounted for. She took a deep breath. Well, even if they were, no one could prove she had been down there.

Scarlett took a breath (which she instantly regretted due to the smell permeating the room) and grabbed a new blanket, nappy, and the box of wet hand towels. Scarlett located a trash can in the corner and threw the soiled materials in there. One hand towel in each hand, she attacked the child's bottom, cleaning it as well as she could. She had changed a diaper once before when she had helped with the Tinies, but it had not been nearly as bad as this one. Scarlett tried to breathe only through her mouth. With one last moist hand towel, she rubbed the few spots of fecal matter that had splashed on her suit and on the monitor. The child seemed amused by her frantic movements, watching her and not at all upset by the cold nature of the hand towels.

Scarlett sighed and re-dressed the child in her nappy and blanket. It didn't look quite right. She took the blanket off and re-did it. Still not quite right. As she tried to do it a third time, the child squawked at her in protest.

"I'm sorry," Scarlett apologized. "I don't exactly know what I'm doing. But I'm trying my best. I guess it's good enough." She pulled the corner of the blanket over farther and laid the baby on her resting place again. She frowned then started crying.

"No, no, no," Scarlett said. "I just cleaned you up. What else could you need?"

The child, of course, did not answer in a reasonable manner. She continued crying. Scarlett stroked the child's cheek softly, then ran her hand over the child's fuzzy head. She paused at an especially soft spot. Feeling terribly uncomfortable but following her internal instincts, she bent down and planted a soft kiss on the child's forehead.

The child had stopped crying, but she still looked up at Scarlett.

"I bet it gets a little scary down here all by yourself, huh?" Scarlett asked. "I wish I could take you out, but I can't. I'm not important enough yet to even know about you really." Scarlett continued to stroke the baby's head until her eyes drifted closed. "You sure do sleep a lot," Scarlett concluded. She felt tired herself, and she knew it had to be after one in the morning. Time for rest. As cautiously as possible, she crept out of the room and back into the kitchen. No one saw her.

Chapter 22

Scarlett was assigned to Rhys for their shift that afternoon, and she couldn't have been more relieved. She didn't trust Devon, and the thought of talking with Phan again disconcerted her.

"Let's head this way," Rhys said as though they actually had a choice in the matter. They followed the same route every day. However, Scarlett couldn't say it ever felt boring because there was always something unexpected happening.

Scarlett wanted to tell him about what she had found out, about the baby, about herself. She couldn't get rid of the thought that a female had birthed her, and then she had been taken to the training center when she was so small she didn't even remember. It made her feel different. She knew it shouldn't, though. Just because she had recently discovered the truth didn't mean it was a new truth. It had always been the story of her beginnings; she simply hadn't known it. Scarlett wondered if the Blues at the training center knew and just didn't tell her.

"We're supposed to go do a surprise inspection of houses forty and forty-three today," Rhys said after they had walked for a few minutes. Scarlett looked at him, confused.

"I didn't hear that. You and me?"

Rhys shrugged. "I guess. That male, Marle, I guess, looked at us when he said it."

"Marse?"

"I don't know. I think that's his name."

"I haven't met anyone named Marle, so I'm pretty sure it was Marse."

"Okay, Marse, whatever. Weren't you listening?"

"I was listening, but I didn't hear that. Okay, so, when? Now?"

Rhys shrugged again. "I don't know. He didn't say."

Scarlett didn't like the unclear aura of the order, so she thought it over for a few minutes, trying to pinpoint the moment she must have zoned out. But she trusted Rhys. "Okay, let's do a round first." Maybe when they passed by the houses, it would be clearer to her when they should do an investigation. She immediately thought back on the investigation she had done with Marse, finding the male dead. She shuddered.

"It's not that cold out here," Rhys said when he saw her shudder.

Scarlett grimaced. "Thanks, it's not that. It's just that I guess I'm not ready to find someone else dead."

"Dead?"

So Scarlett spilled the details about finding the dead male and what Marse suspected. "Have you ever heard of that before? Suicide? Is it a disease only here in the Cities?"

Rhys looked thoughtful for a few moments. "I know I've heard about it before, but I honestly don't remember what it is. It's never something we've caught in the training center, anyway."

"I had to take some liquid to the compound," Scarlett explained. "I washed my hands really well, but I guess I'm just paranoid that I'll get sick with suicide now."

Rhys shook his head. "No way. Marse wouldn't have given you something that could make you sick like that."

Scarlett nodded. They were just reaching house number forty. "Should we go in?" she asked.

Rhys shrugged then nodded. "Let's do it." Scarlett stood on a lower step as Rhys gave a cursory knock before pushing the door open. The female was standing over the burner, her face red as she stirred a large pot. She looked surprised, her eyes darting back and forth between them. Then, she smiled, though Scarlett didn't feel it was genuine.

"How are you both doing today?" she asked, giving the pot a last stir before drying her hands on her apron. Rhys nodded, his eyes glancing around. Scarlett felt out of place. They had no idea what they were looking for or what they were doing here, only that surprise visits on these houses were necessary.

"We would like to take a look around," Rhys responded politely, stepping toward the closet beside the bathroom. Scarlett gave a cursory poke under the bed and in the cabinets. The female watched with an almost amused look on her face. In five minutes, they were done. Scarlett knew they should say something but didn't know what. She placed her three fingers over her heart and repeated the pledge. "May the Government's wisdom and power live forever." She and Rhys left.

"This would be a lot easier if we knew what we were looking for," Rhys said, echoing her thoughts.

Scarlett nodded. "I guess just keep our eyes open for babies stuck in drawers or under the bed."

Rhys laughed slightly. "Yeah, that's it." As Scarlett looked around, hearing a noise behind them, she saw Kendrick limping in their direction, much slower than them. They were leaving him behind little by little. Scarlett's heart started beating faster. She wanted to talk to Kendrick again. She wanted to know more about life in the Cities and not Malak's perfectly scientific knowledge either, but something first hand. Scarlett began searching her mind for excuses to be separated from Rhys.

"Hey," she finally said. "I forgot that Marse told me to meet him at 18:00 to talk about the results of the suicide examination."

Rhys frowned. "When did he tell you that?"

"It was before our shift started, this morning, after . . . we washed the dishes."

Rhys nodded. "Okay, where are we supposed to meet him?" He looked at his timepiece. "Depending on where it is, we should probably begin walking."

"Well, he just wanted me to meet him," Scarlett responded. "Because he didn't want both of us to neglect our duties, but, I can fill you in on the details once he tells me."

"Oh," Rhys frowned. "Okay, well, I guess I'll let you know where to meet me. Just radio me when you're done."

Scarlett sucked in her cheeks. If they radioed that they were meeting and where, then their whole team would know they had split up. And without any official orders to do so, that would be hard to explain.

"How about I meet you on the easten side in half an hour? It shouldn't take me long. Or if it does, then I'll radio you."

Rhys shrugged his okay. Scarlett made a big show of checking her timepiece, then she turned and hurried back the direction they had just come. She made eye contact with Kendrick who was some distance behind them now and nodded ever so slightly toward the space between houses thirty-seven and thirty-six. She continued down the walkway and turned the corner as she normally would then cut back behind the houses to meet Kendrick. Her heart beat quickly as she hoped Rhys would continue on and not see any reason to linger.

She slipped between the houses, hoping it was the right alley as she couldn't see the house numbers from the back. She breathed heavily as she glanced out between the houses. It was just starting to grow dark. Good. Someone might get suspicious seeing a Blue squatting between the two buildings.

Kendrick limped around the corner but stopped when he saw her. They sized each other up for a moment, then Scarlett motioned for him to sit. He awkwardly collapsed to the ground before righting himself and leaning against the wall of one of the houses.

"Hey," she said. He scooched over so that their shoulders were almost touching.

"For a second there, I couldn't tell if it was you or not," Kendrick said, heaving out a large breath. "In the dark, you all look the same."

Scarlett got straight to business. "You said you wanted to talk, and I have maybe twenty minutes before my partner will be expecting me."

"So you lied to him, eh, to talk here with me?"

Scarlett frowned. She didn't like the way Kendrick said that, as if he had been listening to their conversation. Of course he couldn't have heard them, but still, Scarlett felt as though her privacy had been infiltrated.

"So," Scarlett said, suddenly feeling awkward around him. "What did you want to know?"

Kendrick shrugged. "I don't know. If I knew it, then I wouldn't want to know it. I would already know it." Scarlett untangled his words and smiled just a little.

"Fine, I'll tell you about being a child in the training center, and you tell me about being a child here. Fair?"

Kendrick nodded, using his hands to reorganize his legs.

"Well, when you grow up in the training center, you're always assigned a color. That's your level. And you have to pass a certain test before you can move up. So, there's Tinies, they don't have a color nor a test. But when they turn four years old, they get to be Reds. You can be a Red forever if you never pass the test, but the oldest Red I ever remember was a ten-year-old, and she hated being with the four-year-olds so much that she studied and practiced every day until she could pass the test."

Scarlett smiled as she remembered how much everyone had cheered when she had graduated to a Yellow.

"So, yeah, after Red is Yellow then Green then Blue and White."

"So, why aren't you a White?" Kendrick asked.

Scarlett shrugged, not wanting to explain that she wasn't legally a Blue either. "I haven't been a Blue long enough to receive the honor of being a White."

Kendrick gave a short chuckle.

"What? Why are you laughing?"

"Because don't you realize that you're killing us? Killing the Citizens?"

Scarlett frowned. "I haven't killed anyone. And I know that Phan shot you, but that was totally an accident. But just because that happened doesn't mean that I go around shooting people."

"Yeah, not yet," Kendrick said. "Just wait. The guards who come are always nice at first. That one who shot me." Kendrick snorted. "We used to be friends."

"Friends?"

Kendrick nodded. "Well, not like, best friends—let me tell you all my secrets. But we got along. We could joke around a bit. But then, he got promoted to White, and everything changed, like he wasn't the same male at all anymore. You saw the way he was determined to shame me, like he's a better person."

Scarlett thought about all of the expectations and worries that were constantly flowing through her mind. She hated the pressure that was on them as guards to get everything right. "Well, I didn't know him before, so I don't know about that. Everyone's different." Who was Phan? He had talked like he wanted to save the babies. But his actions with Kendrick and the other male . . . Scarlett felt like she couldn't be sure of anything.

Kendrick didn't respond, so Scarlett prodded him for more details about his childhood. Kendrick shrugged. "It's just like everyone else here in the City. I lived with my family, and I have an older sister. She's married now and has her own family." Kendrick shook his head, and Scarlett remembered his statement before about not being able to get married or work a job now. "As a kid, I went to school—"

"School?" She was also storing "sister" into her mind to ask about, but she figured only one question at a time would be best.

Kendrick looked at her, the whites of his eyes glowing in the falling dark. "Please don't tell me you don't go to school at the training center."

Scarlett shrugged. "What do you do there?"

"You learn about boring things like history or numbers or—"

"Oh, classes," Scarlett confirmed.

Kendrick still eyed her. "Yes, classes. So, you did have classes? Or school?"

"Yes, we had classes, but I've never heard them called school before."

Kendrick was silent as he watched her in surprise. "Anyway, then at ten, just like everyone else, I got a job as a chopper. When you're a child, they don't expect you to do a whole lot; it's more just learning and seeing where you fit. But by the time you're fifteen or sixteen, you're putting in a full day. So, that's it. That's all I know." Kendrick was quiet for a few moments as Scarlett soaked in his story.

She took a deep breath as though the fresh air would clear her confusion. "So, once assigned a position, then that's your position for life?"

Kendrick motioned to his leg. "Well, unless something like this happens."

"Can't you be assigned to a different position?"

Kendrick pressed his lips into a firm line. "Unfortunately, once you have been trained in a position, it would be very rare for a supervisor to accept you for something you have no training in. I mean, you don't see a lot of eighteen-year-olds like me training in a new position. And especially because that White behind this, well, you can bet he won't go pulling any strings."

Scarlett tried to imagine how pulling strings would be helpful for getting a job. Was there some kind of job that involved string-pulling here? There certainly wasn't anything like that at the training center. Scarlett just nodded anyway.

"Maybe, you can be one of those people who hands out the rations. You don't have to move that much," she suggested, trying to be helpful. Kendrick shook his head.

"I don't need you to come here and solve all my problems," he said. "I can figure that out myself."

Scarlett frowned. He had sounded like he wanted help, and she didn't think her suggestion was a bad one. But she knew from experience that when males said they didn't want help, they really didn't want it. "So," Scarlett responded. "I should probably head back. Rhys will be expecting me." Scarlett started to rise. But as she did so, Kendrick reached up and grabbed her knee.

"Hey, don't go yet." Scarlett pulled her knee out from his grasp and stared at him wide-eyed. Not only was he a Citizen setting hands on a guard, but she was a female.

Kendrick laughed at her wide-eyed expression. "What is that supposed to mean?"

"But, uh, you t-touched me."

Kendrick laughed again, this time louder. Scarlett looked around to see if he was attracting any attention.

"Why are you laughing?"

"I don't get what the problem is. What? You're too high and mighty, being a Blue? I thought you were actually a little more real than the rest of them."

"But . . . I'm a female."

"O—kay," now Kendrick looked just as confused as she felt.

Scarlett crossed her arms, her brows knit. "Well, you're a male." Kendrick shook his head slightly, the strange idea confusing him even more.

"Males can't touch females," Scarlett said, putting it out in the open. "Isn't it the same here?"

Kendrick made a strange guffawing sound. "Um, no, there's kind of the need to keep producing children."

"What?" Now Scarlett was really confused. "What does that have to do with touching a male?"

"Why is that a rule?" Kendrick asked.

"Because . . ." Scarlett thought. "I don't know. That's just the way it is. I don't question every single rule. Why is there a rule that I wear Blue?

Why don't the littles wear Blue and we wear Yellow? That's just the way it is."

Kendrick screwed up his lips, concentrating on getting to his feet. "I think you should ask about that rule, because there's no such rule here." Kendrick was on his feet now, leaning slightly against one of the houses.

"I'm not really the kind of person to start questioning the rules," Scarlett said then thought to herself as long as the questioning involved being verbal. She would sneak around and be curious all day long.

"How about we do an experiment?" Kendrick suggested, taking a hop-step forward.

"I'm not very good at science," Scarlett responded. "I mean, I passed, because I had to, but maybe someone else would prefer to try experiments."

"How about this one?" Kendrick said with another hop-step. He reached his hand out slowly, Scarlett's eyes following it like it was an approaching snake. "I touch you, just slightly, here, and you tell me what you feel."

Kendrick's fingers brushed her face, trailing toward the back of her neck and touching her hair. Scarlett smiled without meaning to. Kendrick smiled back at her, pressing the nape of her neck softly. Scarlett shuddered then backed away, but she didn't stop smiling.

"So?" Kendrick asked softly.

Scarlett felt her face reddening, as if she had been caught doing something wrong. "I don't know," she responded.

"You—"

"What are you doing?" a harsh voice interrupted. Scarlett's hand reached for her pistol in surprise. Kendrick whirled around, his goofish smile gone. Rhys was blocking the faint light from the walkway. His hands were clenched into fists by his side. "What are you doing here?" he asked Kendrick, his eyes drilling into him as though they could do real damage.

Kendrick didn't back off, and Scarlett's stomach curled. She didn't want a repeat of three days prior when Phan had shot Kendrick.

"Let's get back on track with our round," Scarlett said, leading the way back to the wide walkway. She hoped Rhys would follow her and leave Kendrick alone. She bet correctly. Rhys's longer strides quickly caught up with hers.

"What were you doing?" he asked, making no attempt to keep his voice low.

"I—nothing," Scarlett said. She scrambled to come up with a story that would be plausible. "I met with . . . Marse, and on my way back, I saw Kendrick, and—"

"You know his name?"

"Well, yeah, I was there when Phan tried to kill him. I kind of got to know him as they were arguing, so . . ."

Rhys shook his head. Scarlett glanced at him out of the corner of her eye. She could see his jaw tight, the muscles flinching ever so slightly.

"Yeah, I'm sure that's what it was, and you just let a Citizen pull you into a dark alley when he was shot just days prior while you were there? That seems like a brilliant move."

Scarlett sighed. "That's not what happened."

"Then tell me, huh? What happened? You took an alley to come back, and he just happened to be there?"

That didn't sound like such a bad idea. "Well, kind of. Not exactly, but yeah, I wasn't expecting him there. So, I just saw him and decided to be polite and ask him how his leg was feeling."

Rhys stopped suddenly. He waited for Scarlett to turn and face him. "Yeah, after your meeting with Marse? The same Marse I ran into not a quarter hour ago who asked where my partner was? That same Marse? You *obviously* lied to me. For what? To talk to *him*?" Rhys scoffed and shook his head. "No way you're *that* stupid. Or are you?"

Scarlett's eyebrows turned inward. "Stop! Stop acting like you know everything! Look, I didn't meet with Marse, okay? Is that what you wanted to hear?"

Rhys nodded. "The truth would be nice. But who knows with you? Apparently, I can't trust your word anymore." Then, as if they had ended the conversation, he started walking again. Scarlett huffed and followed him. She didn't have much of a choice now. What had Rhys said when Marse asked where she was? Had Rhys told the truth? Would Marse be coming after her? What would Phan think? As her worries floated around her, Scarlett couldn't help allowing her head to dance back to how it had felt when Kendrick touched her. She wished they had been able to finish their conversation.

Rhys refused to speak to Scarlett for the rest of their shift, and it annoyed Scarlett. Sure, he was mad. Let him be mad. But don't act like she didn't exist. That was the stuff of three-year-olds.

"Hey, did you see those Citizens over there?" Scarlett asked at one point. The Citizens had slinked behind a house when they saw Scarlett and Rhys coming. Rhys didn't even acknowledge her question. He did go over to the Citizens and make small talk for a minute as though he wasn't looking to cause any trouble but just looking for a conversation. They moved on, and Scarlett felt even angrier.

"Oh, so you're allowed to have casual conversation with Citizens, but I'm not. That makes complete sense."

No response, which only made Scarlett angrier.

"Okay, fine, whatever, don't say anything."

Rhys continued to be silent. Scarlett started goading him, just wanting to make him respond.

"So, Kendrick told me something interesting," Scarlett said, her voice angry and nasty. "Apparently, here, touching between males and females isn't forbidden." She half-scoffed, half-huffed. "So, looks like Haman was right about something for once."

Rhys still didn't respond.

Scarlett considered seeing if it would make him angry when she told him about Kendrick touching her neck and how it had made her feel, but she didn't know how to explain it, and she wasn't sure anyway if she wanted to share that moment.

Scarlett stayed silent until the end of her shift, forcing herself to stop several times before she said something to Rhys. If he was going to be silent, she could be silent, too.

When they reached the compound again, Scarlett was hungry. She grabbed her food and shoveled it down her throat. Following her normal routine, Scarlett went to the exercise room for a short workout before bed. The room was nearly deserted. Darlin was there, though, and Scarlett found a spot next to her.

"Anything to report today?"

"No," Scarlett responded, and this time, she was being honest. She had barely seen Phan all day.

Darlin made a sort of scoffing noise, and Scarlett looked at her with a frown. "What?"

"Nothing," Darlin responded. "Just working out." She gave another puff of air as though to prove it. Did Darlin have reason to believe that Scarlett wasn't being forthcoming about everything she knew? Scarlett had been careful, not even telling Rhys about her conversation with Phan, so there was no way that Darlin could know, unless . . . the idea didn't sit well with Scarlett, but she had to consider it. What if Phan had made up this fake story about the baby to test her, to see if she would rat him out as a sign of loyalty to the Government or if she would keep quiet and betray the Government? What if Phan and Darlin were working together?

Chapter 23

Scarlett followed the pattern of the night before, sneaking down the kitchen stairs and entering the tiny human's room. She couldn't keep herself away, though she promised this would be the last time. The baby seemed to recognize that she was there, fussing when she heard Scarlett coming into the room. Scarlett quickly scooped the child up to quiet her. This time, she didn't smell like a dirty explosion. Scarlett felt relieved. She didn't really want to change another diaper.

Scarlett scanned the room, but nothing looked out of place. No one had noticed her intrusion. "Good," Scarlett whispered to the little female. "Because I like visiting you. I hope that you're doing okay, and that you know I'm here for you, okay?"

The female didn't respond, but Scarlett freed one of her hands and played gently with the tiny fingernails and fingers. Everything about her was so perfect.

"Do you have everything you need down here?" Scarlett asked. The female didn't respond, but her eyes finally opened and moved around randomly before fixing on Scarlett's face. "Do you remember me?" Scarlett asked another question. Then, she smiled. She was crazy, talking to a human who wasn't able to respond.

Scarlett spent only a quarter hour with the small female, before she began to feel anxious. Scarlett looked toward the little window but couldn't see through. Still, she felt uneasy and decided she should leave the little female and get to bed.

Scarlett set the female down carefully, but still the female protested with tiny whimpers. "It's alright," Scarlett told her. "I promise I'll be back before long. Okay? But you have to be quiet now."

The female didn't seem to understand reason. Her whimpers turned into wails. "Okay, it's okay," Scarlett told her, her level of alarm rising with each cry. Scarlett stroked the fuzz on her head, which seemed to calm the child. Each moment, Scarlett glanced anxiously at the door, but no one appeared. No one noticed.

Scarlett set the child down in the bassinet and continued to stroke her head as the child lay quietly. A beep caused Scarlett to freeze, and she looked up to see Phan entering the room.

Their eyes made contact, and Scarlett didn't move as though if she were still enough, Phan wouldn't notice her there.

"What are you doing down here?" he asked, his voice low.

"I . . . was checking on her."

Phan shook his head. "You don't listen, do you?" Phan let the door close behind him, and he strode over to the sleeping baby. Scarlett took a step back as Phan removed a bag of liquid that was attached to the child by a tube. Scarlett watched as he added some liquid to the bag.

"What are you doing?" Scarlett braved to ask, since she hadn't been arrested or reported yet.

"Putting her in a deep sleep," Phan said. "She's leaving tonight."

"Where is she going?" Scarlet continued conversing with Phan's back as he adjusted things.

"Away from here." Phan turned and locked eyes with Scarlett. "And when she's gone, you are to forget about her. She was reported dead, and that is what everyone believes to be true. Her mother killed her when she knew she would be taken."

Scarlett's eyes darted to the clearly alive, though sleeping, baby.

"If you tell anyone what you have seen, you won't serve here another day," Phan threatened.

"I wouldn't—I wasn't going to tell anyone. I just want to know what's happening."

"You don't need to know what's happening. Knowledge is danger." Scarlett nodded as Phan picked up the child. She would never have described him as gentle before, but with the child, all of his features changed. He placed a hand on her chest then over her eyes. She was sleeping deeply. He placed her in a lined bag and zipped it almost all the way closed. "Go back to your dorm," Phan commanded. Scarlett turned immediately, ready to carry out the order as she always did. But as she marched down the hallway and toward the door that led to the kitchen, she wondered what would happen if she followed Phan and the baby. She wanted to see what would happen to the child. But, she couldn't risk the child losing its opportunity, even though Scarlett didn't exactly understand what that opportunity was.

* * *

Scarlett crept up the stairs to the dining hall. Standing by the top of the stairs was Rhys. Scarlett froze, hoping he hadn't seen her yet. But he had. Of course.

"What are you doing?" Rhys asked, his jaw set in anger.

Scarlett opened her mouth to respond, but she was truly at a loss for words. She didn't have any excuse that made sense, and it was too late at night for her mind to work quickly. She just wanted to shush him.

Rhys's jaw flinched. "Tell me," he said, each word loud and deliberate.

"I . . . uh—it was nothing," Scarlett said.

"Your words clearly mean nothing," Rhys responded, his arms crossed and his eyes narrowed. "Come on. How *stupid* do I look? You were down there visiting that child. Stop lying to me. And stop sneaking around, doing things you're not supposed to do!" His voice was rising, and Scarlett looked over his shoulder to see if anyone else was nearby. She couldn't see the full dining hall but feared that someone was coming to put her in solitary confinement.

"Be quiet," she responded somewhat hushed. What if someone came out to see what all the noise was about, and someone found out what Phan was doing?

"Why should I?" Rhys asked, his voice above the normal tone of conversation. "Hmm? You don't seem to trust me anymore. You don't listen to me anymore. You obviously think you've got this on your own. So, do it on your own then."

"If you want me to do everything on my own, then why are you here, spying on me? I didn't ask you to check up on me. Just be quiet, and I'll tell you about it tomorrow."

Rhys shook his head. "You never think before you do anything. You just do what you wanna do. You don't think about anybody else. You're too stupid to even think about yourself."

"Stop. I'm not stupid!" Scarlett responded, still keeping her voice in a whisper, which seemed to annoy Rhys even more..

"Mmm, sure, okay," Rhys's non-committal words annoyed her.

"Why are you following me around?" Scarlett asked.

"Maybe because I wanted to talk to you, and I thought you would be in the exercise room. You weren't, so I started wondering what you could be up to at one in the morning."

"Maybe sleeping," Scarlett responded. "So you were just going to wander around looking for me while I was sleeping?"

"Clearly you weren't sleeping though, so I was right."

"It doesn't matter." Scarlett said, hating that he thought she couldn't take care of herself. "I don't need you following me around. I don't need you telling me what to do. I've got this."

"No, you don't! Anyone could see you here, and what do you think someone else will do?"

"Be quiet!" Scarlett said. "You're so loud! If you're so worried about me, then why are you shouting at me in the middle of the night? Leave me alone." Scarlett stomped past Rhys, into the dining hall, glad to see it was empty and the lights were dimmed. Rhys followed her loudly.

"I don't have to be quiet just because you tell me to. I'll be as loud as I want!" Rhys said, proving his point by ending his declaration on an especially loud note.

"Shut up!" Scarlett shouted back. "Stop following me!" She walked purposefully toward the hall with the bathrooms and dorm rooms. Her stomach dropped as she saw Malak coming out of the Blue male room and another head peering out of the room after him.

Scarlett froze as Rhys continued babbling behind her.

"I'll do whatever I please. As you expressed so eloquently before, you can do whatever you want and so can I."

"If you wouldn't mind," Malak said as he approached them. "Some of us are trying to sleep. And by some of us, I mean everyone except the two of you."

Scarlett pointed at Rhys as though she was a Red and the Blues had just broken up a baby fight. "Get him to leave me alone. I can't even go exercise without him stalking me."

Malak turned to Rhys, but before he could say anything, Rhys scoffed. "Exercising? Clearly, exercising if you consider—"

Scarlett leaped toward Rhys, determined to make him stop talking. What had gotten into him? Was he determined to get her in trouble? Did he care if she disappeared forever? He didn't even know what was at stake here. Malak grabbed Scarlett's arm as her fist swung toward Rhys.

"Scarlett," he said, his voice firm, but not in the judgemental way Rhys's was. Malak may look reedy, but his grip was steely. "Let him be."

Rhys was smiling at them both. "Let her hit me," Rhys said. "I don't need you to protect me, Malak, though I appreciate the sentiment."

His words only made Scarlett angrier. She lunged toward Rhys, but Malak held her back once again. Two female Blues came out of the dorm room, angry looks on their faces.

"Shut up!" one of them yelled loudly enough to make everyone else who may have still been sleeping wake up. Scarlett hated all the attention and feared it would draw more surveillance to her. She backed away, only because she feared consequences from higher up, not because she felt scared or calmed.

She gave Rhys her angriest look and turned away seething. She was not done with this conversation. Just the sight of his teasing smile was enough to make her feel vomit rising in her throat.

Chapter 24

Scarlett had lain awake for what felt like two hours the night before. She kept running through Rhys's words in her mind. He had always been her best friend, at least for the last four or five years. He was the only one she really trusted here, and she couldn't stand the thought of him hating her. The anger in his eyes kept playing through her mind. Scarlett's fingers rubbed the mole halfway up her stomach, annoying it as her thoughts turned her in circles.

She saw the way he had looked at her, as though she had betrayed him, the same way she had looked at Devon. She still didn't trust Devon, and their lack of friendship to begin with meant no love lost. But with Rhys, it was different.

Scarlett tried to think of what she could say to make everything better, but she couldn't just ignore what Rhys was doing. She had to find a way to explain calmly that her visiting the baby wasn't as forbidden as it might seem. Besides, the baby was gone now. As her eyes drifted shut, Scarlett was sure her plan to remain calm would work.

The next morning, the rustle of first shift getting up at half past six was enough to wake her up. She'd slept only four hours, but there was no way she was going back to sleep now.

Scarlett couldn't stand lying in her bed staring at the ceiling anymore, so she got up and wandered the facility, hoping for a glimpse of Rhys. Nothing. He was probably sleeping in pure bliss, not at all bothered by their fight. Or too angry to be bothered. He wouldn't still be angry, would he?

"Hey!" a female voice behind Scarlett shouted. Scarlett turned around, as did everyone else in the dining hall. "You were the one waking everyone up last night!" the Blue female said moving forward and crossing her arms. Scarlett had never spoken to this Blue before; she had already been here when Scarlett's group arrived a few weeks ago.

"Mm, yes, sorry," Scarlett said, not looking for another fight. Everyone was looking at her, and the other Blue didn't seem to mind the attention.

"Next time, have your little quarrel somewhere else. Or maybe I'll come wake you up in the middle of your sleep. Some of us actually have to get up early."

"I'm up early, too," Scarlett said. As in, she didn't get much sleep so she didn't need anyone annoying her.

"Yeah, well, maybe I'll wake you up early every day," the Blue said.

"Leave her alone," Gayla said, a Blue that Scarlett hardly knew from first shift.

The other Blue turned on Gayla. "Just because you sleep like a rock doesn't mean the rest of us do."

"Chill," a White male said. "Enough of this." He stepped between Scarlett and the other female. Scarlett held up her hands innocently.

"I'm not doing anything."

The White didn't look as though he believed her. "We have enough fighting among Citizens. We don't need everyone here at each other's throats. If you have a problem with someone, you can deal with it quietly. And if you continue to have problems, then we don't need you here. Got it?"

The other female smiled sweetly at the White. "Sure, we get it. Where can I go to file a report of someone breaking the rules? Looks as though this one is a troublemaker."

The White didn't buy her sweet demeanor. "You know where the Black's office is. Now get on with your business." The Blue female turned away without even a parting look at Scarlett. Scarlett's eyes tried to find someplace in the room to rest, someplace where another set of eyes wasn't boring angrily or curiously into her. She saw Rhys watching from the doorway into the dormitory hall. Scarlett's heart jumped slightly, and she took a step toward him. But as soon as he saw her coming, he turned away and headed back toward the male's dormitory.

Scarlett sighed. She *would* talk to him. At least he didn't look angry anymore.

After breakfast, Scarlett headed down the stairs toward the kitchen for dish-washing. "You're assigned to laundry," a White said, stepping in front of Scarlett just as she reached the bottom of the steps. Scarlett recognized the White. He was on her shift, on a different squadron. But why was he changing her chore when everyone else she normally washed dishes with was still in the kitchen?

"O-kay," Scarlett said. "Is everyone switching chores?"

The White shrugged one shoulder. "I was just told to tell you you have a new assignment. I don't have all the details."

"Who told you?" Scarlett asked.

The White narrowed his eyes. "So many questions. Do as you're told." Scarlett left the kitchen, finding the laundry room down another stairway near the exercise room. Why had she been picked out? Was that a good sign or a bad sign? Did someone know what she had been doing after washing the dishes?

A White in the laundry room told her how to sort the clothes and wash them. There were no machines; everything was washed by hand. After two hours, Scarlett's biceps were hurting, and her hands were raw.

While doing laundry was taxing on her body, it had left her mind free to wander. And she was more than ready to talk to Rhys when she finished.

Rhys wasn't anywhere she could find, which meant he was in the male's dormitory. What could he possibly be doing there? Scarlett grabbed a book from the library and camped in the hall, ready to pounce on Rhys whenever he came out. Devon was who came out, though.

"Hey, what are you doing?" he asked, as though he couldn't see the book opened in front of her.

"Reading," Scarlett responded curtly.

"About what?" Devon tilted his head so he could see the title, but Scarlett tilted it away from him. He turned his head the opposite way as though not getting her hint. "Ah, that's fiction. I wondered at you reading. It's not like you're Malak or something."

Scarlett frowned. "So I'm not allowed to read because I'm not as smart as Malak."

"Hey, I didn't say that."

Devon sat on the floor next to Scarlett. She sighed and rolled her eyes, but he still didn't get her hint that she didn't want him there. "So . . . last night?"

Scarlett pressed her nails down one at a time, counting them to keep her patience. "I don't really want to talk, Devon," she responded as politely as she could.

"Hey, you don't have to tell me about it. Rhys already gave me an earful."

"Really? What did he say?"

Devon laughed. "I thought you didn't want to talk about it."

"Stop, Devon. I've been through enough in the past couple of days. Just be normal."

"Normal? Can you define that for me?"

"Ask Malak," Scarlett responded. "Hey, have you seen Rhys recently? I was hoping we could kind of . . . fix things, you know, without shouting."

Devon shook his head. "Nope."

"He's not in the dorm?"

"Nope, is that why you're camped out here? Waiting for him? That's creepy."

"Okay, well, whatever." Scarlett stood up. If he wasn't in the dorm, there was no way he had been in the bathroom that long. He had to be in the exercise or entertainment room. Scarlett started toward the closest one, and Devon stood up and started walking with her.

"Please," Scarlett said as politely as she could. "Let me just go talk to him."

"I have nothing else to do," Devon said, "at least until feeding time at fifteen hours. So I think I'll head to the entertainment room."

As Scarlett turned toward the exercise room, Devon started to follow her, but she gave him a dirty look. He finally took the hint and left her alone. But Scarlett still couldn't find Rhys, and it was starting to bother her. She didn't like how people could just disappear.

Finally, just as her shift was getting ready, Scarlett spotted Rhys coming through the dining hall, sweaty and clearly just finished exercising. But where had he been exercising? They weren't allowed to just go take a stroll around the City.

Scarlett scanned in at the machine and grabbed her assigned pistol. After tucking it into her waistband, she felt Rhys come into the entrance area. He was right behind her. She could smell the familiar scent of his sweat mixed with musk. She watched his dark hand on the scanner, and she felt such a desire to reach out and grab his hand. She remembered how it had felt when Kendrick touched her neck yesterday. She wanted to touch Rhys's neck and see if he felt that same knot in his stomach that she had.

When she turned to look at him, he didn't make eye contact. Scarlett's cheeks reddened slightly. Could he tell what she was thinking? Of course not!

Scarlett followed Phan. "Same as yesterday," Phan announced without any anticipation. Then, he turned and marched over toward the first shift Whites. Scarlett looked toward Rhys. Rhys wasn't looking at her.

"You guys can get a head start," Rhys said to Malak and Devon. Rhys and Scarlett stood there, looking in different directions. Scarlett nodded politely to a Citizen who was carrying a small child down the walkway. She didn't return the nod.

"Let's go," Rhys said when enough time had passed. Scarlett ran through what she wanted to say in her head again.

"Rhys," she said, keeping her eyes on the path ahead of them. "I just want to say that I trust you. I do. And I'm sorry if you didn't feel like that. But just from now on, let me do what I want to do. Okay? I don't need you turning me in. And . . ." Scarlett had to think about it. Of course she could trust Rhys, but it still felt wrong to admit what she knew about Phan.

Rhys was silent for so long that Scarlett opened her mouth to repeat herself.

"I know you think you've got everything under control, but did you know that someone saw you go down to the kitchen last night? I'm not talking about myself either."

"Who?"

"Marse, or whatever his name is."

"Yes, Marse. Did he say anything? Did he see you?"

Rhys shrugged. "I wasn't going where I wasn't supposed to go. It doesn't matter if he saw me or not. The point is that he saw you, and if you keep breaking the rules and doing whatever you want, you're going to end up in trouble. You could lose your opportunity to become a White. You could be shipped back to a training center. Or . . . if it's seen as treason, you could be executed."

Scarlett sucked in her breath. "Okay, I know the consequences. But I'm not okay with everyone keeping secrets. I . . ." She was about to argue that she hadn't specifically been told not to visit the baby, but she had been told not to go through the door again. By Phan. And Phan hadn't seemed too bothered by it the night before. "It doesn't matter. Worry about yourself." She snapped.

Rhys moved so quickly that Scarlett didn't have the opportunity to react. He grabbed her arm and pushed her between two of the houses. "Stop!" he said. His voice was harsh but barely above a whisper. "Stop, okay? What do you hope to gain from this? Do you *want* to die?"

Scarlett's surprise turned into anger as she peeled at Rhys's grip on her arm. He held on, more tightly than before.

"The only thing you're going to get from digging into things is trouble. Trouble. Not a high position or a hope at a nice future. Trouble. Or death. So stop."

"You stop!" Scarlett said, his grip distracting her. She used her slightly long nails to claw at his hand. He dropped his hand slowly as if to let her know that he was deciding to let her go, not being forced to do so. "Stop telling me what to do! Stop, Rhys! You've never been like this before, so stop acting like you're so high and mighty now."

"You really are dumb. You think I'm trying to tell you what to do because I think I'm better than you? You are so wrong! If I didn't care about you, I wouldn't be here trying to convince you to stop sneaking around."

"Yeah, right, if you actually cared about me and respected what I thought, then you would just listen and be okay with it. Instead, you're so selfish that you're more worried about getting in trouble instead of actually caring about the small human that has been left all alone in the basement of the facility!" Scarlett's voice had risen as she spoke. "All you care about is just doing exactly what we're told, and you're not the same person I used to spend time with at the training centers."

"I've changed? I've changed!" This outraged Rhys. "If I follow the rules more, or you know, care about not dying, that's because I'm a Blue now. It's not the same as when you're a Green or a Yellow. Now, there are serious consequences—"

"You think I don't know that? I'm the one who has spent a day in isolation! I'm the one who has seen the females being questioned about where the child was. I was responsible for beating a male my first day here. So enough of you acting like I don't know anything." Scarlett stepped further into the alley, closer to the backstreet. She didn't care what her orders were. She couldn't stand next to Rhys for another minute. She had to clear her head. The anger rushing through her felt so explosive. He had better not try to stop her.

"Scarlett," Rhys said. She turned and headed toward the backstreet. She could hear his footsteps.

Leave me alone, leave me alone, leave me alone, she willed him in her head, but her teeth were gritted, and her jaw was too tight to say anything at that moment. Then, Rhys's hand was on her left shoulder, tight as before.

Scarlett gave a strange, angry grunt as she whirled around and drew her pistol in one swift motion. Almost in automatic response, Rhys drew his. They both stood there, staring down their barrels at each other. Scarlett's eyes darted back and forth between Rhys's finger on the trigger and his eyes. Would he really do it? Would he shoot her? She felt scared, upset. He couldn't. He wouldn't. Scarlett wanted to lower her gun, but she couldn't. She was afraid to give up her advantage. Who was this man staring at her through the sight of his gun?

"Hey!" a shout made Scarlett jump, and her finger pressed the trigger. The gun bucked back slightly in her hands, and she smelled the acrid scent of used gunpowder. Scarlett watched Rhys fall to the ground as the loud sound of a gunshot rang in her ears. She fell to the ground, too. Was someone shooting at them?

Once on her stomach, Scarlett felt the gun's warmth in her hand, in the piece of metal pressed against her fingers. Scarlett turned her head slowly as though she couldn't quite take in everything at once. She saw a white-uniformed set of legs coming toward both of them. Was a White shooting at them? Surely not. Was he trying to warn them of something?

Scarlett saw another White behind the first and a third turning into the alley from the main walkway. A Citizen was farther back. Something was happening, but Scarlett didn't seem capable of processing it. Maybe Rhys would know. She looked to where he was crouched on the ground, but he wasn't moving. Scarlett army crawled her way over with a cacophony of shouts in the background. Then, it was as if the shouts broke through an invisible curtain and fell upon her ears.

"Stop moving!"

"Put the gun down!"

"Stay where you are!"

"What happened?"

Scarlett started to get to her knees, her gun dangling loosely at her side. "We need your help," Scarlett said to the nearest White. She was relieved to see a face she recognized in Marse. "Something happened. There was a shot—" but Marse interrupted her.

"Put your gun down now."

Scarlett hadn't realized it was still dangling from her hand. She moved to replace the gun in her waistband, but Marse shook his head, his eyes hard.

"On the ground."

Scarlett frowned. "But there was . . . someone—" She placed the gun on the ground and stood back upright.

"Hands behind your back," Marse said. Scarlett's eyes flicked around at the faces, all looking at her.

"But, he needs help," Scarlett said, motioning toward Rhys. "Somebody needs to help him. I don't know where—"

"Help is on the way for him. Worry about yourself," Marse said. Scarlett wasn't resisting as Marse circled her and handcuffed her hands behind her back. She kept looking at Rhys, waiting for him to move, waiting for him to stand up and laugh it off. Then, her gaze fell on her pistol on the ground, and she felt the cold handcuffs against her wrists. She hadn't done anything wrong. It was an accident. She would never shoot Rhys.

Chapter 25

Scarlett was in her old cell, the one she had occupied only two weeks before. The dank smell instantly made her stomach turn over. She had been marched there without ceremony but with many questioning eyes. Haman had let out a nervous giggle as she was marched into the entryway. She hadn't looked up long enough to note how everyone else was reacting.

Now, she sat, wondering how long she would be left there. Would she be fed? She hadn't seen or heard anyone since they had left her. It had felt like hours and hours ago, but her shift probably wasn't even over yet. Among these small worries danced the image of Rhys laying on the ground. Where was he? Had the doctor been able to attend to him right away? Had he fallen unconscious? Was he awake right now? Did he know it was her who had shot him?

Even admitting that to herself didn't seem right. It seemed like a strange dream. Scarlett tried to recall the details, but it seemed hazy. She just wanted to get out of there and see where Rhys was.

Scarlett dozed off and woke again several times throughout a long stretch of time. Finally, the door opened. Scarlett's stomach grumbled, but there was no food. Two Whites from the third shift were standing there, watching her. Scarlett stood uncertainly, waiting for them to tell her what she should do.

One of them motioned her forward. Scarlett stepped forward, one of them letting her pass in front of him, so she was walking between the two of them. As she passed in front of the male, he leaned forward and said in a low voice. "I hope you're executed."

Scarlett shuddered and looked back at the male. Had he really just said that? His face was impassive, as though she had imagined the whole episode. The White in front of her started leading her up the long flights of the stairs.

She knew where they were taking her. She would talk with the Black. He would know everything that had happened. He would ask her to explain herself. Suddenly the hours passed in isolation seemed wasted. She should have been trying to think of an explanation, something that would show that everything was an accident. But whatever he decided, Scarlett couldn't think about what that might be, she had to see Rhys.

They stopped in the doorway of the Black's office. He motioned them in. The two Whites came in. Scarlett looked at the floor, her heart beating hard.

"You may leave," the Black said. Scarlett looked up to see he was motioning the Whites out of the room. They shut the door behind themselves so that Scarlett and the Black were alone. Her stomach dropped. What was he going to do to her that no one else could witness?

The silence was unbearable. Scarlett's palms started sweating. She glanced up to find the Black's eyes boring into her. She stared down at the floor again, swallowing hard as the excuses welled up in her. Silence was always best, better than the confusion of words in her brain.

"You shot and killed a Blue," the Black said. His words hit Scarlett.

She looked up, her eyes wide. "I . . . what? He's dead?"

The Black just stared back at her, without even so much as nodding to answer her. Scarlett felt her strength fade. She fell to her knees, pressing her face into her hands. She tried to mumble something, some sort of excuse, but the grief rushing over her took away her ability to speak. After a few minutes, she was aware of the Black's eyes boring into her. She wiped her face harshly and looked up at him from the ground, the way a Tiny would look up to ask for more snacks.

"Why?" the Black asked, no sign of grief or sympathy in his features.

"I didn't mean to," Scarlett said. "We were . . . arguing. Someone shouted at us, and my finger slipped on the trigger. I was never going to shoot him. I wouldn't do that."

"You did it," the Black confirmed.

"It was an accident. Someone surprised me, and I wasn't expecting that."

The Black stared at her for a few minutes. "Why should I not have you executed immediately?"

"Uh—"Scarlett groaned and knotted her hands into fists. She couldn't think. Her mind was clouded. Was Rhys really dead? He hadn't moved, but that didn't mean he was dead. He had to be alive. She needed to see him, to tell him she was sorry.

"Your last chance," the Black said. "Or do you realize that you deserve death for what you have done?"

"I . . . it was an accident. I've never shot someone or done anything like that before," Scarlett said. "I wouldn't hurt Rhys. Never—" her last word was said in a soft whisper. "Please, I want to see him."

"Who?"

"Rhys."

"The one you shot."

"Yes, please, I . . . " It sounded dumb to say she needed to say goodbye. But she had never known anyone who was alive and then who . . . wasn't. He couldn't hear her maybe, but she just couldn't wrap her mind around the possibility.

"His body is being disposed of as we speak."

Disposed of? What did that even mean? Scarlett looked up at the Black. He didn't have anything like sympathy in his eyes. Would she die?

Would it really be so bad if she did? She felt his gaze on her for a few more minutes as she looked at the ground, her head pounding with a sudden migraine that distracted her from all else.

"You will be executed tomorrow," the Black said. "At noon." Scarlett couldn't swallow the bile she felt rising in her throat. She couldn't die. She hated everything, all the secrets about this place, but she didn't want to die, to cease to exist.

"Please, Sir. Please," Scarlett said. "I don't want to die. I'll do anything. I understand what I did was wrong. I'm sorry."

The Black regarded her for a few more moments. He pressed a button on his desk, and the same two Whites entered his office again. Scarlett wondered if they had been listening to the conversation from the hallway.

"Take her back to isolation. And give her a plate of food." Scarlett was marched back to the dank room. Both Whites appeared impassive about what was happening. But the one in front of her made eye contact with her when she passed by him. He didn't look angry. He looked sorry for her. Scarlett waited, but no food was brought. She stared at the dark wall for hours, wondering what it would be like to die. Would she feel pain? Would it take a long time? Scarlett didn't want to find out.

Suddenly full of energy, Scarlett began to pace the room, covering the distance in three long steps. She couldn't die. She couldn't die. Not yet. Scarlett walked over to the door. She tried the knob and almost didn't believe it when it opened. The door squeaked as Scarlett gaped at the stone stairs. The stairs. But what could she do? Try to sneak out? And go where? Stay there and wait to die? No, that wasn't an option. She wouldn't passively accept an execution. She would fight.

About the Author

Laurel Solorzano has enjoyed writing since she was in middle school, exchanging manuscripts for years with her best friend. After traveling the globe for a time, Laurel set her goal to become a published author. As she worked teaching English and Spanish, she wrote stories in her free time. Laurel currently lives in Raleigh, North Carolina.

You can get to know Laurel more by visiting her at www.laurelsolorzano.com.